"I'll go w...

One sharp shake of his head and Gabriel Klein headed for the curb. "Not a good idea."

"Regardless." She hurried to keep up. "I need to observe everything you do."

"You might observe a whole lot more than you ever wanted to. Accident near the mountains could be vehicular, could be hunting, could be feudal." She snorted as if he were kidding. But then, she was from out of town. "It could be damn near anything, and if they asked for paramedics, you can be certain there's blood involved."

"I'll manage. I might even be able to help."

Klein took in her pristine-white blouse and neatly pressed khakis, her slim soft hands, ponytailed hair and youthful demeanor. "Somehow I doubt that."

Her eyes narrowed; her lips tightened. "I'm not just decoration, Klein. You'd be surprised at what I can do if you look a little deeper than my skin."

Isabelle held Klein's gaze. He hesitated.

Klein opened the door of the squad car. "All right," he said. "Surprise me."

Dear Reader,

Thank you to all the readers who have written to me about my first three Superromance novels. Many of you asked for more stories with animals after reading *Doctor, Doctor.* Many also asked for the story of Gabe Klein after reading *Leave It to Max.* I'm happy to say that with *A Sheriff in Tennessee* I'm able to grant both requests.

Gabriel Klein has a new job as sheriff of Pleasant Ridge, Tennessee. He's hoping to live the quiet life. Unfortunately, Pleasant Ridge isn't very quiet.

Between his deputy, a Barney Fife clone who arrests folks at will for outdated nonsense, Klein's gun-shy hound dog, Clint, and an insane Chihuahua with horrible fashion sense, he has his hands full. Then he discovers he's been volunteered to teach Isabelle Ash, former supermodel-turned-television-actress, how to be a small-town sheriff.

What's a poor guy to do? Why, fall in love, of course.

I had great fun with the characters in Pleasant Ridge, both human and canine. I hope you do, too.

And for those of you who wrote asking for Kim Luchetti's story—I'm working on it!

For information on future releases and contests, check out my Web site at www.lorihandeland.com

Lori Handeland

Books by Lori Handeland

HARLEQUIN SUPERROMANCE

922—MOTHER OF THE YEAR
969—DOCTOR, DOCTOR
1004—LEAVE IT TO MAX

A Sheriff in Tennessee
Lori Handeland

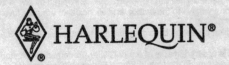

HARLEQUIN®

TORONTO • NEW YORK • LONDON
AMSTERDAM • PARIS • SYDNEY • HAMBURG
STOCKHOLM • ATHENS • TOKYO • MILAN • MADRID
PRAGUE • WARSAW • BUDAPEST • AUCKLAND

ISBN 0-373-71063-1

A SHERIFF IN TENNESSEE

For my editor, Beverley Sotolov,
who always knows just the right words.

Thanks.

CHAPTER ONE

"WHAT DO YOU MEAN there's nothing I can do about it?"

Sheriff Gabriel Klein leaned over the desk and scowled, but Malachai Smith, the mayor of Pleasant Ridge, Tennessee, was unimpressed.

"I made this deal long before I hired you. Not that I'd have asked your opinion about it even then." Chai tapped Klein's big knuckles with what looked like a check. "Get off my desk and sit down. You don't scare me, Sheriff."

And therein lay the problem with Mayor Smith. He wasn't scared of much because he knew it all. Too young to be mayor and too pretty to be alive, Chai drove Klein to distraction, which was a pure pain in the behind when the man was his boss. Klein had been the sheriff of Pleasant Ridge for only a month and already he wanted to quit.

He sighed heavily and sat the same. Chai put the check on his desk and pushed it across with one long finger. Even the man's hands were handsome—manly, yet unmarked by strife. His golden hair was just a bit long, so he appealed to the younger crowd. But his seventy-five-watt smile and his trusty blue eyes had won him the elderly vote, and his runner's physique had won over women of all ages. Or perhaps it was the running attire itself. Everyone knew the mayor jogged through town every morning at seven in skimpy running shorts.

Malachai Smith was the chosen child of Pleasant Ridge. He'd received a track scholarship to the University of Tennessee, gotten a degree in business and come home to assume the job his father had held on to—until Chai returned. It was enough to make a grown man gag.

Life just wasn't fair. But men like Klein learned such truths at a very young age. Knowing them had made him a good cop. He expected the worst and he was rarely disappointed.

"Take a gander at the check, Klein, and tell me I'm stupid."

Klein counted the zeros, then looked at Chai. "You're stupid."

Chai blinked. The one thing he did not have was a sense of humor. So Klein couldn't resist making jokes at the mayor's expense—jokes the man rarely got. Which made things all the more fun for Klein.

Chai snatched up the check and tucked it into the inside pocket of his summer suit. The calendar might read April 21, but in southern Tennessee the thermometer ran the show and at ten a.m. it said seventy-seven degrees.

Klein's dirt-brown uniform was already damp beneath his gun belt. He was a big man, six feet four inches and nearly two hundred and fifty pounds, but having a belt around his middle that sported a side arm, ammunition, handcuffs, walkie-talkie and keys made stronger men than Klein break a sweat much earlier in the morning.

From day one he'd refused to wear the hat that went with the uniform, not only because it made him resemble the sheriff in *Smoky and the Bandit,* but because he couldn't bear to add one ounce of unnecessary weight to his increasingly beleaguered body.

Chai patted his pocket as though afraid the check might disappear if he didn't keep his hand on it. "Pleasant Ridge needs this money. The only profitable business left in town is the Smith and Son Winery."

"Convenient," Klein murmured.

Chai ignored him. He did that a lot. "With this check I can upgrade the schools, loan to new businesses and assist some of the old ones. Not only that, but the extra people in town will increase our revenue. It's win-win all around."

"Not for me." Klein had been through it all before. He'd come to Pleasant Ridge from Savannah, Georgia—a beautiful town, with far too many people. "More people, more trouble. For crying out loud, my police force consists of me and Barney Fife."

The mayor's eyebrows drew together. "Virgil Gumm has been the deputy in Pleasant Ridge since he was my age."

"I'm sure he was as good at his job then as you are at yours now."

Chai opened his mouth, then shut it again. He wasn't sure what to make of that comment. *Good.*

"I can handle things when it's just us folks," Klein continued, "but add Lord knows how many strangers, and California strangers to boot, well, then I don't know. There's gonna be trouble, Chai. Mark my words.''

"What kind of trouble can there be with a television crew and some actors? They stay a while, get the flavor of the town, film their pilot and leave.''

"You promise?"

The mayor's gaze slid away. Klein fought the urge to grab Chai's perfect chin and force the man to look him in the eye.

"What did you do?" Klein asked softly.

"Well, uh.'' The mayor stared at his desk calendar as if it were the most fascinating piece of paper on the planet. "There's a clause in the contract.''

"What kind of clause?"

"If the show is a hit, they film here a few months out of every year.''

Klein cursed. "What were you thinking?"

The mayor finally looked at him. The expression in his eyes was as mulish as the set of his mouth. "I was thinking that we'd get another check with every year the show is renewed. With the money, we can improve. With the extra population, we can grow.''

"Did you ever consider that the extra attention, the added publicity, the money might ruin this town?''

"Why would they?"

Klein couldn't sit still any longer so he stood, and Chai leaped to his feet, too. They were nearly the same height, but the mayor was at least sixty pounds lighter. Klein could easily kick his ass, and right now he was having a hard time remembering why he shouldn't.

He moved to the large window behind Chai's desk. This second-story office had the best view in town. From it Klein could see all of Pleasant Ridge and the mountains beyond.

"Look at that, Chai." The mayor joined him at the window. "For a minute just look at it and tell me we need fast-food hamburgers, pizza and tacos. Tell me we need a miniature golf course and a water park. Explain why a chain department store and hotel would be good things."

"They couldn't hurt."

"Yes, they could!"

With a sigh of disgust, Klein turned away from the window and the sight of the town he'd picked from a list of so many others. Pleasant Ridge could be the home he'd been searching for all his life— if the Mayor Wonder didn't screw up the place first.

"Pleasant Ridge is special. That's why they want it. You said this show is a modern-day *Mayberry RFD*. When these people get through with us, we won't be special anymore—we'll be a joke on national television."

The mayor remained silent. Had Klein managed to get through that thick head? But when he turned around, Chai was again seated at his desk with his back to the town. Maybe if he had to face the place and the people he worked for, the man wouldn't be so quick to ruin everything.

Klein toyed with the idea of sneaking into Chai's office under dark of night and rearranging the furniture—then nailing it to the floor.

"One more thing about the contract."

The mayor still wasn't looking at him. Now he appeared fascinated with the gold-engraved pen his daddy had given him when he was elected.

Klein sighed. "Am I going to have to hurt you, Chai?"

"Maybe." *Click, click, click.* His thumb jabbed the top of the pen until the office sounded like the site of a Morse code jamboree. "But it won't change anything."

Klein growled and yanked the pen from Chai's hand, then held it out of reach. He considered snapping the thing in two, just for the hell of it—but then he'd have to deal with Daddy. Anyone who thought Smith Jr. was a pain in the behind had not met Smith Sr.

"Talk." Klein ordered. "And this time tell me all of it. What's this show about?"

"Just what you said."

"Then, why might I have to hurt you? Not that I mind, but I'd like to know why."

"Do you remember *Mayberry RFD?*"

"Do you? You seem a little young for it."

"Reruns are a wonderful thing. Mayberry, North Carolina, will become Pleasant Ridge, Tennessee."

"I got that."

"And Sheriff Andy Taylor will become…"

Klein had a horrible idea. "Not me. Oh, no. Uh-uh."

Chai laughed. "You? On television?" The mayor's gaze met Klein's. "I don't think so."

At thirty-five, Klein should be used to the way people looked at him, talked to him, as if he had no feelings, as if he didn't care that he was not a handsome man. Klein knew what he was—tall, strong, smart, capable and kind. A regular Boy Scout. But handsome? Not even close.

"Then, who's the sheriff? Drew Carey? No wait, Martin Sheen. He'd be good."

"It's a new millennium, Klein. The television sheriff of Pleasant Ridge is a woman."

"What woman?"

"Isabelle Ash."

Klein searched his memory, then shook his head. "Never heard of her."

"You may not know her name, but I'm sure you've seen a lot of her."

Klein scowled. What did that mean? He should have known Chai couldn't wait to tell him.

"She's a model. Victoria's Secret. *Sports Illustrated* swimsuit edition—she was on the cover last year."

"I never look at those things."

Chai quirked a brow as if he didn't believe it. "We *all* look at those things."

Klein didn't bother to explain the difference between twenty-three and thirty-five, between handsome as hell and plain as porridge. Age had given him insight; homeliness had given him a sarcastic view of life and a lot of the people in it.

"This show sounds more like *Baywatch* comes to Mayberry, if you ask me."

Chai's face went dreamy. "Wouldn't that be nice?"

Klein stifled another sigh. This *kid* was his boss. This *kid* was the mayor. But Klein remembered twenty-three very well, and while he at that age had already learned his lesson about women, lost his dreams, joined the marines and grown up, most of his buddies hadn't. The twenties were a time for foolishness, bad choices, playing when you should be working, dreaming impossible dreams, because for kids that age there was still a chance dreams might come true.

But a twenty-three-year-old mayor? Klein contemplated the expression on Chai's face and shook his head. There oughta be a law.

"So they're giving the lead in a spanking-new television series to an underwear model?"

The mayor blinked and fell back to earth. "Who better?"

"Someone who can act?"

"Who says she can't act?"

True enough, and none of Klein's concern, anyway. His concern was keeping the town and himself from going insane.

Klein headed for the door. "When can I expect the fun to begin?"

"Tomorrow."

He rested his forehead on the scarred mahogany door and resisted the urge to bang it a few times. "Tomorrow? The horde will descend tomorrow?"

"Not the horde. Just Isabelle. Her being here early is supposed to be a secret. Though in Pleasant Ridge, I doubt she'll stay a secret long. They don't want any media following her while she's having her lessons."

Klein wasn't a good cop because he could shoot straight. He was a good cop because he knew people; he could hear every nuance in their voices, even when he wasn't looking at them. Especially when he wasn't looking at them. Right now he could tell, even before he turned around, that Chai was grinning.

"What lessons?"

"Did you forget the final contract clause we were discussing?"

Klein wanted to spit. He *had* forgotten. And before he'd fully discovered what it was, too. Shame on him. "The one I might have to hurt you for?"

Chai's smile faded. "That would be the one."

"Spill it, pretty boy."

To the mayor's credit he didn't hesitate or try to shuffle around the issue, probably because he knew Klein was on the edge of reason and had no patience right now for bullshit.

"According to the contract, you'll be teaching Isabelle Ash how to act the part of a small-town sheriff."

BELLE STARED into the window of the bakery and contemplated everything chocolate. She couldn't decide—cookie, brownie, cake or pie? What she should do is buy one of each. It wasn't as if she couldn't afford to.

The thought of all that dessert, just for her, made Belle light-headed with hunger, or perhaps it was a sham sugar rush. What would people think if they saw a woman sitting alone eating all that she could grab? Since Belle was thin, people would probably figure she was just going to throw it up as soon as she finished.

And they'd be right.

She shook her head. They'd have been right several years ago, but not anymore. She was better now. In control of her life, her career, her health. She wouldn't be throwing up all the desserts, because she wouldn't be having all the desserts. She'd buy one and then she'd continue to explore the town.

No one could ever learn her secret; no one could ever uncover the weakness beneath her show of strength. That would be worse than the weakness itself.

Belle stepped back from the window and caught sight of her reflection. No wonder people on the street rarely recognized her. Amazing what a good hairstylist and makeup artist could do for a woman. With her long, artificially enhanced blond hair stuffed beneath a baseball cap, no concealer to cover the dark smudges beneath her eyes or blush to give her naturally pale complexion a hint of peach, the fine bones of her face appeared stark and strained.

Her overalls were the smallest size she'd been able to find back in Memphis, and still they bagged at the seat and gaped at the waist. She loved them.

Rarely did she get to wear clothes that were too loose. She'd come to loathe the tight belts, tight pants, tight shirts, the skimpy, confining *everything* of her profession. They made her feel like sausage stuffed into a casing. When she wore clothes like those, she could remember too well a childhood spent as the fat kid.

She'd covered her ample breasts—yes, they were

hers, thank you very much—with a loose, hot-pink tank top, and the heated spring breeze brushed her bare shoulders. For a moment the stresses of the past few months lifted, and she almost felt like herself again. Or what self she could remember from the time before she'd let them stuff her into the casing that was Isabelle Ash.

To be honest, *let* wasn't exactly the word she should use. She'd wanted this career; needed it, too. That hadn't changed in the years since she'd left home. In fact, the wants and the needs had only become more pronounced....

Belle narrowed her choice to the brownie with cherries on top or the marble cheesecake with the chocolate icing. *Decisions, decisions.*

She'd come to Pleasant Ridge early because she'd been too anxious to stay in California one more day. This show was her big chance, and could make or break her budding acting career. If she didn't do well, she'd be back modeling thong bikinis in thirty-degree weather.

She could think of worse things. But being a model was probably not the best career choice for a bulimic. Even an undiagnosed, self-counseled, secret bulimic.

"The brownie," she muttered. "Definitely."

A buzzer announced her entrance into the bakery. Seconds later an elderly woman bounced in from the back. Her spritely step belied the lines on her face and the gray in her hair.

"Can I help you?" She smiled as her glance swept Belle from head to toe. "I'd say yes. You need a cake."

Belle raised her eyebrows. "A whole cake?"

"Well, sure. Doesn't everyone?"

The accent made Belle nostalgic. It had been a long time since she'd heard the cadence of the South. She'd just spent the past few years erasing it from her own voice. Ironic that she'd have to recover that accent for her very first part.

"What if we start with one of the cherry-topped brownies I saw in the window?"

The woman's smile fell. "I'm sorry, sugar. Those are plastic. I've only got what you see in the display case right here." She tapped a fingernail on the glass in front of her.

"Why would you put plastic brownies in the window?"

The woman's cheeriness faded and her shoulders sagged. "It's no secret that business isn't the best these days. Folks are having a hard time making ends meet in Pleasant Ridge, and when that happens the first things to go are the luxury items. Bakery, for instance."

Belle nodded. One of the reasons this town had been picked out of so many others was that Pleasant Ridge was dying but not dead yet. The place still looked prosperous, but it could be bought.

"There's no point in baking all that I can and then throwing it out every night, now is there?" The woman indicated her display case with a regal tilt of her head and a sigh. "So I have samples, and I only make certain things on certain days. Monday is brownie day."

"I'll have to remember that." Belle hunkered

down and stared into the case. Wednesday appeared to be cake day. "Can I have a piece of cake?"

"You bet. Which one?"

Belle picked the chocolate cake with chocolate icing—as close to her original choice as she could get. The woman handed her a slice big enough to rival one of the mountains on the horizon, atop a plate the size of the moon.

"Uh—" Belle was treated to a smile of such expectation that she found she couldn't ask for a smaller serving. What would be the point of asking, anyway? She wouldn't eat all of a smaller piece, either. "Thank you," she said, instead.

After paying a miniscule amount for such a large piece of cake, Belle returned to the street. Before the door closed behind her, she heard, "See you Monday, sugar!"

Belle waved before heading toward the tiny apartment the production company had rented for her above the five-and-dime. Private stairs from alley level gave her access to a clean-but-sparse kitchenette, bath and living area. Her favorite part was the bed that pulled out of the wall. She'd always wanted one of those.

Folks had been apologizing for the accommodations since she'd arrived, and while the apartment was much less than what she'd had in the past few years, it was much more than she'd had in the years before that. The important thing was the window through which she could watch the streets below. That had been her only requirement for a living space in Pleasant Ridge.

Belle would immerse herself in the town, its people, her part. She would *become* Sheriff Janet Hayes. She could do this. All she needed was some guidance from Gabriel Klein. Both her director and the producers had assured her she would get it.

The man was new to Pleasant Ridge, but he'd been in law enforcement for a very long time. Belle paused on the sidewalk to cut off a morsel of cake and popped it into her mouth. As she rolled the sweet around on her tongue, making one bite last before she took another, she considered what she knew about the sheriff.

The Citadel for college, then eight years in the marines, where he'd been an MP. After his service, he'd worked in Atlanta, become a detective, then, oddly, taken a job in Savannah for less than two years before coming here. He was a fascinating man, and Belle couldn't wait to meet him.

She swallowed her last bite of cake and glanced at the paper plate. Without realizing it, she'd already cut the rest of the slice into tiny pieces and moved them about to appear as if she'd eaten more than she had. Old habits were hard to break.

Before she could be tempted further, Belle tossed the remains into the nearest trash can and hurried on so she wouldn't have to hear the *thud* as the great, big, beautiful treat hit the bottom of the barrel. She hadn't gone three steps when a hand descended on her shoulder.

"Hold it right there, missy."

A sun-leathered, sinewy old man scowled at her. The expression only deepened the myriad lines in his face. He slid his hand from her shoulder to her elbow, as if afraid she might run. The sleeve of his rumpled and baggy brown uniform bore the insignia of the Pleasant Ridge Law Enforcement.

Belle's eyes widened. *This* was Gabriel Klein? She'd thought him a younger man, but then, she'd only heard the highlights of his career. Perhaps he'd worked in a dozen other cities as well as Atlanta and Savannah—two dozen by the looks of him.

He was barely her height of five foot nine— didn't the marines have some macho height requirement?—and she probably outweighed him, too. But his gaunt fingers were strong as they ground into the sensitive skin above her elbow. She tried to tug away, but he was having none of it.

"Hello," she began. "I'm—"

"A 4-25," he announced in a high-pitched, nasally voice she knew right off was going to be far too annoying to listen to for long.

"I'm sorry. What did I do?"

His thin lips tightened and he jabbed a bony finger at the ground. Belle followed his direction and discovered her cake all over the sidewalk. She frowned. "I must not have hit the hole in the trash can quite right. I'll pick it up."

She made a move toward the cake, but he yanked her back. For a skinny, little old guy he was incredibly agile. "Too late now, missy. We take littering seriously in this community."

Before she could ask how seriously, she learned. The sheriff pulled her hands behind her back and shackled them in handcuffs with an ease born of practice.

"Hey, wait a minute. I said I'd pick it up."

"But you weren't gonna until I caught you. You

just marched right on and never glanced back. That cake is pure evil."

"Don't I know it," Belle muttered.

"To a dog. Didn't you ever hear that chocolate is dog poison? What if I hadn't been here and Miss Dubray's Chihuahua ate that? Can you imagine what would happen if the yapping twit up and keeled over right here on Longstreet Avenue? While some days I wish he would, I'd rather not have to listen to his mama. Miss Dubray treats that Mex puppy like her baby. Even dresses it in baby clothes."

"There oughta be a law."

The sheriff scowled at her. "There is. Against people like you. Let's go."

Belle could have argued. She could have told him who she was. She could have screamed for the mayor, a lawyer, her producer. But then she wouldn't find out how it felt to be arrested like a common criminal, how extremely embarrassing it was to be dragged directly to jail. She'd never experience an arrest from the side of the arrested.

But no sooner had they entered the police station than the sheriff's radio crackled static.

He cursed and spoke into the contraption, which appeared to be a walkie-talkie as old as he was. "Ten-four. I'll be there in five."

"You understood that?"

"'Course. It's a 10-91D." At her blank expression, he continued. "Cow standing in the middle of Highway B, about seven miles outside town, tangled with a semi. Only known casualty the cow. We don't get it off the pavement, there's gonna be

BBQ before sundown. I'll have to put you in a cell and book you when I get back.''

He was already forcibly encouraging her toward a gray cement-block hallway at the rear of the police station. There, a room opened off the hall, with two cells inside.

''You're just going to leave me here? Don't I get a phone call?''

''When I get back.''

''Don't you have a secretary or something?''

He snorted. ''Yeah, but she's out havin' lunch with my butler.''

He twisted the key in the cell door, removed the cuffs and hustled her inside. The closing clank of the iron door made her flinch. Somehow this wasn't so interesting anymore.

''What you see is what you get, missy. This ain't Memphis.''

''I could sue you.''

''You could?'' He shrugged. ''Sue me later.''

The sheriff walked out, leaving Belle alone. The outer door closed, then silence settled over the Pleasant Ridge police station.

Belle didn't mind being alone. She was alone a lot. As a child she'd had no friends; as an adult she didn't have any, either.

She sat on a surprisingly comfortable cot and looked around. She was starting to feel just a bit claustrophobic. Funny, she'd never known that about herself. A life of crime would not be her thing. If she had to stay in this small, locked room much longer she was going to scream—and if she started to scream, she wasn't sure she'd be able to stop.

A door opened somewhere, then closed. "Hey!" she shouted, the sound ricocheting around the cell.

Footsteps approached. Belle geared up to give the sheriff a piece of her mind. But the man who stepped in wasn't the sheriff.

Belle couldn't help it; she blinked and her mouth fell open. He was huge—at least six foot and then some of solid muscle—and the way he walked, confident and sure, with a hand on the butt of his pistol, the other swinging free and loose...

She couldn't stop staring at his large, capable hands. Belle shut her mouth and swallowed. She had a thing for nice hands.

She allowed her gaze to travel up his wide chest, over to a pair of great biceps, then up again to meet his curious blue eyes. He had nice eyes, too—determined but kind, and intelligent. He wasn't the handsomest man she'd ever seen; in fact, she'd bet most folks would call him downright homely. But Belle knew a thing or two about the value of a pretty face—a commodity, nothing more.

His short salt-and-pepper hair gave her pause. As did his brown uniform.

Huge. Muscular. Crew cut. Well, duh.

"You're—"

"Gabriel Klein," he said, his voice a sexy, Southern rumble from the depths of that incredible chest.

Now, that's more like it, Belle thought.

CHAPTER TWO

KLEIN WAS IN NO MOOD for trouble. He'd had a morning full already. Unfortunately, the young woman in the cell looked like trouble on a platter.

He'd just spent the past half hour walking the streets of Pleasant Ridge, nodding to the folks who greeted him, walking and walking, trying to calm down enough to come back here.

He should have learned by now that arguing with the mayor only gave him a headache. Chai was his boss, plain and simple. And as Mayor Smith had pointed out, if Klein didn't like the way things were in Pleasant Ridge he could go straight to…another town.

Klein ground his teeth, a new habit courtesy of Chai. Obviously he still wasn't calm enough and should walk another mile or so until he was. But he'd heard Virgil answer the call on the dead cow and knew he'd better return to mind the fort. He wished Virgil had told him they had company.

"What did you do?" he asked.

Might be any one of a hundred things, with Virgil. The man remembered the code book better than he remembered what he'd had for breakfast. Klein spent a lot of time releasing people Virgil arrested for outdated nonsense. It gave them both something to do.

"I believe it was a 4-25."

Klein frowned. Her voice was odd. Pleasant, but odd. The overtones were flat Yankee, yet the sound of the word *four—fo-ah*—made him wonder— Damn, he had far too little to detect in Pleasant Ridge if he was pondering the accent of a college kid who'd wandered off the interstate.

The way she'd shouted "Hey!" and the tense manner in which she held her shoulders did not bode well. That he couldn't see her face beneath the shadow of her Titans cap made Klein edgy. He liked to look into a person's eyes. But her baggy clothes and high-topped tennis shoes assured him she was just a kid, despite the mature, somewhat sexy tenor of her voice.

Klein rubbed his eyes. *Sexy?* Great, he was starting to stalk the cradle.

"A 4-25?" He dropped his hand. "Jaywalking?"

She snorted. "Not according to your sidekick. Littering seems to be a federal offense around here."

"A lot of things are."

"I'll have to remember that. I'd think that if you locked people up for every little thing you'd have more jail cells—or at least, fewer empty ones."

"Well, we sort of have a system here. Virgil locks folks up—" Klein unhooked the ring of keys from his belt, twisted one in the lock and opened the door "—then I set them free."

"Interesting system."

She stepped out and took a deep breath, as if she needed fresh air. She wasn't going to get it in here, where the overriding scents were old paint and ancient coffee.

However, *she* smelled fresh and sweet, like sunshine and chocolate. Two of his favorite things.

Klein took a giant step backward, away from temptation. He needed to get a grip. Or maybe get laid. Because what else could explain his attraction to a sweet young thing? Gabe Klein knew better.

"If you'll follow me." He led the way to the front office. "We'll just light a small ceremonial fire with your paperwork and you can be on your way."

"Your friend—"

"Deputy."

"Fife was it?"

"Gumm," he snapped. It was okay for him to call his deputy by the name of the infamous screwup from Mayberry, but no one else had better try it. "His name's Virgil Gumm."

"Even better," she murmured. "There *was* no paperwork. Deputy Gumm got called out on the suicide cow before he could book me."

Suicide cow? Klein almost laughed. He had an odd sense of humor himself, but most of the time he was the only one who got his jokes. Chai certainly couldn't be counted on—for anything—and Virgil, well, not much was funny to Virgil Gumm. The law was a serious business.

Klein stopped just inside the office doorway, and she bumped into him. The difference in their sizes caused her to bounce back several steps. "Hey!" she said. "Your brake lights are busted."

"Sorry." He continued to his desk and glanced at the surface. No papers, just as she'd said. None on Virgil's desk, either. *Damn.*

"So you're telling me my deputy put you in a cell and never read you your rights?"

"He didn't even ask my name."

Double damn. Virgil was losing it, and this time they could have a lawsuit on their hands.

"I apologize, miss. We're a small town and sometimes things get muddled."

"Fascinating word choice, Sheriff." Her lips curved. "I think I'm going to enjoy working with you."

Klein's gaze leaped from her mouth to her eyes. They were still shadowed, and he could see little but the line of her cheek and the slant of her jaw.

Then she pulled off her Titans cap and shook out a mane of long, curly, blond hair. He forgot all about her face as the mass tumbled to her waist, drawing his eyes to the tank top that exposed pale skin on either side of her overalls. The sight was the most erotic thing he'd encountered in a long time.

He yanked his eyes from her hips to her face, and froze. She wasn't as young as he'd thought. But that wasn't what had his ardor waning quicker than ice melts in springtime.

It was the sight of a beautiful woman.

BELLE WASN'T USED TO men staring at her with no expression in their eyes. Over the past several years she'd viewed a gamut of emotions—appraisal, admiration, avarice, lust, even love—but she had to say, she couldn't recall any man looking at her as Gabriel Klein was right now: as if he had no interest in her at all.

She might think he was gay, except there *had* been interest at first. Not only in his eyes but in his body language, until she'd taken off her hat and let him see her face. That usually reduced most men to gibbering slaves. This one merely turned his back and walked to the window. She had to admit, she was intrigued.

"*You're* Isabelle Ash?"

"You don't recognize me?"

"Sorry. I'm not much of a Victoria's Secret buyer. No matter how many times I ask, they refuse to carry my size."

Belle choked. He threw a glance that was almost admiring over his shoulder, before he caught himself, sobered and focused his attention outside once more.

He didn't know who she was! He'd never drooled over a picture of her in satin and lace, not even spandex and a smile. Why did she find that more appealing than eight dozen white roses?

"Are you going to sue us?" he asked the window.

Ah, so that's what he's worried about.

"Sue the department that's teaching me all I need to know for the chance of my lifetime? I don't think so."

"Swell."

Funny, he didn't sound happy about it, and she

had a feeling she knew why. "You don't want us here, do you?"

"I never said that."

"Specifically, you don't want *me* here. You don't want to help *me*."

He turned, and his gaze met hers. Annoyance made his eyes shine like blue neon against his sun-bronzed face. "Fine. I don't. But I've just been informed I have little choice in the matter. So the point is moot."

Belle slapped her hat against her thigh, annoyed herself. Having the man she needed in her corner pissed off at her—and the world, it appeared—was not a good way to start. But how was she going to change his attitude? She didn't think smiling and flipping her hair would carry much weight with Gabriel Klein.

What would? Perhaps the honesty her mama had always preached—the honesty that had never done Belle a lick of good in L.A.

"What have you got against me? You don't even know me."

He raised his eyebrows at her demanding tone. "Nothing personal. I just don't think all the attention, all the people will be good for this town."

"From what I understand, Pleasant Ridge needs the money."

"Money can't fix everything, Ms. Ash."

Something she understood to be true better than anyone.

"Call me Isabelle." She hated that "Ms." crap, and only her family called her Belle.

"I don't think—"

"Good. Don't think. Just call me Isabelle. And I'll call you Gabriel." He grimaced. "Or not."

"You can call me Sheriff, or Klein if you like, even Gabe if you must."

"Just don't call you late for dinner." She made the motions of a silent drumroll. *"Ba-dump-bump."*

Klein's mouth twitched. She could *really* like this guy—if he let her.

Belle didn't know how long they stood in the office staring at each other, trying not to smile, but before they could continue their conversation, the sound of running footsteps drifted in the half-open window. Klein looked out, groaned and banged his head once against the wall.

The door opened and a tall, very well-dressed man stepped inside. He was clearly agitated. His eyes searched the room. When he saw Klein, he frowned, then strode over to Belle and, without leave, took her hands.

"Ms. Ash, I apologize. I just heard what happened. Please forgive us. We're small. Yokels, practically. This mistake will never be repeated. You have my word."

He was handsome, most likely the handsomest man in town, and he knew it. But the way his gaze swept her face, touched on her bare shoulders, skittered over, then away from, then back to her breasts—

Belle resisted the urge to growl as his thumbs rubbed lightly, suggestively along the sensitive skin between her thumb and forefinger. As her mama always said, handsome is as handsome does, and in that vein this man was very unattractive. She glanced at his hands on hers—just as white, just as smooth, just as slim and pretty. Yuck. Regardless, he was obviously someone with clout in Pleasant Ridge or he wouldn't be giving her his word.

So she unclenched her teeth, smiled sweetly, and as he stood dazzled, she removed herself from his grasp and his reach. "And you would be...?"

"Malachai Smith. Mayor of Pleasant Ridge."

The mayor. Well, she was glad she'd resisted the age-old urge to kick him in the shins.

Belle hadn't realized she'd moved closer to Klein until he spoke right above her left shoulder.

"What do you want, Chai?"

The mayor scowled at the sheriff, and the expression made his pretty face sour. "You're fired."

"See ya." Klein strode toward the door.

"Wait!" Belle shouted. The mayor froze; Klein kept going. "Please?"

The sheriff stopped with his hand on the door, but he didn't turn around. For some reason Klein didn't like looking at her, and Belle wasn't sure what to do with a man like that.

So she dealt with the one she did know what to do with. "I need him, Mr. Mayor." She smiled again, and the mayor's jaw went slack. "I've only got two weeks to learn how to be a small-town sheriff. From what I've observed of the deputy, he won't be much help."

"He's fired, too."

Belle shrugged, but Klein was suddenly right there. "No. If I stay, so does he."

"Just this morning you were complaining about him." The mayor sounded exasperated.

Belle glanced back and forth between the two men, who seemed to have forgotten all about her.

"I can complain, but no one else had better try it. Besides, I'm going to need him."

"What for? To arrest folks like poor Ms. Ash?"

Poor Ms. Ash? She'd never been described just that way before. She'd been poor Belle, the fat girl. And the poor little Ash gal—as in dirt poor and ignorant. But since she'd become Ms. Ash, no one had called her poor. She found she liked it no more when it was just a figure of speech than when it had been the truth.

"I'm fine," she said. "No harm done. In fact, experiencing an arrest has been very helpful."

"But you weren't—"

She glared at Klein, and he snapped his mouth shut. He didn't need to blab that she hadn't actually been arrested, merely incarcerated.

"If Gabe says he needs his deputy—"

"Gabe?" The mayor scowled at the sheriff, who shrugged.

Belle resisted the urge to point out the mayor's rudeness in interrupting her. Men like him did not appreciate being corrected, especially by a woman. Besides, it *had* felt funny to call Sheriff Klein "Gabe." From the mayor's reaction, no one else did. Maybe she'd just stick to calling him late for dinner.

"I need Virgil," Klein reiterated. "He knows the rules."

"Too well."

"Which will come in handy with the increase in population." At Mayor Smith's confused look, he sighed and rubbed the back of his neck as if it ached. "The more people in an area, the more the rules need to be enforced. What might be silly today won't be tomorrow if a hundred people are doing it."

"Like littering," Belle put in.

Klein smiled at her, and Belle tried not to preen. She had a feeling Klein didn't smile much. "Or jaywalking. If it's just us folks, such arrests are silly. But if you've got fifty people throwing trash on the street and twenty walking against the light..." He lifted, then lowered one massive shoulder and spread his incredible hands.

"You've got trouble," Belle finished.

"And how."

The mayor cleared his throat, and they glanced his way. He looked annoyed. Klein seemed to have that effect on him, and the feeling appeared to be mutual.

"Fine. You're not fired. And neither is Virgil. But try to refrain from arresting the bread-and-butter, would you? Tell your deputy the same."

The bread-and-butter? How flattering. At least he hadn't called her the T and A. Although it wouldn't be the first time, nor the last time, she would have to ignore it.

"Ms. Ash."

The mayor took her hands again. He was really quite smooth at the maneuver. She'd bet her first month's salary that Malachai Smith had pledged a fraternity and spent some time squiring Southern sorority sisters to cotillions. With that face and body, she'd bet her second month's salary he'd often charmed those same girls out of their panties in the back of his overly large luxury vehicle. Men like the mayor always drove big cars. She'd discovered it was a compensation for other, smaller things.

"Anything you need, you just call me."

He handed her a card with one hand while still holding on to one of hers with the other. Too smooth by far.

"Anything, y' hear?"

I hear you loud and clear, Belle thought, *and I won't be calling you. Ever.*

She took the card and put it in the front pocket of her overalls, then patted the pocket with a smile and a wink. The mayor grinned and released her.

"Back to work," he said, and exited with a wave.

Belle kept her smile fixed until the door closed behind him.

"You do that well."

Her gaze flicked to Klein. He'd retreated to the chair behind his desk. He no longer smiled at her with approval; instead, his face was expressionless again. She was coming to understand that meant he disapproved. Since leaving home at seventeen, Belle had rarely been disapproved of. She hadn't missed the feeling it gave her.

"I do what well?" she asked, though she was pretty sure she didn't want to know.

"I'm sure you've had a lot of practice."

She crossed the short distance to the desk, put her palms on his blotter and leaned forward. "Practice at what?" she said in a deceptively quiet voice.

"Getting your way by batting your eyelashes and flashing those teeth. Tell me, Isabelle, if that doesn't work, do you always lean over and give us foolish men a view down the front of your shirt?"

Pointedly he lowered his gaze. Belle followed his direction and discovered that her overalls and shirt were loose enough to flash half the town with a choice view of her unadorned, white cotton brassiere. Belle straightened as heat rose up her chest, spread across her neck and settled in her cheeks.

"I didn't mean—"

"I'm sure you do it unconsciously."

"I do not!" Or did she? Belle wasn't so certain anymore. And she wasn't sure which was worse— consciously using her looks to get her way, or using them without even knowing she did it.

What she didn't like was being judged by a man who had no idea what she'd been through, or what she still had to go through before all was said and done.

Belle lashed out. "If a man's dumb enough to give me my way because I'm pretty, he deserves it."

"Maybe the man isn't the one who's dumb."

She stared at Klein. How could he know? Did everyone know? It wasn't as if her education, or lack of it, was a secret. But so far the tabloids hadn't shrieked that Isabelle Ash was a high school dropout.

"Y-you think I'm dumb?"

His eyes went shrewd, and Belle wanted to curse the neediness in her wavering voice. She lifted her chin, stared him straight in the eye. What did she care what some small-town sheriff thought of her?

Except she did. Much, much more than she ought to, though she couldn't say why.

"On the contrary, I think you're a lot smarter than anyone, including you yourself, gives you credit for. Who told you that you weren't?"

Your face is gonna get you out of here and save us all. There are hundreds of smart girls, but how many look like you do? Use what the good Lord gave you, Belle, and forget about school—

"Isabelle—?"

She blinked as Klein's voice overrode that of her mama.

"Why don't you use your brain instead of your body? It'll last longer."

He continued to judge when he had no idea what drove her. Even if she hadn't used all the money she'd made to help her family, even if she'd saved it and gone to college, a doctor couldn't earn near what she earned modeling. Pathetic but true. And the fact was, the fact had always been, she needed the money now, not ten years from now.

"Why don't you mind your own business," she snapped.

He shrugged, unfazed. "Just trying to help."

"Just trying to get me to quit and leave your precious town. But the contracts are signed. Both you and Pleasant Ridge are bought and paid for."

Anger flashed, turning his eyes from sky blue to midnight storm, but she was too mad to stop now.

"We'd better try to get along, because for the next two weeks, you and I are going to be closer than honey on bread."

CHAPTER THREE

"PEACHY," Klein muttered, as Isabelle Ash slammed the front door behind her.

Two weeks in the company of that woman? He wouldn't live that long. Or she wouldn't.

Beautiful girls rubbed him wrong. So why did this one call forth every protective instinct he had?

Isabelle could take care of herself. She'd shown that already. It was no skin off his nose if she chose to manipulate with her face, her body, that voice—as long as she didn't try it with him. He'd been manipulated that way before, and he would never let himself fall for such a lie again.

Once, he had loved a pretty woman, and he had believed she loved him. He'd learned then, and never forgotten since, that beauty of the flesh rarely went any deeper, and that beauty of the soul was far too difficult to find.

So why was he drawn to Isabelle? Why did he imagine he saw insecurity lurking in the depths of her cinnamon-brown eyes? Why did he hear vulnerability in that voice that shouted Yankee one moment, then whispered Mississippi the next?

Because he was a fool. Isabelle needed no one, nothing. She already had it all.

Klein had become a cop because helping people

was what he did best. His father had taken flight long before Klein knew what a father was; as a result, he still didn't know. His mother was a woman in need of a man—always. Pretty, flighty, not the brightest light, she could charm anyone with a wink and a smile, even her son.

At fifty-five, Luanne Chalmer Klein Delaney Seaver Johnson Duffy Krakopolis could still tempt the pants off any man, and often did. Thankfully she was mid-husband these days and had no use for her son. If number six went the way of numbers one through five, Klein would find his mother on the doorstep within a day of the next funeral, disappearance or divorce. And he'd be unable to refuse her.

Because as a child, the only time she'd loved him was between men. Klein had come to cherish when it was just the two of them, when she needed him and no one else.

As a teen he'd even done his best to get rid of the husbands and the men friends. He smiled as he remembered a few of his pranks. He was lucky they'd been decent guys, or that he'd grown mighty big by the time he was thirteen; otherwise, his life could have turned out completely different.

Older and wiser now, Klein knew his mother loved him as best she could and that it was silly to feel whole and important only when he was helping others. But knowing something intellectually and knowing it emotionally were two different things, and being able to change who you were at this late date was nigh onto impossible.

He'd been a caretaker practically from the day of

his birth, and he'd no doubt be one until the day
he died. Duty, first to his mother and later to his
country and those in need, had defined both his life
and himself—

His deputy chose that moment to slam into the
police station. Virgil did everything at top speed,
rarely thinking about the consequences, only concerned with what was wrong and how quickly he
could make it right again.

"Hello, Chief."

Virgil refused to call him Sheriff, Klein, Gabe or
anything but Chief. Klein had given up correcting
him.

Why bang his head against that particular wall?

"How's the cow?" he inquired.

"Hamburger."

"Thank you for that image. And the semi?"

"Dented." Virgil crossed the room and poured
himself a cup of coffee.

One thing the hyper old man didn't need was
coffee. But tell him that.

"Lucky it wasn't a car or we'd have more than
a cow fatality. You don't want to go head to head
with a cow when you're in a car."

"I know I wouldn't."

"Now, a deer's another matter entirely." Virgil
sipped long and hard from his foam cup. "Deer and
a car—car wins." He frowned. "Mostly."

Realizing that if he let this line of conversation
continue, he'd get a lecture on roadkill that he really didn't need, Klein changed the subject. "Is
there anything you forgot to tell me when you went
out on that call?"

Virgil scrunched his face and thought. Then he crunched the coffee cup in one heavily veined hand. "4-25."

He started for the jail, but Klein waved him back. "Never mind."

The deputy's shoulders sagged. "Again, Chief? If you're just gonna release 'em all, why should I even fill out the paperwork?"

"What paperwork?"

The old man scowled harder. "No? I must have been too excited about—"

"The suicide cow." Klein smirked.

"I don't think she tried to get hit." Virgil's voice was deadpan. "Do you? Should I write it up as a suicide?"

All amusement fled. No one got his jokes in this town. Except—

Klein stood. He needed another walk. "No. Just write the report the way you'd planned to, and forget about the 4-25. I took care of it."

"You always do," Virgil grumbled.

Klein ignored that. "Next time remember—arrest, charge, rights, paperwork. Okay?"

"I always remember. Just sometimes I remember things later than others."

"And someday we're gonna get sued for that."

"Everyone's sue-happy these days. There oughta be a law."

"There is. It includes arrest, charge, rights and paperwork."

Klein stepped outside. The day was fine—sunshine, not a trace of rain. The sky was so blue his eyes hurt to look at it. But if the sky had gone dark with a storm, his eyes would hurt from the beauty of that, as well. Because when a storm rolled over the mountains, the trees and the grass became so intensely green as to be surreal, and when lightning split the midnight sky and thunder rocked the farmhouse he'd bought just outside town, Klein would stand on his wraparound porch and partake of the Tennessee hills.

He might not be handsome, but that didn't mean he couldn't appreciate beauty and long for it. Perhaps he longed for beauty more because of the lack of beauty in himself, or the lack of beauty he'd discovered in the world at large. Klein had a soft spot for pretty things—bright colors and lights, fabric and flowers. His favorite pastime—heck, his only pastime—was redecorating his house. Lucky he was so big and scary. No one dared call him a sissy—to his face.

He walked down Longstreet Avenue, which would be Main Street in most other small towns. He knew; he'd lived in enough of them. As a boy he'd been dragged from town to town on the whim of his mother's man of the month. Then Klein had always been the biggest kid, the ugliest kid, forever the new kid.

But he had high hopes for Pleasant Ridge. He could grow to love this place. He could belong here in a way he'd never belonged anywhere else.

Each day he walked the streets, making his rounds on foot rather than in his car. During his years in law enforcement he'd discovered the personal touch worked better, no matter where you went. If he could say, *Joey Farquardt, quit throwin' stones at that garbage can or I'll tell your mama,* he got a far sight better response than if he had to say, *Hey you, kid, knock that off.*

He was a cop because he wanted to help; he needed to be needed. When he'd first left the marines, he'd taken a job with the Atlanta PD, figuring there'd be a whole passel of people who needed help there. What he'd discovered was that there were too many of them and not enough of him. He'd wound up feeling like a failure, becoming more depressed with every passing day.

So when he'd heard of the opening on the detective force in Savannah, he'd moved there. Smaller town, fewer problems, he'd thought, but still a big enough place to need him.

Wrong again.

Savannah had big-town problems as a result of more tourists than Klein ever cared to see again, not to mention the movie crews in and out of the city and surrounding area, filming the movie of the moment. With that many strangers, trouble was rampant. Once again Klein had felt he was fighting a battle that could not be won.

He'd made friends there—Livy Frasier, her mother, Rosie, and her son, Max, as well as her business partner, Kim Luchetti. He missed them, but in truth, he'd been on the outskirts of their busy lives—a guy they saw sometimes, even if he was a guy they liked.

By the time Klein moved to Pleasant Ridge, Livy had married Max's father, the bestselling horror novelist Garrett Stark, and she had another baby on the way.

Klein hadn't liked Stark at first—the guy *had* run off and not returned for nine years—but once Stark had come back he'd turned out to be all right. Klein had made sure of that before he'd left. Garrett Stark loved his wife and son more than Klein had believed him capable—

Yip. Yip. Yip.

Something tugged on his pants leg. Klein looked down to find Miss Dubray's Chihuahua, Tid Bit, growling viciously as it fought the battle of the trouser cuff. Some men might boot the pipsqueak into the next county. The dog *was* a menace. But Klein didn't have the heart. Instead, he paused in front of the Pleasant Ridge Civil War Museum and waited, as he did every day.

"T.B.? T.B.?" Miss Dubray skidded from the front door, frantically searching the street for her baby.

At least the thing wasn't wearing a lace bonnet today. That always gave Klein the creeps.

"Oh, hello, Sheriff. I should have known it was you by the tone of T.B.'s voice."

"Miss Dubray." He nodded politely, standing still while she disengaged T.B. from his cuff.

Once released, the miniature monster trotted back toward the museum, throwing a haughty glance over its shoulder and, Klein could swear, a smirk.

Considering his experiences with the Chihuahua, Klein wasn't sure what had prompted him to get a dog of his own—except a lifetime of loneliness. A dog's devotion had nothing to do with a master's charm, looks or bank account. Klein could use a little everlasting dog love in his life.

At home, Clint waited—calm, patient and huge—the perfect animal for a man like Gabe Klein. Perhaps he should bring Clint into town to meet T.B. Klein grinned at the image. He didn't think T.B. would be smirking anymore.

"My, my, what a nice smile." Miss Dubray observed. "I hardly ever see you smile."

He'd heard that often enough. He found little in this world to smile about. Law enforcement was funny that way.

"Did you hear, Sheriff? I'm designing a new display for the artifacts from Shiloh. You'll have to stop in next week and see what I've done."

Miss Dubray had a nice smile of her own, and she used it often. Even though her hair was still jet black, her skin lined but smooth and her figure pretty nice, too, she was seventy if she was a day. She'd never married—maybe she'd never wanted to—and she had more energy than her blasted dog. Which was lucky, since she owned and ran the museum all by herself.

Not that there was very much to do in the Civil War Museum, except dust and take money for tickets—the latter only if someone happened off the interstate for a night and slept at the Pleasant Ridge Hotel-Motel, which itself most likely dated from the War of Northern Aggression. But Miss Dubray had a fascination with the war that she felt never should have been lost.

Not only had her great-granddaddy left her this building on Longstreet Avenue, but he'd left her the artifacts he'd brought home from the war. Miss

Dubray made a small but adequate living with her museum, and she was doing what she loved.

That most of her artifacts were junk or worse held no weight with her. Kids liked to see the forearm bone of a Yankee, and the news-at-five from Chattanooga had once come and done a spot on the bloody sash of Nathan Bedford Forrest. Miss Dubray had not been amused when the news made mention of General Forrest's postwar activities. Just because they'd blabbed everything in *Forrest Gump* didn't make it acceptable to discuss the KKK in public. Down here, such embarrassments simply weren't verbalized.

Miss Dubray still stared at him expectantly. "I'll be sure and stop by next week," Klein promised. *Maybe I can find some chain-mail pants by then.*

Klein moved on down Longstreet Avenue. As a result of his conversation with the mayor, he peered at the business district and cataloged the empty storefronts. There *were* far too many. He'd never noticed before, but the main drag of Pleasant Ridge was looking a bit shabby. To him, the place had seemed quaint, homey. Now he knew better.

The schools did need work. Heck, they had one computer per building. These days, that was as bad as having one book per classroom. The floors needed fixing and there was asbestos in the ceiling tile. He didn't even want to think about the safety hazard in the outdated playground equipment at the elementary school or the prehistoric science lab at the high school. Perhaps a little progress wouldn't hurt. Nor would a lot of money.

Klein sighed. If he blew this deal and the town died, he'd have no one but himself to blame.

At the end of Longstreet Avenue he paused. A few hundred yards outside of town the avenue became Highway B and extended all the way to Knoxville. But near Pleasant Ridge, Highway B was a paved-over dirt road that skirted the mountains and curved past a lot of farms, his included. Klein could see the white roof of his house over the next incline, and coming down another slope, just past his place, ran a solitary figure.

He frowned. Who was out there alone, and why was this person running?

Klein lifted his walkie-talkie and let Virgil know where he was going. Then he set his feet on Highway B.

BELLE RAN until her heart rate rose to one hundred fifty beats per minute, then she ran some more. The first ten minutes were always the hardest, anyway.

After her argument with the sheriff, she'd returned to her apartment. Restless, she'd gone over and over her conversation with the man, trying to pinpoint what he'd said that had made her crazy. That comment about her being dumb? *Probably*. She couldn't recall any cracks about her weight, her talent or anything else personal. Just her mind.

When the wheel in her head that went round and round whenever she felt a lack of control—and oh, did she feel a lack of control around Gabriel Klein—kept spinning, she'd cursed, tossed off her clothes and rummaged through her bags for shorts, sports bra and T-shirt. From past experience, she knew she had to run and run until the madness went away.

She'd headed straight out of town so she wouldn't have to make chitchat with the populace. Running was serious business when she was in a mood like this.

She'd always been sensitive; the most offhand personal comment would haunt her for days. After having been called ''Big Belle'' for years, she ought to have acquired a thicker skin. Instead, losing weight seemed to have made her skin thinner, too.

Why was it that people felt it was all right to ask a thin person how much she weighed? To ask if she'd gained weight, lost weight, eaten for a year? Questions that they'd think twice about asking a heavy person they announced in the middle of a crowd to her, never realizing that could send her to the scale, and from there to a binge-and-purge cycle that might last for days.

She'd learned to control that cycle by jogging whenever the mad wheel began to spin. She'd come to crave the runner's high whenever she felt inadequate. Run long enough and you received an incredible head rush, a sense of well-being and power better than drugs, alcohol or sex. Or at least better than most sex she'd had. Not that she'd had very much.

Belle had jogged in cities all over the world. The change in scenery made for an interesting workout. She had to say, jogging outside of Pleasant Ridge was as appealing as jogging along the Seine and more peaceful than running through a foggy dawn in London.

Those mountains—they reminded her of home.

Belle shook her head and picked up the pace. No use mourning what she couldn't go back to. For the next little while, home was going to be Pleasant Ridge, Tennessee. Or rather, she'd live in Pleasant Ridge. Belle had learned long ago that home was where your loved ones slept, and hers were in Virginia.

When she was a good distance out, Belle glanced behind her and pulled a U-ie to the opposite side of the highway. She'd calmed down enough to really look at things now. As well as mountains and new grass, there were working farms and play farms—as her daddy always called those the rich folks bought on a lark, then fixed up and sold at a loss.

She wasn't sure what to make of the farm she approached now. The land hadn't been worked in a long while, and the outbuildings and the house weren't being fixed up, either—at least, on the outside. The whole place had a lonesome air, almost abandoned. But the curtains in the windows—there were so many the place had to have twenty rooms—the red, white and blue peonies marching along the sidewalk and the paper in the paper box nixed that theory.

The main building was huge—three stories, with a lived-in attic from the appearance of the highest window, which was also curtained. A wraparound porch sported rocking chairs at every corner—another indication the farmhouse had not been abandoned.

Belle swallowed against a sudden thickness in her throat. Her mama would love this house. Shoot, Belle was already half in love with it, and she had no need of such space when there was only her, and probably always would be.

She was so interested in the house that she didn't see the man on the other side of the road until he spoke.

"Like my place?"

Belle tripped over the toe of her running shoe and tumbled headfirst into the ditch. Lucky for her it was a grassy ditch. The only things skinned were her pride and her elbow.

She lay there for what seemed a long time, staring at the clouds and muttering every curse word her brothers had ever taught her, until Klein's head blotted out the sun. His eyes were the same shade of blue as the sky and as calm as the sea at midnight.

The observation annoyed her enough that she snapped, "What did you do—stroll over here? I might have killed myself."

"I could hear you cursing. No one with breath left to curse is seriously hurt."

Klein put one foot on the incline, leaned over and held out his hand. He was so tall he could reach her with that minute movement. For some reason, the thought calmed Belle more than her run had.

She placed her palm in his. He hauled her to her feet, straight on out of the ditch, then released her so abruptly she stumbled again. He caught her, steadied her—fascinated her.

Even though he must have walked out from town—a distance of several miles—he still appeared crisp and clean in his uniform. His ebony hair sparked blue and silver in the sun and his bronzed skin shone. He should be sweating, as she was. He should smell, as she probably did.

Belle took a deep breath. He did smell—terrific—a combination of sun and wind and grass. Or maybe that was just the sun and wind and grass—although those things had never smelled quite so good before. She swayed.

"You twist something?" he barked. "Knee, ankle, arm?"

She shook her head. "Why?"

"Tripping, stumbling, falling—you don't seem the type."

Belle narrowed her eyes. "What type do I seem?"

"The smooth type. I doubt you got where you are today by tripping down the runway or stumbling through your screen test."

True enough. She lifted one shoulder, then lowered it again. Her T-shirt stuck to her chest. *Lovely.* "I didn't do a screen test."

"No? Thought that was standard."

"They came after *me* for this show. It was mine before anyone else was even cast. The director and I have a rapport. The producers knew what they wanted."

"*Baywatch* comes to Mayberry," he grumbled.

The sweat trickling down Belle's spine turned cold. "Is that what they told you?"

"Isn't that what it is?"

Good Lord, she hoped not. But it wouldn't be the first time people in the business had lied to get her to do what they wanted.

Belle patted her chest, trying to soak up some of the sweat and get rid of the annoying trickles. "I was told *Mayberry RFD* meets *Picket Fences*. We tap the good memories for the senior set and the kids who watch a lot of *Nick at Night* with the Mayberry angle, and we gain the mid-age group with the *Picket Fences* aspect. That show was brilliant—funny and dramatic. Didn't you watch it?"

Klein stared across the road at the big, white house and not at her. "I don't watch much television."

"No VSC, no SI, no TV. What *do* you do for fun, Klein?"

"I don't do fun."

"I'll just bet you don't."

He snorted, and she could have sworn it was a laugh, but when she sharpened her gaze on his face, there was no humor to be seen. How did he *do* that?

Belle was very good at emotion—both real and pretend. What she couldn't get a handle on was how to remain stoic in the face of disaster. She needed to learn, and she wasn't too proud to beg.

"Listen, Klein, I'd like your help. I know we didn't start off on the right foot, but could we try again? Maybe be friends?"

Friends? Had she actually said that? She couldn't recall meeting a less friendly man.

"Friends?" he murmured, and looked at her at last.

The idea of friendship must seem as outlandish to him as it did to her. But he also appeared intrigued, which only made her wary.

Belle knew what she wanted from him, but what did Klein want from her? With most men, she'd know. With Klein, she might never be sure.

CHAPTER FOUR

"YOU SAID you weren't hurt."

"I'm not."

Klein took a step closer and reached for her arm. "Then, what's this?"

He turned her elbow, big hands gentle and sure. Running down Belle's forearm was a bright-red trickle of blood.

"Hmm," she said, and raised her gaze to his.

He was watching her face in that way he had that made her think he was trying to see inside her. Belle's youngest brother looked just that way at machinery—large and small—right before he took it apart to discover what made it tick.

"Hmm," he repeated. "Funny, that's just what I thought."

She smiled, and amazingly, he smiled back. Perhaps their being friends wasn't such a foolish, far-fetched idea after all.

But as quickly as he'd smiled at her, he stopped. As quickly as he'd reached for her arm, he dropped it. As quickly as he'd moved toward her, he turned away.

"You'd better clean that out and put a bandage on it before you get blood all over your designer sneakers."

Belle's own smile faded. "Thank you for the advice, but I could figure that out for myself. And I have other sneakers."

"I'll just bet you do."

Why did that sound like an insult?

"Come on," he grumbled, and headed for the white farmhouse on the opposite side of the road.

Belle hesitated. "Come where?"

He stopped, turned and stared at her as if she were dim. "*My* place." He jabbed a thumb at the farmhouse. "Remember?"

Suddenly she heard clearly what he'd said before she fell into the ditch. "Oh! So this is yours?"

His nod was slow and deliberate. Though she really should turn up her nose and jog on back to Pleasant Ridge, the idea of dripping blood behind her like Hansel and Gretel's trail of bread crumbs held very little appeal. Her elbow was starting to sting, and in truth, she really wanted to see the inside of that house.

Belle hurried across the road and joined him at the gate. There was actually a white picket fence around the yard. It could use painting, perhaps not white this time but sky blue or yellow, with ivy, stenciled or real, winding up every third picket.

Lost in her dream decorating, Belle didn't realize at first that Klein hesitated outside the fence. She glanced at him just as he unloaded his pistol and tucked the clip into one pocket.

She frowned. Did he have children? That would make him married, something she hadn't been told. The disappointment that flowed through her should not be so strong. Shouldn't be, but was.

Her confusion deepened when he drew a large bandanna out of another pocket and wrapped the gun in the cheery red material. Then he unlatched the gate and stepped into the yard.

Belle opened her mouth to ask what on earth he was doing, but before she could, the air was filled with the braying bark of a hound dog.

Expecting to see it tear around the side of the house toward them, ears flapping madly, huge feet pattering wildly, tongue lolling, jowls dripping, Belle was bewildered when no dog appeared.

"Quiet, Clint," Klein ordered, and the braying stopped.

"Where is he?"

"On the porch."

Belle peered at the house, and sure enough, a hound dog lay at the top of the porch steps, head on his paws as he calmly observed them with sad, sad eyes.

"He isn't going to greet you properly? Run down here, knock you over, drool on you a little?"

"Knock *me* over?" Klein slid a glance her way. "I don't think so."

Belle let her gaze wander over Klein. "I see your point."

Klein grunted and stalked toward the house, presenting her with his back—and a very nice back it was. The uniform hugged him in all the right places. He certainly was a big man. When had she become attracted to tall, strong, broad, undoubtedly hard bodies like his? She couldn't quite recall when she hadn't been.

The dog kept his eyes on the bandanna and not

on Klein. As soon as Klein's foot hit the bottom step, the animal leaped up and ran to hide behind the nearest rocking chair, where he peeked around the corner, trembling.

Klein sighed. "Relax, Clint. It's not loaded."

Confused, charmed, amazed, Belle hung back and watched as Gabe Klein hid his bandanna-shrouded gun in an old milk bucket next to the front door, then went down on one knee and beckoned to the dog.

Clint crept out from behind the chair and meandered over to Klein. Belle's lips twitched. What was that saying about people resembling their dogs? These two were quite a pair—sad eyes, relaxed manner, steady and sure, trustworthy.

Klein rubbed behind the dog's ears, and the animal lifted his nose and laid his cheek along Klein's. Closing his eyes, Clint sighed. Belle's heart did a slow roll. She knew love when she saw it.

After a single quiet moment, Klein stood. "Take off, boy," he ordered. With a dubious glance in Belle's direction, the dog wandered over to the cool shade beneath the eaves, circled once and collapsed in a heap of loose skin and russet fur.

Belle looked at Klein. Eyes wary, he shrugged.

"Let me guess," Belle said. "He's gun-shy."

"Big-time."

Her father and brothers had a pack of dogs for hunting. She'd been around them all her life. "You know, some dogs have to be eased into hunting, not forced."

"Really? I'll have to remember that the next time

I take a puppy out and blast my shotgun over his head until he cries and hides under the truck.''

Belle frowned. She couldn't imagine Klein doing any such thing. But, then how——?

Klein opened the front door, and Belle forgot about the dog for a moment. "You don't lock your door?"

Klein, halfway in and halfway out of the house, paused. ''Not in Pleasant Ridge, Ms. Ash. That would be an offense against myself. Besides, Clint's here all day.''

"Oh, I bet he's a lot of help. They pull a gun— he hides behind the rocking chair.''

Klein winced, then glanced at Clint as if he expected the dog to understand. Unable to help herself, Belle looked that way, too, and was immediately contrite when she met the sad, sad eyes of the hound dog. He seemed to have understood her words and been crushed by them.

Foolishness. The dog didn't understand her. *All* hound dogs appeared sad *all* the time. Sad was what they did best.

"Lesson number one." Klein held up a finger. ''Any thief who knows his business knows it doesn't pay to carry a gun on a job like this. You get a lot more years if you're caught with a weapon. And any burglar worth his salt would pass on by a house with a braying hound dog and rob the one without. It's not worth the noise or the trouble. Besides—'' he swept his arm out in a ''be my guest'' gesture ''—I have nothing worth stealing.''

Belle raised her eyebrows as she entered the cool, dark interior of his home. He was right. There was very little inside worth stealing. No stereo, no VCR, no television, not even a CD player graced the living room, and there was no computer in sight. Maybe he kept his electronics upstairs.

But she had to say, the lack of ultramodern conveniences did not detract from the beauty of the place. Though the outside looked untidy, the inside was fresh, clean and remodeled.

The walls of the living room were a muted white, the furniture navy-blue leather, the coffee tables chrome and glass. They definitely had not come with the house.

The entryway had been painted to resemble fading redbrick. She reached out and touched the walls. They were even rough like brick. That must have taken hours—she followed the design all the way up along the curving oak banister to the second level—make that *days* to accomplish.

Unaware that Belle stood in the hall with her mouth hanging open, Klein strode ahead of her toward the back of the house. The place was quiet; it felt deserted.

"You live alone?" she called.

"Nope." Klein kept on walking. "I live with Clint."

Relief washed over her. No wife, no girlfriend, no kids—just the gun-shy hound dog and the sad-eyed man. Belle told herself her relief merely stemmed from knowing that a wife or a girlfriend, even kids, would not be happy to let Gabe Klein spend two weeks in her company, but deep down she knew better. Belle hurried to keep up with him, glancing into rooms along the way.

The kitchen had a Formica table, which might have been left from older days, except that the entire room had been remodeled like a fifties diner. Across the hall was a library—all four walls covered with black chrome bookcases filled with books. In the center sat a giant bean bag chair and a funky reading lamp.

She'd never seen so many books together outside of a public library. Had Klein read them all? The possibility only made her feel more inadequate.

Belle glanced away from the books just as Klein disappeared through a door at the end of the hall. She hurried after him, nearly slamming into his back when she came through the door. Leaning over a sink, he peered into the medicine cabinet behind the mirror, then glanced over his shoulder.

"Take a seat."

Belle looked around. They stood together in a half bath, and the only seat was one she didn't plan to take with Klein in the room.

"I'll stand."

He shrugged, and the movement of his wide shoulders so close to her nose made Belle realize how small the room was. She stepped away, and her back bumped the door casing. The place just wasn't made for a man of his size and anyone else, let alone a woman who might be slim but had never been small.

"Suit yourself." He returned his attention to the medicine cabinet and snatched out a white tube. "The only antiseptic I've got is going to sting."

"I'll live."

He muttered something she couldn't quite catch,

but she didn't ask him to repeat himself. She had an idea that anything he muttered she really didn't want to hear.

"Scoot up on this." He patted the smooth expanse of ceramic around the sink.

Avocado green and gold, this room obviously had not been visited by the remodeling fairy—unless of course she had a penchant for seventies chic. Belle really couldn't see anyone purposely decorating a room with avocado velvet wallpaper. She shuddered.

Klein's sharp blue eyes pinned her. "Cold?"

"No."

She didn't want to insult him, just in case he planned on leaving the room like this, so she didn't elaborate. Inching past his large body to get to the chipped gold vanity, she was unable to prevent her breasts from brushing his wide chest. Belle gritted her teeth to keep another shudder, of a completely different type, from racking her body. Damn, this room really was too small for the two of them. She hiked her butt onto the sink's edge and lifted her gaze, to find him scowling at her again.

"What?" she growled. She had *not* done that on purpose, even if she had enjoyed it.

He shook his head and reached for a washcloth on the towel rack to her right. The movement brought his chest close to her face. For an instant she imagined what it would be like to have him in the same position, minus the sheriff's shirt. It was a very nice image.

What had gotten into her? She was not the type of woman who indulged in sexual fantasies about strangers. She certainly didn't indulge in sex of any kind—real or imagined—with men she had to work with. That made for very bad business and a tackier reputation than the gossips had already given her.

Bummer, because Belle had a feeling Klein might be worth all the trouble he would cause. She expelled a breath on an irritated sigh, and he leaped away from her as if she'd slapped him. The scowl still in place, he jabbed the cloth at her.

"Here. Wash it off first."

She did as he ordered, fumbling a bit since the scrape was on her right elbow and she was right-handed. Her left hand had never been good for much more than balance.

Additional muttering erupted from Klein, and he snatched the cloth away. Grabbing her wrist, he twisted her arm so he could do what she'd been playing at.

Belle braced herself for the onslaught, but instead of scrubbing the cloth over her wound, he dabbed and pressed, patient, gentle and sure, until the blood had disappeared.

When he reached for the antiseptic, then squeezed a dollop onto the callused tip of one finger, she tensed.

"Why Clint?" she blurted, hoping that if she talked about the dog, she'd forget about that long, elegant finger smoothing over her quivering, injured skin.

He glanced up, and she could have sworn he blushed, but it was hard to tell in the dim light of the room. He grasped her wrist, squinted at her arm. "He doesn't seem like a Clint to you?"

Belle resisted his ministrations until he looked at her once more. "I'd really like to know."

Their gazes warred, then he shrugged and tugged on her arm again. This time she let him twist her until she was positioned like half a pretzel.

"Somebody dumped him." He dabbed the antiseptic on her raw elbow. Belle hissed and he stopped. "Sorry."

She tried to blow on the sting as her mama always had, but couldn't reach the affected area. Klein leaned over and did it for her. The sting faded as goose bumps rose across her skin, and a buzz started low and deep in her belly. What *was* it about this man that made her feel like a woman and behave like a hormone-crazed teenager?

She pulled on her arm, then inched away from his mouth before she gave in to the temptation to press her own to his. "I'm okay." She sounded hoarse, with a trace of the twang she'd worked so hard to lose, and not okay at all. Belle cleared her throat. "Go on."

That was better, crisp and clear, down to business. No trace of an accent, no more of that lingerie-model huskiness.

Seemingly unaffected by the intimacy of their situation and the too-close quarters of the room, Klein went on with the first aid and his story. "Virgil brought him in. Poor thing was shaking and staring at Virgil's gun like it was going to bite him. I was new here, had this big place, and I always wanted a dog."

"So you took him home."

"Someone had to."

That single sentence said more about Klein than any FBI profile. He'd adopted a gun-shy hound dog because he thought someone had to—probably because he knew what would happen to the dog if no one did. He wrapped his gun in a bandanna and hid it in a milk pail to soothe a poor beast's fear.

And she'd accused him of wrecking the animal. Belle—who ought to know better than to judge folks based on how they appeared. She'd met enough people who saw Blond, Busty Model and assumed brain dead followed. Just because Klein looked big and strong and macho didn't mean that he was a puppy-kicking son of a bitch.

"So, why Clint?"

He glanced up from his frowning perusal of the bandage box. Belle reached over and plucked out two. "This should do it."

Slow and sure, he accepted the offering and picked at the ends to open them. For such a large man he had nimble fingers, and he was able to pull the annoying tabs on the wrappers much more easily than Belle ever could have. His dexterity made her wonder just how talented he would be with other tasks—like unbuttoning buttons, unzipping zippers, unsnapping snaps.

Her hormones were getting out of hand here, so she offered her arm before he could reach for her again. As he positioned the bandages over her scrape, she stared at the top of his shorn head and resisted the urge to run her free hand over the dark stubble. She'd never seen such short hair. Would it be soft like the hair on his chest, or bristly like the hair on his chin the morning after?

"You remember *The Beverly Hillbillies,* don't you?" He glanced up, eyebrows drawn together.

Belle blinked, hoping her lustful thoughts did not show on her face.

"Maybe you're too young," he said.

She snorted her opinion of that. He returned his attention to her arm, but not before she caught the glimmer of a beautiful smile. Belle never would have considered that she of all people would lust after someone on the basis of appearance alone. It was embarrassing.

"The hound dog was named Duke," he continued.

"I remember. But he wasn't gun-shy."

"No. He was movement challenged. Did you ever see that dog move any faster than slow motion in reverse?"

Belle searched her memory. "Not that I recall. I don't see how that applies to Clint, though."

"It doesn't. But when I got him I thought he could use a tough-guy name. Couldn't hurt, right? So I came up with Duke, which made me think of John Wayne, and then—"

"Clint Eastwood!"

"Exactly." He patted her bandaged arm as if she were a child, and stepped back.

"Why didn't you name him Dirty Harry? He'd be tough enough then."

"No self-respecting, small-town law enforcement officer would own a dog named Dirty Harry. That would give folks the wrong idea."

"'Go ahead, make my day'?"

"Yeah. We frown on that kind of attitude in tiny-town Tennessee."

"Is that lesson number two?"

He shrugged. "Sure."

"Does that mean you're going to help me?"

His warm blue eyes cooled. "Did I ever have any choice?"

Belle stifled a sigh. "I want you to *want* to help me."

"We don't always get what we want, Ms. Ash."

"We're back to 'Ms. Ash'? I thought you were going to call me Isabelle."

"That name doesn't fit you."

She blinked. She'd always thought the same thing. "Uh, well, my family calls me Belle."

As had everyone else who "knew her when." Though she, too, thought of herself as Belle, she'd never liked the nickname, especially when *big* preceded it, as it so often had.

He shook his head. "You're not a Belle, either."

Their eyes met, and she felt a camaraderie with Klein she couldn't recall having felt with anyone else. What was his name? *Gabriel.* He certainly didn't seem like an angel. "Klein" fit him better. Strong, succinct, with a soft center. Yes, Klein was the perfect name for Klein.

They were still staring into each other's eyes, and suddenly the moment became something more than a mere look. The air seemed difficult to breathe—hot, almost steamy.

She was being silly. She might be attracted to him, but he considered her an annoyance, nothing more. Belle had spent most of her life as an annoy-

ance to virtually all the men she cared about. First
to her three younger brothers, who were mortified
to have a sister like her, then to any boy she might
have a crush on. Big Belle liking him was an em-
barrassment to any teenaged boy, as if her affection
somehow made him less instead of more.

Of course, things were different now, but Belle
had never forgotten how it felt to be rejected, and
she didn't ever want to be again. Since Klein appeared to care for brains more than beauty and he
thought she was a dim decoration, not the brightest
light on the Christmas tree, she would not make a
fool of herself by believing a look was anything
more than a look.

Belle jumped down from the sink just as Klein
pushed away from the wall. She bumped into him.
He stumbled back, hands coming up to catch her
and clasping her elbows.

"Ouch!" she squeaked as his palm slapped
against her scraped, though bandaged, skin.

Immediately his hold gentled, but he didn't let
her go. Her nose practically pressed to the firm wall
of his chest, she raised her head to find him staring
at her with his familiar scowl.

"Izzy," he muttered.

"Huh?"

"You look like an Izzy."

Klein's mellow Georgia drawl caused a resurgence of goose bumps on her skin. When his gaze
lowered to her mouth, she caught her breath.

"You can call me Izzy if you like," she whispered.

Something flickered in his eyes, then was gone

so fast she couldn't identify the emotion. He released her with a little shove, then slipped from the bathroom far too quickly for a man of his size.

Belle stared at the ugly-as-sin velvet wallpaper while the pain of rejection washed over her. A long time might have gone by since a man had turned away, but the feelings were as familiar as her favorite shade of lip gloss. One touch had made her forget all her good intentions.

Tears pricked her eyes, but she refused to let them fall. She had learned the hard way that showing people they'd hurt her only made them hurt her all the more.

WHAT IN HELL had come over him?

Klein stalked down the hall and out the front door, putting as much distance as he could between Isabelle and him. He would not, *could not,* think of her as Izzy. In that direction lay far too much danger.

Because Izzy was the name of the tousled, bleeding, vulnerable woman in his bathroom, the woman he'd rescued, the one who'd needed him. For Izzy he'd felt far too strong a liking, far too intense a physical longing.

No. Better to think of her as Isabelle, as she'd asked. Isabelle, he could resist. Isabelle, he could work with and not want.

Klein always got into trouble when he thought a woman needed him.

He sank down on the top porch step, and Clint heaved himself to his feet with a groan. The dog's youthful body housed an ancient soul.

Clint padded the short distance across the porch and laid his snout on Klein's shoulder. His sigh of commiseration blew bubbles of drool into Klein's ear, which was the most action Klein had seen since long before moving to Pleasant Ridge.

He sat up straighter at the thought. *That* was why he'd responded to Isabelle as he had, not because he'd lost his ever-lovin' mind.

Clint lifted his head an instant before a soft footfall announced her arrival. Klein didn't bother to turn around. He would let her set the tone of the conversation.

"Will you help me?"

Klein sighed. What had he expected? Hot sex and eternal devotion? *Right.* She wanted something from him; she wasn't going to rest until she got it.

She must have sensed he was attracted to her, even though he'd thought he'd done a pretty good job of hiding it. Hell, he'd had years of practice. But some women could smell a man's interest a mile away. His mother was one of them. Obviously Isabelle was another.

"I already said that I'd help you."

"Because you have to."

"Doing that won't make me want to."

"Doing what?"

She sounded genuinely confused, so he turned and looked at her. His movement made Clint meander back to his cool corner, where he collapsed with a groan that might rival Virgil's on a chilly morning in December.

Isabelle's face appeared as uncertain as her voice. Well, she was an actress, or so she said.

"Come now, Ms. Ash. The room *was* small, and your breasts are..." He let his gaze wander over them. *Magnificent,* he thought. What he said was "Big."

She gasped.

"But how many times did you have to brush them against me?"

Her mouth opened and closed, then opened again. "You think I—I—"

"Didn't you?"

"No! Yuck! How disgusting. I'd never—"

"As I said before, you don't need to do that. In fact, you'd be better off to save it for someone who cares—like your boyfriend."

"I don't have a boyfriend."

He found that hard to believe. Years of answering domestic dispute calls had taught him that women like Isabelle usually had big, bad-ass boyfriends ready to crush to a pulp anyone who looked at them crosswise.

"Whatever." He shrugged as if the news about no boyfriend hadn't made his heart beat a little faster. "Save it. I have no choice but to help you."

He saw once more a hint of vulnerability in her eyes, and he could have sworn her lip trembled. He felt like a jerk. Maybe because he was. But he'd been played for a fool too many times before, and he couldn't bear to be played for one again.

"Some woman really did a number on you, didn't she."

His gaze shot to hers. Any trace of vulnerability was gone; shrewd intelligence and a hint of sympathy had replaced it. He didn't need anyone to feel sorry for him, least of all someone like her.

He stood and moved closer, crowding into her space, forcing her to tilt her head up to see him, using his body to intimidate as she'd used hers to ensnare. He had to give her credit—she refused to retreat; she did not glance away.

"What the hell," he growled. "It's no skin off my nose if I teach you everything I know."

And maybe, just maybe, if he taught her about the people and the place as well as the job, she'd fall in love with Pleasant Ridge, too. Maybe she'd leave it, and him, alone.

But as he gazed into her determined brown eyes, Gabe Klein knew such a hope was as much a fantasy as every other hope he'd ever had.

CHAPTER FIVE

SHE'D HAD MORE GRACIOUS offers. But since Klein's grudging acquiescence was most likely the best she was going to get, Belle snapped it up before he could change his mind.

"Terrific."

Stepping away from his intimidating height and breadth, she gave him a dazzling smile to show she held no hard feelings over his insulting belief that she'd been using her body to get what she wanted. Not that she didn't secretly harbor them—but she knew better than to let such feelings show. Pissy women did not get far in a man's world.

She wasn't so slow that she didn't notice Klein had avoided her question about women by changing the subject to the one she wanted to hear. Some woman *had* done a number on him, and Belle was getting to pay the price.

She dodged around Klein's exceptional body and skipped down the porch steps, turning at the bottom to look up at him. He studied her with the usual scowl. "What time should I meet you tomorrow? And where?"

His eyes narrowed, and she had a suspicion he was going to tell her where to go, right now, instead. But he closed his eyes, sighed, then opened them again.

"Six o'clock in front of the station."

"Six o'clock in the morning?"

He smirked. "Problem?"

"No." She'd always been an early riser. Her mama would have had it no other way. "I'll just have to go for my run at night instead of in the morning."

"You run at six a.m.?"

"Someone has to."

He didn't crack a smile. "No, no one has to. You don't need to beat yourself up jogging. Why don't you let it slide while you're here?"

Just the thought of letting her exercise program slide was enough to make her edgy.

"Do you let your weight lifting program slide?" she snapped.

"What program?"

"Don't tell me you got muscles like those riding in a cop car."

"Okay, I won't tell you."

Belle frowned. "Seriously. You have to lift weights."

"No one ever told me that rule. Is it in the life handbook?"

"Ha-ha. Explain to me how you stay in that kind of shape if you don't lift weights. You don't look like a runner."

"I never run when I can walk. Never stand when I can sit. And I never, ever lift something as foolish as a barbell. What's the point?"

"Muscles? Cardiovascular health? Ability to run down a suspect if the need arises?"

"I can count on one hand the number of times I've had to chase anyone."

"I suppose you just shout 'Halt!' and they do."

He shrugged. "Pretty much. The gun does help." His probing eyes met hers. "Didn't anyone ever tell you that walking is as good for the heart as running? And it's a lot easier on the knees."

Someone *had* told her that; she just didn't believe it. How could strolling possibly be as worthwhile as pounding the pavement? But as she let her gaze wander over Klein, for the first time she wondered.

"Okay, maybe you don't lift weights, but you must lift something."

"Yeah, doughnuts to my mouth."

He had to be kidding, yet his face was as deadpan as his voice.

"You'll see tomorrow," he continued. "Six a.m. in front of the station. I'll bring the doughnuts."

With that parting comment, he whistled to Clint, nodded to Belle and disappeared inside.

Belle strolled to the road, glanced back at the house, considered the doughnuts and began to jog toward Pleasant Ridge.

She slept well that night, her window open, a pleasant mountain breeze blowing across her bed, across her. A long time had passed since she'd been able to sleep beneath an open window. She hadn't realized she'd missed it.

When her travel alarm went off at five-thirty, the sky was still dark, though the eastern horizon glowed a lighter shade of blue behind the indigo hills. She sat on her bed, watching the sky and the mountains as the cool dawn air ruffled her hair. If not for the dreams of Gabe Klein still tangled in her brain, she would say she'd found the greatest peace she'd known since leaving home.

Unfortunately, those images of Klein *were* disturbing. She'd slept well, but she'd slept with him. Her brothers would say she needed to get laid, preferably by Klein, and then all the fantasies would go away. They'd no doubt be right. Thus far in her life, Belle had never found real sex as enthralling as the illusion.

She headed into her tiny bathroom and stepped beneath the tepid, trickling shower spray. The apartment felt more like home every day. Little things like lack of water pressure took her right back to the foothills of Virginia. Those memories made her feel like a kid again. Too bad her youth was not something she cared to recall. In those days she had been uncertain, off center, alone.

Alone. That could explain her unreasonably strong attraction to a man she should not be attracted to. She was lonely. Nothing more, nothing less, nothing she had not lived with all her life.

She could not sleep with Klein. He already thought she was a dim-brained tramp. She wasn't going to prove him right, no matter how much she might want to touch the chest he kept hidden beneath the dirt-brown uniform and the badge.

Twenty minutes later, still-damp hair slicked into a ponytail and face devoid of makeup, Belle stood in front of a dark and desolate police station. The morning air was already heating up, despite the fact that the sun had not yet broken above the mountains.

She'd considered wearing shorts and a tank top to offset the coming spring day but had opted, instead, for capri-length khaki trousers and an oversize white T-shirt. The less attention she drew to herself the better. She was nervous enough already, without having people point and stare at her all day. Even though her presence in Pleasant Ridge was supposed to be a secret for the time being, she knew better than to count on that.

Expecting Klein to arrive in a squad car or maybe even a pickup truck, she didn't at first notice the solitary figure ambling in from Highway B. Once she did, she just watched Klein move.

He walked the way he did everything else—slow, sure, determined. The man was like the mountains at his back. Did anything ever move him to anger, to joy, to passion?

"'Morning," he said as he crossed the deserted street.

Annoyed at her inability to keep her mind off things it had no business thinking about, Belle blurted, "Where're the damn doughnuts?"

He laughed, the sound loud in the still of the morning, but comforting just the same. His laugh, too, was like him—strong and deep, uncommon— and she found herself smiling in response. Maybe today wouldn't be so bad after all.

"Lesson number three." Klein pointed down the street. "To know the job, you have to know the people. Watch Pleasant Ridge wake up."

Lights sparked against the mountain backdrop, like stars coming awake in the sky.

"Lucinda Jones," Klein murmured as he pointed to the bakery. "Her husband died when she was forty, and she never remarried. Her kids scattered, and she's devoted herself to the business. It's been standing there since Pleasant Ridge was little more than four houses and a general store. There's been a Jones baking in that kitchen for the better part of two centuries."

The back of Belle's neck prickled. Imagine—the same family doing the same thing for two hundred years.

"If none of her kids come back and take over, she'll be the last," Klein said. "And that'll be a shame."

Belle nodded in agreement just as her stomach growled, protesting her supper choice the night before—a can of tuna eaten in front of the TV during the six o'clock news, before she spent the rest of the evening making notes about her first day in Pleasant Ridge.

She glanced at Klein to see if he'd heard, but he still stared at the lights of the bakery. "Thursday is cherry turnover day. My favorite."

"No doughnuts?"

"You'll learn, Ms. Ash—"

"Isabelle," she said automatically, then winced at the memory of the last time they'd had this conversation. Too close in too small a room; gently touching; secretly yearning; his heat and his scent surrounding her, enticing her. She didn't want to remember his deep voice calling her Izzy. She'd already remembered it all night long.

"Isabelle—"

He lowered his head, a gesture that made her think of lords and ladies, courtly manners, times long past, then continued as if she had just invited him to call her Isabelle for the very first time. Perhaps he didn't even recollect what still haunted her.

"You'll learn that being a cop in Pleasant Ridge is a whole lot different from being a cop anywhere else. Right down to the doughnuts."

"Is that why you're here?" she asked. "Because it's different?"

He shot her an unreadable glance. "What does it matter why I'm here?"

"I need to know why a man like you, a man with your background, your training, would give it all up and come here."

"Why do you need to know that?"

"It goes to character."

"Mine?"

"And mine. For the show."

"I see." He rocked back on his heels, but he didn't answer.

Belle stifled the urge to sigh or snarl. She had a feeling she would be dragging information out of this man for the next few weeks; therefore, she'd better learn how to do it without annoying him, regardless of how much he annoyed her.

"So, why *did* you give it all up and come here?"

"Give what up?"

Aargh! Belle took a deep breath, let it out slowly. Sometimes that helped.

"The excitement, the danger, the opportunities for advancement?"

He shook his head. "The violence, the drugs, the kids with guns. A never-ending wave of people I couldn't help."

Any lingering sense of annoyance fled as understanding dawned on her like the sun bursting over the far mountains. Klein—bless him—had just handed Belle the perfect motivation for her character to come to a little town in Tennessee.

He was already walking down Longstreet Avenue without her. Belle hurried to catch up. "Do you think you can help people here?"

"Hope so. This is the end of the line for me."

"End of the line? What does that mean?"

"If I can't find a reason here, I'm not going to find one."

"A reason for what?"

"Being me."

Belle stopped; Klein kept right on walking.

"Wait!" she called. He paused, turned. "I don't understand."

"Never mind. I get maudlin when I'm hungry."

Maudlin? What small-town sheriff used the word *maudlin* in conversation? What *man* used it? A man like Klein, who was no doubt better educated than anyone Belle had ever met.

Belle studied Klein's profile, wondering how much he would tell her about himself, today or any other day. Before she could come to a conclusion, irate barking began behind the door of the building they stood in front of. Klein mumbled what sounded like a curse and walked more quickly than she'd ever seen him walk. Belle glanced up to read the sign, just as a light came on upstairs.

Civil War Museum. Well, that sounded interesting. She'd have to check out the place later.

Headlights blazing, a truck roared into town, then parked in front of the grocery store. Belle caught up to Klein just as he began to talk, as if he hadn't even noticed she was no longer at his side.

"Jesse Wright, son of Joseph Wright—"

Belle's gaze skidded over the Wright Grocery Store sign and back to Klein's pensive face.

"Jesse would like to move to the big city, as would most of the young people here, but he doesn't have the money for college or the training for any other job except the one he has—driving the truck to Knoxville and bringing back produce. His father did it before him and his father before him."

"And before that?"

Klein slid a glance her way. "Before that, they used a horse and wagon. But the son brought the supplies and the father ran the store."

"I'm beginning to see a pattern here."

"I thought you might."

"What if there's a daughter but no son?"

Another truck pulled out of the alleyway next to the newspaper office and headed out of town. "Cassidy Tyler owns and operates the *Pleasant Ridge Gazette*. Cass is the daughter you asked about. Runs the paper mostly on her own now. The circulation in this neck of the woods isn't big enough to warrant a publisher *and* a truck driver. Her father started the *Gazette* in 1984. She's a newcomer."

"Nearly twenty years here and she's a newcomer?"

"She wasn't born here." He spread his hands. "Newcomer."

"Will her children be considered 'from here'?"

"Of course. Although I wouldn't hold my breath waiting for Cass to have any children. She wants more than Pleasant Ridge. Always has. A lot of folks want out." His gaze drifted to the mountains once more. "And then there're some folks who just want in."

Like you, she thought.

"What did Pleasant Ridge do for news before 1984?"

"Picked it up at the back fence like any self-respecting small town. Gossip has always moved much faster than any printing press."

"Don't I know it," Belle murmured. Gossip moved faster in large towns, too, and in the entertainment industry even faster.

"Been the subject of nasty gossip, have you, Isabelle?"

She shrugged, not willing to elaborate on her past experiences with the press. She'd learned to keep her mouth shut about anything she didn't want to see splashed across the front page of every smut rag in the country.

"There was a monthly newspaper," Klein went on. "Owner passed on. No son or daughter, so Tyler bought the building, then began publishing a weekly. Most folks didn't think it was necessary. They'd been doing without a weekly paper for centuries. But Tyler came from a family of newspapermen and he knew what he was doing. Took a while, but he won 'em over. Now I don't think there's a house in town or a farm outside that doesn't get the *Gazette*."

They continued to walk the streets of Pleasant Ridge. There weren't all that many. Belle learned the names of the business owners; the troublemakers—there weren't all that many of those, either; any folks who might need more help than most.

"You make rounds like this every day?" she asked as they headed down Longstreet Avenue once more.

He gave an affirmative grunt. "Morning, noon and night."

"Seriously? And your deputy?"

"Uses the squad car."

"Why don't you?"

"Because I'm not older than dirt."

"True."

Belle waited for a serious answer to her question. Eventually, after they'd walked past several empty storefronts, he answered. Perhaps she was making progress.

"The only way to hear the gossip is to talk to the people, and that's pretty hard to do if I'm in a car passing by."

"You don't strike me as much of a gossip-monger."

"Gossip is how I find out what kind of trouble is brewing. There's usually some truth in all the hype. If I hear that Betty Jo Trumpen is sporting a black eye from running into the door..." He rolled his eyes.

"You know you'd better have a talk with Mr. Trumpen."

"Damn straight," he growled.

Belle smiled. "And I bet one talk is all it takes, too."

He grunted. "With guys like that, not hardly."

His shoulders slumped a bit, and Belle was reminded of Clint's droopy demeanor. She wanted to cheer Klein up, make him stop thinking of guys like Trumpen who picked on those who wouldn't or couldn't pick back.

"Hey," she said brightly, pointing to the front window of the bakery. "I think the turnovers are done."

His head went up and his eyes brightened as they lit on the sugar-coated dough wrapped around plump juicy cherries. He gave her a glance that told Belle he knew what she was up to, but he opened the door of the bakery anyway and waved her inside.

TEN MINUTES LATER, after Isabelle had signed autographs for Lucinda's grandchildren, two customers and their children and grandchildren, Klein carried a bag with half a dozen cherry turnovers and a thermos full of coffee out of the bakery.

"That'll go on for the rest of the day," he grumbled. "Everyone's so pleased you're here."

"Except for you."

He shrugged. Truth was truth. He wanted her gone. Fat lot of good that wanting it did.

"They'll get used to me," she said. "The more I'm around, the more normal I'll seem."

Klein looked her up and down. Despite the fact that she was dressed plainly, she didn't fit in. "You couldn't be normal if you took lessons."

Something flickered in her eyes, and he felt bad, even though he'd thought he was giving her a compliment. But the emotion, whatever it had been, was gone quickly, and when she spoke, her voice was bright, her smile the same.

"Isn't that what I'm doing? Taking lessons?"

"Yeah." He sighed. "Let's sit over here."

She followed him to a small picnic table in front of the bakery. Taking out a turnover for each of them, he tipped the thermos in her direction. She shook her head.

"How can you not drink coffee?" he demanded. "I suppose you're one of those people who doesn't eat anything with a face, either."

"That's vegetarian. Or maybe it's vegan. Whatever. I'm not one of *those*." She smiled. "How un-American."

He had to keep himself from smiling back. She'd been annoyed with him yesterday, but this morning she was back to smiling and teasing. He had to admit she forgave much more easily than he did. If she'd said to him what he'd said to her... Well, that was over and forgotten, it appeared. Today they'd start fresh.

"Not drinking coffee." He lifted his cup and took a deep drought. "Now, *that's* un-American."

"Haven't you read the latest studies? Coffee causes wrinkles."

Klein snorted. "I never read that stuff. They change their minds every other day about what's good and bad for a body.'' He slugged back more coffee. ''Mmm-mmm *good*.'' He waved the cup underneath her nose. ''How can you resist? Lucinda makes the best in three counties.''

Isabelle took a healthy sniff. ''I always did like the smell.'' When he offered her his cup, she shook her head. ''If you had to make your living off your face, you'd give it up, too.''

She'd directed her attention to the turnovers in the bag, so she didn't see him freeze as the hurt washed over him. How could offhand comments like those still hurt after all these years? After so many similar comments?

''I doubt I could make any kind of living off this face.'' He snatched the bag from her hand.

Licking her lips in anticipation of the first bite of the sugar-dough-cherry concoction, suddenly she scowled and glanced his way. ''What does that mean?''

Klein picked up his turnover and shoved half into his mouth. He needed sugar, then caffeine, then more sugar. She could just wait.

But Isabelle was not a woman who waited. Instead, she got up from her side of the table and walked over to his. Sliding onto the bench next to him, she didn't stop until their hips bumped.

Right there in the middle of town he remembered what it had felt like to touch her skin, to catch the scent of her hair brushing his face, to see the bright colors of her shorts and shirt in contrast to the horrendous shades of his soon-to-be-remodeled bathroom.

The name Izzy whispered through his mind,

along with the same delusion he'd had yesterday—
the one where she'd wanted to kiss him—and the
hard-on he'd fought all night long returned.

"Klein—?"

She laid her hand on his knee. His body responded accordingly. He swallowed what was left
of the turnover in his mouth. It lay like a brick in
his belly.

"Tell me what you meant by that."

Man, life just wasn't fair. Why did he always
have to lust after the prom queen when he was the
biggest geek in school?

Klein slid off the bench, away from the warmth
of Isabelle's hip, the weight of her hand. No use
torturing himself all day as he had all night.
"You've got eyes," he said. "I'm not a handsome
guy."

If that wasn't the understatement of the year.

Her gaze clouded with what appeared to be anger. "Who told you that?"

"No one had to tell me. I can see. I'm ugly,
Isabelle. It's not a state secret."

She was shaking her head before he finished his
sentence. "You're a lot of things, Klein, but ugly
isn't one of them."

He stared into her eyes. He'd become adept at
reading folks. Cops back in Savannah had called
the ability his shit-o-meter. But the fact remained,
Klein knew people. With Isabelle he found he
didn't have a clue. She appeared sincere while feed-
ing him the biggest load of crap he'd heard since
high school.

He wasn't sure what to do, what to say—a novel

experience for him. Then a movement from the corner of his vision drew his attention from Isabelle.

Seven a.m. The townspeople could set their watches by the mayor. Right on schedule, women stepped onto their porches or appeared in their windows. Some sights were too good to miss.

"You might not know ugly when you see it—" he nodded at Chai "—but you've got to know pretty."

She followed his gaze, then shrugged, unimpressed. "My mama always said, 'Pretty is as pretty does,' and in that vein, the mayor resembles a molting vulture in my eyes."

Klein choked on his second cherry turnover. He took a slug of coffee to wash it down, then sprayed it all over his hiking boots when he scalded his tongue.

"Of course, right now you aren't too appealing, either," she murmured.

Klein lifted his eyes. She was smiling.

He watched the mayor jogging down Longstreet Avenue in white running shorts, matching tank top, shoes and headband. Hell, if Klein had been a woman, *he'd* have run after him. What was the matter with *her?*

"You don't think he's studly?"

"I think he's a snake in a thousand-dollar suit." She stood, tossed three-quarters of a cherry turnover into the trash and shook her head. "God, Klein, give me credit for a few brain cells."

He opened his mouth to answer that, though what he expected to say Klein wasn't sure—when Virgil's voice crackled from his walkie-talkie.

"Chief, we have a problem."

Klein retrieved the contraption, pushed the button and held it to his mouth. "Where and what?"

"Out near the mountains. Possible 10-57. Definite 11-80."

Klein's head spun. Police codes often differed by area and he'd learned his share of codes. Virgil used a variation on a standard 10-code, but Klein screwed it up more often than not, especially when he was distracted.

"English, Virgil. Now," he snapped.

"Report of firearms discharged. Accident, with major injury. Call came on a passerby's cell phone that kept breaking up. They want paramedics."

Klein cursed.

"What's the matter?" Belle asked.

"No paramedics. No hospital. Not even a clinic."

"Doctor?"

"Kind of." All Pleasant Ridge boasted for medical care was a lone family doctor who'd been practicing here since Virgil was a pup. Klein pushed the walkie-talkie button again. "You called Doc Meyers?"

"Yep. He was already out in that direction, delivering a baby. He'll get on site as quick as he can."

Klein stifled another curse. Doc Meyers's quick was everyone else's yesterday.

The radio crackled again. "I'll pick you up. Location?"

"In front of Lucinda's."

"Roger, that. Over and out."

Klein resisted the urge to roll his eyes at Virgil's radio lingo, which wasn't much different from his regular lingo. The man would have done well in the military, or perhaps NASA.

Klein finished his coffee and tossed the garbage into the trash. Mind on the mystery accident—could be minor, could be major, from the information he had—he started when Isabelle spoke.

"I'll go with you."

One sharp shake of his head and he headed for the curb. "Not a good idea."

"Regardless." She hurried to keep up. "I need to observe everything you do."

"You might observe a whole lot more than you ever wanted to. Accident near the mountains could be vehicular, could be hunting, could be feudal." She snorted as if he were kidding. But then, she was from out of town. "It could be damn near any-thing, and if they asked for paramedics, you can be certain there's blood involved."

"I'll manage. I might even be able to help."

Klein took in her pristine-white blouse and neatly pressed khakis, her slim soft hands, ponytailed blond hair and youthful demeanor. "Somehow I doubt that."

Her eyes narrowed; her lips tightened. "I'm not just decoration, Klein. You'd be surprised at what I can do if you look a little deeper than my skin."

The squad car slid to a stop at the curb. Isabelle held Klein's gaze. The annoyance in her eyes gave way to hope as he hesitated.

"Chief!" Virgil snapped. "Today."

Klein opened the back door of the car. "All right," he said. "Surprise me."

CHAPTER SIX

NOW THAT KLEIN had called her bluff, Belle was uncertain. She didn't know much, except that she was tired of being just a pretty face. But if she wanted to be seen as more, she'd have to prove that she was. Or at least pretend.

Belle climbed in the back seat and Klein slammed the door. She glanced at Virgil through the crisscross gate that separated her seat from his. As their gazes met in the rearview mirror, he nodded solemnly.

"Four-twenty-five," he greeted her.

"Virgil." Klein slid into the passenger seat and tossed his thermos onto the floor. "This is Ms. Ash. Remember? The mayor asked me to teach her about my job for the television show."

The old man grunted. "Fancy-girl actress. Fancy-man mayor. I remember. I ain't senile yet."

Although *fancy girl* was a much nicer way of describing her than she'd heard in the past, Belle wasn't certain she appreciated being likened to Chai Smith. She didn't think the mayor had ever ridden in the prisoner section of a squad car to help with an accident.

Belle settled back in her seat and absorbed the experience. She couldn't say she liked it. No handles on the doors; no seat belts, either. She was trapped. And while that was the entire idea, the lack of control over her environment was not a big plus for Belle's state of mind.

The murmur of Klein's deep voice from the front seat brought her attention back to him. She recalled the strength of his hands, the gentleness of his fingers, the warmth of his body, the way hers had been drawn to his. Frowning, she considered their interrupted conversation and let her gaze drift over his wide shoulders, square jaw, the curve of his earlobe.

Klein thought he was ugly. What idiot had given him that idea?

Belle could see the mayor turning up his snooty nose at Klein; however, she could not see Klein giving a damn. But the way he'd looked when he'd said he was ugly... Belle shook her head. Someone had hurt him. Someone who mattered.

The belief that he was nothing special went deeper than an acquaintanceship, beyond Pleasant Ridge, probably all the way back to his childhood. Though Klein's problems were none of her business, Belle discovered that she wanted not only to know who had hurt him but to make his hurt go away.

She gave herself a mental shake. She had to stop thinking that way about him, because he certainly didn't think that way about her. To Gabe Klein, Isabelle Ash was an annoyance, nothing more. Someone he would endure until she left, and once she did he would no longer think of her at all.

A drop of sweat ran down her cheek, and she

brushed at it impatiently, glancing at the doors with
no handles. She hated being trapped back there.
What if Virgil rolled the car, the gas tank burst and
she was stuck inside with no way out?

See the bright side, Belle, advised her mama
practically. *If he rolls this car, and you with no seat
belt, there'll be no worryin' about a way out.*

Needless to say, by the time they arrived at the
foot of the mountain, Belle was squirrelly. As soon
as Klein opened the door for her, she leaped out.

And landed in a horror movie.

What else could noise, crowds, twisted metal,
bullets and blood be? Folks had stopped at the
scene of the accident, which made for both a mob
and a traffic jam.

Virgil trotted off, waving at the gawkers still near
their cars, ordering them in a high, thready voice to
"Move along now. Nothing for you t' see here."

A lie if she'd ever heard one. There was so much
to see, and so much to be done, Belle didn't know
where to start. So she stood frozen next to the car,
unable *to* start. Klein had no such problem. He
waded right into the disaster.

Even without the uniform and the gun, the crack-
ling walkie-talkie, the crowd would have parted for
him. The aura of command dwelt in his bearing, his
walk, his stance. Command clung to him, preceded
him, defined him. His sharp blue eyes flicked over
the scene, assessed what needed to be done, and
then he did it.

"Anyone here a doctor? A nurse?"

Heads shook. No one came forward.

"Anyone with any first-aid training at all?"

He received the same response.

"Son of a—" He bit off the rest, lowering himself to one knee and placing his fingers on the neck of a victim.

In a smooth, confident motion, he began CPR. No one helped, but everyone gathered closer to watch.

Belle glanced at Virgil, but he had his hands full clearing the road and keeping any more gawkers from assembling. She hadn't realized she'd followed Klein, until he glanced up when she paused at his side.

"Go back to the car, Isabelle," he snapped. "There's nothing you can do here except get in the way."

Ignoring the spark of resentment his summary judgment caused, she, too, dropped to her knees, replaced his hands with hers and began compressions. "I can do this," she murmured, as much to him as herself. "It's just been a while. You go on."

After watching her work a moment, assessing that she did in fact know what she was doing, Klein gave her a nod of approval that settled into her belly like a cup of tea on a chilly day, then moved off to help the others.

Morning bled toward afternoon. Doc Meyers arrived, took one look at Belle pressing a compress to a gaping wound without a quiver and commandeered her for his own. She lost track of how many times he grabbed her hand and showed her something she really didn't want to know.

As a child Belle had often pretended she was someone else to make her forget for a while the misery of being herself. As she worked amid the blood and the pain, she began to pretend she was a competent nurse so she could forget the uncertainty, the fear and the dread. The longer she pretended, the better at it she became. Though always, in the back of her mind, there was the thread of panic that accompanied any situation beyond her control.

Klein moved in and out of her vision—first here, then there, eventually swallowed up in the increasing swarm of people, cars and things to do. But he was the calm in the chaos. Serenity swirled around him like the clouds atop the mountains, creating beauty, dispensing peace, while leaving the mountain untouched.

KLEIN DID HIS JOB. His job was what he did best. But he had to say that in a tiny corner of his mind he was screaming. Violence and tragedy—they were as much a part of life as death. He knew that. But that didn't mean he had to like it or accept it.

So Klein walked faster, talked louder, worked harder, trying to stave off what tragedy he could. He'd always dealt with the uncontrollable in life by butting his head against it until every aspect that could be controlled by him was. That was the only way he could keep doing his job without losing his mind.

Doc Meyers tried, but there were too many injured, and help took too long to arrive. By the time a helicopter landed, he'd lost one patient. By the time an ambulance pulled up, another was perilously close to the end. The old man continued to labor gamely, but Klein could see the situation weighed on him.

Sometime after noon the urgency diminished. Serious injuries had been routed by air or land, minor wounds dealt with on site. Statements had been taken, weapons confiscated, arrests made. Klein had sent Virgil back to the station with the moron responsible for it all.

Isabelle had laughed when he'd referred to a feudal accident, but that was what this was. In the South—hell, most likely in the North, too—feuds between families still raged. Some were worse than others—leaving burning dog crap on the porch as opposed to leaving dead folks on the lawn—but a feud was a feud. They did not fade with time, and it was rare for any of the participants to know what had started them in the first place. However, everyone knew how to keep them going. Land disputes, boundary arguments, romantic entanglements—he'd have to sort this one out later.

Walking around the perimeter of the disaster, Klein made sure all the others were doing their jobs. He stopped dead near the makeshift clinic when he saw a familiar blond ponytail bobbing among the injured. Somewhere along the line Isabelle had covered her pristine-white blouse with a mint-green scrub shirt.

Occupied with other problems, he'd lost track of her, but he'd figured that once the doctor showed up Isabelle would get back to Pleasant Ridge— somehow. He couldn't say he hadn't been shocked that she'd known CPR, and that she'd gotten right down in the dirt and used it, but he had been grateful. Meaning to thank her and then send her on her way, he headed in Isabelle's direction, only to halt and go still when he realized what she was doing.

"Here," Doc Meyers said, taking her hand. "Pressure there. Don't make a face."

"I'll make a face if I have need to. You just keep on talkin' so I don't puke."

Meyers snorted. "I've never seen anyone less of a mind to puke than you, Belle."

Klein scowled at the easy way the man said her name. Klein certainly couldn't manage it.

"You held up today like an army nurse. In my opinion, you've got balls of steel, girl."

"Why, Dr. Meyers, sir, you flatter me."

There it was again, a hint of the South in her flat Yankee voice. Klein had forgotten that little mystery in the midst of so many others. Unable to stop himself, he inched closer and observed.

Except for the shrouded body in need of a hearse, only those awaiting family members to come and take them home, or one last check from the doctor, remained in the makeshift clinic. Klein refused to look at the body, instead focusing on Isabelle, the doctor and the unconscious elderly gentleman, who by virtue of the gash on his forehead would resemble Frankenstein if not for his snow-white hair.

"Hold together the ends of the wound so I can stitch him up," Meyers growled. "Stubborn old bird. I told him to wait for his daughter, but he had to stand up on his own."

"I don't think the standing up was the problem. More the falling down," Isabelle murmured.

Klein smiled at her wit, but Meyers merely nod-

ded and began to stitch the man's head. From where
Klein stood, the task was not at all pleasant. No
wonder Isabelle had made a face.

Head wounds bled like a bitch, and her gloved
fingers were soon slick. As Meyers had predicted,
she did not pale or flinch. She did what she was
told quickly, and when it was over, she cleaned the
blood off the old man, as Meyers moved on to
check another patient, then snapped off the bloody
surgical gloves and tossed them in a nearby recep-
tacle.

Klein took a step forward, planning once again
to thank her for her help, then quiz her a bit. Where
had she learned CPR and first aid, for instance? And
why did a woman who spoke as if she was from
Minneapolis twist certain words toward Mississippi?

Before he could ask, Cass Tyler appeared from
nowhere and stuck a camera in Isabelle's face. The
whir of the shutter made Isabelle flinch as the blood
had not.

"Ms. Ash," Cass said, still clicking picture after
picture, "you're a heroine. Tell me how it feels to
get your hands dirty."

Half expecting her to revel in the publicity, he
was surprised when she cringed and turned her face
away.

Cass got it all. Circling her prey like the wolf she
was, the newspaperwoman shot an entire roll of Isabelle Ash standing in the middle of the worst
disaster to hit Pleasant Ridge in years.

"What?" Isabelle asked, her voice as shaky as
the hand she used to push back her hair.

That hand did him in—the contrast of strength and fragility, pale skin beneath the brown slash of old blood on her forearm and the red slash of new blood along her wrist. Technology was a wonderful thing, but surgical gloves only extended so far.

Klein strode forward, snatched the camera from Cass's hand, flipped open the back and yanked out the film.

"Hey!" she shouted, making a grab for it. "Give that back!"

But Klein hadn't danced through the marines. Assume, assimilate, adapt. While he held Cass off with a shoulder, he grasped the hanging end of the film and ripped the reel out of the canister like a ribbon.

"Here you go," he said, agreeably placing the ruined film and the open camera in her hands.

"Dammit, Klein—" She poked him in the chest.

She did that a lot. One of these days, she was going to do it one time too many.

"What the hell do you think you're doing?"

"My job."

"Ruining perfectly good film is your job?"

"Nope. Serve and protect. That's my job."

Cass scowled. "I should sue your ass."

"Knock yourself out."

She sighed and stared at the ruined film. "You know I won't."

"Uh-huh."

Cass was another in a long line of Gabe Klein's female friends. Pretty in an edgy way, tall and solidly built, with sharp gray eyes and chestnut hair, Cass was also intelligent and ambitious. She'd taken one look at Klein and pronounced him a pal. That happened to him a lot.

"Isabelle's presence in Pleasant Ridge is supposed to be a secret."

"Isabelle, huh?"

Klein scowled, and she held up one hand in surrender.

"All right, all right. Isabelle Ash isn't any secret, Klein. Everyone in town knows she's here."

"Let's keep it in town, then, shall we?"

"Good luck."

Klein sighed and kicked the dirt with his boot. That was what he'd thought.

"Where did she go?"

Cass's question brought Klein's head up. He scanned the steadily decreasing crowd at the site. There was no sign of Isabelle. He shrugged, both disturbed and relieved to find her gone.

Why had it bothered her to have her picture taken? Today she was a heroine. Wouldn't a woman like Isabelle crave the publicity?

Klein sighed at the echo of his thoughts. *A woman like Isabelle.* When had he become the exact type of person he despised? He had judged her at face value, even though he'd already seen there was a lot more to Isabelle than met the eye.

Cass stomped away, muttering. He barely noticed she had left. Instead, he focused on a rapidly diminishing figure to the west, which he hadn't seen at first because he'd been looking for a car. He hadn't considered that Isabelle might jog back to Pleasant Ridge. What lunatic would?

By the time he cleared the area, then called Virgil

to drive him back to town—he was not up to walking back just now—Isabelle must have reached home, because there was no sign of her on the road. Though he had a pile of paperwork to do and a hundred phone calls to make, nevertheless Klein ordered Virgil to drop him off in front of the five-and-dime.

He glanced up at Isabelle's apartment, but he couldn't tell if anyone was in.

He bent and leaned through the open squad car window. "You go ahead and keep the wheels rolling, Virgil," Klein ordered. "I'm just going to make sure Ms. Ash got back okay."

"10-4, Chief."

For the first time since he'd come to town, Klein didn't have the urge to roll his eyes. The way Virgil talked was beginning to seem as commonplace as rain on a rooftop. In fact, if the old man didn't sound like Barney Fife, life just wouldn't be the same.

He took the back steps as quickly as he could. They creaked beneath his weight, and he wondered briefly if they were up to code, then shook his head. He had a feeling that if he mentioned building codes around here, folks would think he was touched. Buildings were built; then they stood until they fell down. That was the code in Pleasant Ridge.

Since there wasn't a doorbell, Klein knocked. Seconds ticked to a minute and beyond. He shuffled his feet, knocked again, waited some more. *Had* she come home?

The longer he waited, the more concerned he became. There was nowhere else for her to go, was there? She knew no one but him and Chai, and he doubted she'd visit the mayor. Which was one of the things he liked about her.

Liked? When had he started to like her? Before she'd surprised him today? Or after she'd aroused him yesterday?

"Moron," he muttered. "A woman like her is not for you."

He heard again the echo of his earlier thoughts—*a woman like her*—and he was embarrassed, a little ashamed. Isabelle was Isabelle, and she wanted to be his friend; he'd agreed to be her teacher. Right now, he just needed to find her.

Klein whipped out his walkie-talkie. "Virgil?"

"Here, Chief."

Over the static, Virgil sounded more like Maxwell Smart than Barney Fife. Klein shook his head. He was definitely losing his mind—or watching too much classic television.

"Is Ms. Ash at the station?"

"Negative."

"Does that mean no?"

"Affirmative."

Now Klein did roll his eyes. "Thanks."

"Over and out." The walkie-talkie went silent.

She wasn't at the station; she couldn't be at city hall. Maybe she was at Lucinda's, but Klein didn't think so. A bead of sweat rolled down his back; a shiver traced the same path. They might be in tiny-town Tennessee, but shit still happened here. This morning merely proved that.

He never should have let her jog home alone. He

should have run after her, or at least sent Virgil to pick her up. A woman who looked like Isabelle, whose face and body had been plastered all over the media, was a prime target for every nut on the face of the earth.

Standing on her porch as fear and worry mingled, Klein again wanted to protect her from everyone and everything. He wanted to slay all her dragons, banish all her demons. He wanted to be her knight; hell, she was already a princess.

Before he tore the town apart searching for her, he had to make sure she wasn't inside. One last knock and he reached for the doorknob. As he'd told Isabelle yesterday, no one in Pleasant Ridge locked any doors, still, he *had* expected her to. Therefore he nearly fell on his face when her door swung open at his touch.

The interior was shadowed, all the curtains drawn, though the window near the bed was open. A weak breeze fluttered the ancient ruffled material.

She sat on the mattress, legs curled to her chest, her back to him. With every wave, the end of one curtain brushed her cheek. She never moved.

Her white shirt, damp with sweat, stuck to her skin. She must have run all the way back to town. He was surprised she wasn't lying in a ditch somewhere with heat exhaustion. But maybe she'd only made it back to suffer in secret.

"Didn't you hear me knock?"

She didn't answer. The fear that had left him at the sight of her came back when she continued to sit on her bed, too still, too quiet, staring out a window that was curtained.

Klein crossed the room. "Isabelle?"

She turned her face toward him. He didn't care for the zoned-out look in her eyes. Shock? Heat exhaustion? Dehydration? Or all of the above?

At least she recognized him, because she smiled and murmured, "Klein."

If he hadn't been so worried, he might have become aroused by the husky, sleepy way she said his name.

"What's the matter?" he asked.

"Matter?" She blinked, then unraveled her long, long legs and put her feet on the floor.

Klein began to blink, but the sight didn't go away. He thought perhaps *he* was in shock. She'd removed the scrubs she'd donned at the accident scene, and he could see that she'd put them on a little too late. Because her white blouse was spattered with blood. There was a slash of it on her neck. Her forearm and wrist were also still stained. He'd known she'd been helping the doctor, but he hadn't realized how much.

"Don't you think you should take a shower?" he asked.

"Sure."

She didn't move.

"Isabelle." He gentled his voice. "Do you know you've got blood on you?"

He touched her hand to see if her skin was clammy or cold. It wasn't. Perhaps she wasn't in shock after all. But she didn't answer him, and that he didn't like.

"You shouldn't have stayed if the blood was going to upset you so."

"It wasn't the blood. I'm not a ninny."

Her annoyance reassured Klein a bit. She wasn't too far gone if she could get angry.

"If not the blood, what?"

Her hand twisted beneath his, and she clutched his fingers. Her expression was desperate, urgent; so was her voice. "I didn't help them."

"Sure you did. From what I heard, you helped a lot."

"But someone died. I felt so damn helpless. There was nothing to be done."

"Sometimes there isn't."

Her head dipped toward her chest. Her hair, which had been in a neat ponytail all day, now lay across her cheek in damp, sweaty hanks, obscuring her face.

"I can't take it when things get out of control," she murmured.

Klein thought that an odd thing to say under the circumstances. But now was not the time to explore the issue, even though his underused detective skills had gone on alert. Now was the time to get her cleaned up, rehydrated and relaxed.

She still held on tightly to his hand, so Klein pulled her to her feet. "Hop in the shower," he ordered. "I'll get you something to drink."

She released him and headed for what he assumed was the bathroom. Klein crossed to her fridge and peered in. Bottled water, fruit, lettuce, yogurt.

"Party on," he muttered, and grabbed the water.

He'd seen films of marathon runners weaving over the road, stumbling toward the finish line, so dehydrated they appeared drunk. The dazed expression on Isabelle's face made him cross the room, planning to cover his eyes and hand her the water. She could drink it in the shower.

But as he neared the bathroom, he realized he didn't hear the water running. The door was wide open and he could see her reflected in the mirror above the sink. She fumbled almost frantically with the buttons on her shirt; the rasp of her breathing bounced off the tiled walls of the room.

As if she sensed him behind her, she lifted her head. Her eyes were dark in the paleness of her face; her blond hair only made her appear wanner.

She gave a tiny laugh that was nearly a sob and shrugged. "My hands won't work."

Uncertain what to say or do, Klein hovered half in, half out of the bathroom. She took a deep breath, which shook as if she'd been crying. But he could see no trace of tears along her ivory cheeks.

She continued to fumble with the buttons. She managed one, and her shirt gaped, revealing a plain, white cotton bra. Such serviceable underwear should shock him, but it didn't. The more he knew about her the less she matched her leather and lace, satin and spandex image.

Isabelle's hands clenched, then dropped back to her sides. "I can't," she whispered. "Help me."

His gaze met hers once more in the mirror. "Help?" he repeated dumbly.

"Please." She motioned vaguely at her shirt. "The buttons."

The movement made her stumble, and before he knew what he was doing, Klein dropped the water and grabbed her shoulders. The *thud* of the bottle against the floor foreshadowed the leap of his heart against his chest.

The skin beneath her shirt was hot. When he shifted his hands, the material clung to his palms. He glanced into the mirror again. Sweat beaded her lip. She did not look well.

Running through every curse word he'd ever learned in the marines—and there were quite a few—Klein spun her about and made short work of the buttons. She stood there like a child and let him undress her.

Beneath the ruined shirt, the plain white bra—no lace, no ribbons, nothing but elastic and fiberfill—hid more than it revealed. Lucky for him, because undressing her like this, even though there was nothing sexual about it, was making him remember why he'd been unable to sleep last night.

He had to get her to drink some water, then wash off the blood and sweat. But right now he couldn't think past the feel of her beneath his fingers, the echo of her voice asking for help—her need and his both so similar yet so far apart.

She shivered and swayed. Klein snapped out of it. "Dammit, Izzy."

He propped her against the sink, yanked a washcloth from the towel rack and ran it under the cold faucet. Then he plopped the thing on the back of her neck and retrieved the water bottle from the floor.

"Drink this." He shoved it into her hand.

At least she didn't argue. He didn't think she had it in her. Not now at any rate. She lifted the water to her mouth and drank. Her throat moved as she swallowed, once, twice, three times. Suddenly Klein was thirsty, too, and awfully damn hot.

The long line of blood on her neck distracted him. He wanted to wash it away, but he was afraid to touch her, afraid of what she might think. Of what he might do.

Feelings warred within him—one moment lust, the next protectiveness; another instant he yearned; then he had to defend. Beneath it all pulsed the wariness, the uncertainty, feelings left over from his youth, feelings he'd hoped were long dead.

Klein gave up. The blood on her neck was driving him nuts, so he took the washcloth and smoothed it away. Her soft sigh had him groping for something to say.

"You were fine when Meyers was stitching the old man's head. Then Cass showed up." Her eyes flicked to his, and a bell clanged in Klein's brain. *Give the man a silver dollar!*

He tossed the washcloth into the sink. "Was that it? Cass?" She nodded. "But…you get your picture taken all the time. Why would that upset you?"

"Not the pictures, though I'm glad you ruined them. What happened out there today is not something I want splashed across the country. I helped because I could. I don't need or want any publicity for it."

"If not the pictures, then what?"

"She called me Ms. Ash."

"I don't understand."

Isabelle ducked her head as if embarrassed. For a moment he wondered if she'd just realized she

stood in front of him with her shirt completely unbuttoned and her granny bra plainly visible. Her
next words proved she wasn't thinking about the
state of her clothes or even the lack of them.

"I was pretending," she whispered.

"You've still lost me."

Thankfully his libido seemed to have taken a
powder. He was no longer aroused by the sight of
her skin, the slope of her neck, the slant of her
cheekbone. His curiosity was too alive and hum-
ming for that.

"All my life I've pretended to be someone other
than who I am. Today I was Florence Nightingale,
healer of the sick, heroine of the Crimea." Her lips
twisted self-derisively. "Until Cass called me Ms.
Ash."

His mind seemed to be running several seconds
behind his ears today. He took a moment to align
his thoughts. "Let me get this straight. You were
acting like a nurse?"

She tilted her head and peered at him. "Pretty
stupid, huh?"

"*Stupid* isn't the word I'd use. More like clever.
You had me fooled." He shrugged. "Whatever
works."

"Huh?"

"If pretending got you through that mess today
and enabled you to help people, pretend away."

She shook her head as though she couldn't believe what she'd heard, then finished the rest of her
water in one long swig. He studied her, concerned.
Her color was better. Her hands no longer shook.

But she still looked like hell. He should let her get in the shower, yet he had to ask.

"You said you've always pretended to be someone other than who you are. But who wouldn't want to be you?"

Her smile was sad. "Walk a mile in my shoes, Klein, or maybe run a mile."

True enough. He shouldn't assume her life was as fabulous as it appeared.

"What did you pretend to be as a child?"

"A pretty girl."

He frowned. Something wasn't adding up here. "And now?"

"The same."

"But you're beautiful."

"Ah, Klein." She tsked at him. "Didn't anyone ever tell you that beauty is only skin deep?"

"Yeah, ugly people."

She laughed, put her hand on his chest and pushed. "Go on now. I'm okay. I'll take a shower. I'll be fine."

"Are you going to pretend to be fine, or will you actually be fine?"

She raised an eyebrow. "Ha-ha. Get out."

He got out. She closed the door in his face. He waited to hear the click of the lock, but none came.

Klein sighed. She trusted him. She thought he was her friend. She believed he would never walk back into that room, take her into his arms, make her forget a horrible day in the midst of an incredible night.

And she'd be right.

Women forever wanted Gabe Klein as their

friend, and he was a good one. He liked women; he enjoyed talking to them, protecting them, being with them. What wasn't to like? But secretly he'd always resented the fact that he never had a choice in the matter. He was never seen as anything more.

Isabelle was never seen as anything *more,* either. He had to admit that he'd been as guilty as everyone else, putting her into the pretty-blond-bimbo category and being shocked when she turned out to be deeper than she looked.

She made him nervous the way she raced through life, ran everywhere, always pushing, never at ease. He wanted to help her—both in her job and in her life. It was one of his most common failings—the helping—and his greatest strength.

For the first time, Klein *wanted* to be a woman's friend as much as she wanted to be his, and the novelty of that dazzled him.

He could have resisted her beauty. What he couldn't resist was her strength.

CHAPTER SEVEN

BELLE STEPPED OUT of the bathroom. "Oh," she gasped, and practically dropped her towel. Klein was still there.

"Sorry. Didn't mean to startle you, but I wanted to make sure you were okay."

Sitting on the battered sofa that faced the bathroom, he had an arm along the back and an ankle on one knee. He looked as if he'd been staring at the door, waiting for her to appear. Had he thought she'd walk out naked?

Belle sighed. Not Klein.

Clutching the towel with one hand, she crossed the room to her dresser, reached inside and ferreted out fresh underwear. Performing such intimate tasks with him in the room made it seem that they'd been intimate themselves. Her entire body tingled beneath the towel. She glanced at Klein to see if he felt what she felt. He was reading the TV guide.

She yanked a loose-fitting, jade-green sun-dress from the tiny doorless closet that housed her clothes and slammed the bathroom door behind her. The steam of the room brushed her cheeks, whispered along her neck, made her think of lovers she'd had, men she'd known.

Since she'd grown into her face and out of her

fat, men had become attentive. A childhood of being ignored or teased had made Belle relish the attention. She knew it was crazy, but the fact that Klein didn't want her that way was perplexing.

Belle finished dressing and pulled open the door. Klein had finished perusing the TV guide and now stared at her again. How could he be so damn calm, when her entire body was alive and kicking?

"I'll be fine now," she repeated. "I'm sure you have work to do."

He dropped his foot from his knee, and when his boot connected with the wood floor, she started. He raised his eyebrows, but didn't comment on her excessive jumpiness.

"There's always work to be done."

"Then, I'll see you tomorrow."

"And there's a time *not* to do it," he continued as if she hadn't even spoken.

"I don't understand."

"No, I don't think you do, and that worries me." He shook his head. "Isabelle, you need to relax before you leap out of your skin."

"All right."

She sat down at the kitchen table. But now that she'd crashed and gotten past it, she was so wired she could barely sit still. She had felt the same way a few hours before, and jogging home had taken away some of the madness. It appeared to be coming back. Belle shifted to the edge of her seat, and her foot began to tap.

"Oh, yeah, you look practically asleep," Klein drawled.

"I'm fine." She forced her foot to still, but keeping it that way took a whole lot of effort.

"If you say 'fine' one more time, I'm gonna get mean."

Belle considered that. Though Klein was big and could no doubt get mean if he was of a mind, she just couldn't wrap her thoughts around the idea of *Klein* and *mean* in the same sentence.

He lounged on her couch as if he had all day to rest there, when in fact the station must be a madhouse. Just thinking about what *he* had to do was making *her* nervous, and before she knew it, her foot went tapping again.

Klein's gaze lowered to her heel, then returned to her face. "Why did you jog all the way back to Pleasant Ridge?"

She shrugged. "Because it was there?"

He continued to stare at her face, patient as those mountains she'd spent the morning in the shadow of, until she was compelled to tell him the truth—or, at least, some of it.

"Today I was in a situation where all I could do was my best, and it wasn't good enough. The results were out of my control. So I ran, because then I'm in control of my body, my pace, my heart rate. When I push myself harder and farther, the things that are out of control fade because I'm becoming stronger. I feel like I can do anything—"

She broke off at his mystified expression.

"You're big on control?"

"Isn't everyone?"

His lips twisted. "No, honey, not everyone."

When most men called her honey, she wanted to

kick them where it counted. If the mayor had tried it, she might have given in to the urge. But when Klein called her honey, she got the idea that it was an endearment meant just for her. Foolish, but then, she hadn't heard him call anyone else honey lately.

"Let's go for a walk." He stood.

She gaped. "Walk?

"The opposite of run. I'm sure you've heard of it."

"But—but—shouldn't you—"

"Should. Could. But I'm not. Virgil loves paperwork. I'm gonna give him the thrill of a lifetime and let him do it all."

"I don't understand you."

"That makes two of us, but I'm thinking maybe we should try, hmm? You need to calm down, Isabelle."

"I'm fi—"

"Ah!" He held up one hand. "I wasn't talking about just right now. I was talking about the rest of your life. You're gonna have a stroke before you're forty. You ever smell the flowers? Watch the sunset? Walk a dog?"

"Not recently."

"I'm thinking not ever. I said I'd teach you everything I know about being a small-town sheriff. There's more to it than reciting code and scrapin' roadkill off the freeway, although the glamour of that is hard to ignore. Lesson number four—you gotta slow down, honey, or no one will ever believe you're a Tennessee sheriff."

Belle stared at him for a moment. Something had changed, but she wasn't sure what. Klein was talking to her as if he *wanted* to help her, not as if he was being forced to. Since that was what she'd wanted all along, Belle wasn't going to question why.

She stood, too. "A walk sounds good right about now."

His smile soothed her as nothing else ever had. His no-nonsense style, his easy way of moving, his gentleness made her yearn to be near him, or at least to understand him.

Together they left her apartment, and as they headed down the street, Klein contacted Virgil. He'd been right. The old man was delighted to be left in charge of the paperwork.

"I never did hear what happened to cause that mess out there today," she said. "Vehicular, obviously."

"And hunting and feudal. All of the above on my handy-dandy list of possibilities."

Belle glanced at him. He appeared quite serious. "How could it possibly be all three?"

"Busload of tourists ran afoul of a feudal argument being settled with a hunting rifle. Unfortunately, or perhaps fortunately, the moron with the gun is a terrible shot. He missed his target and hit a tire on the tourist bus. Slam-bam, we've got an accident."

"That began with a feud?"

He nodded. "As near as I've been able to decipher, this one is over land, though Lord knows how it began. There are all sorts of disagreements among families and neighbors that seem to last for centuries around here. One thing leads to another, and suddenly folks are doing more than giving one another the cold shoulder. They're actively chasing one another down the mountain.''

"With a gun."

"Which is usually when I become involved."

Belle nodded. Working in a business comprised mostly of women, she had seen feuds aplenty. Women never forgot; they rarely forgave; and they could be downright vicious even without a gun.

Despite the clock, which said late afternoon, people strolled on the street as if it wasn't the middle of the week, the tail end of a workday. Everyone nodded and said hello to the sheriff and hello to Ms. Ash.

"No secrets here," she observed.

"You thought there would be?"

"I guess I thought it would take more than a day for the news to get around."

He snorted. "You've clearly never lived in a small town."

"Not a small town, no."

She'd lived in a small community. News had traveled fast there, too. But with the nearest neighbor several miles away, not quite as fast as news traveled here.

"In a town like Pleasant Ridge, a stranger stands out like a wolf in the middle of a sheep farm," he said.

"Gee, thanks."

Klein lifted, then lowered, his big beautiful hands. "That's one of the things I love about small towns, especially as a sheriff. The second a stranger stays around longer than a day, the populace starts to hum. No one sneaks into a place like Pleasant Ridge, and that makes our little world safe.''

She glanced at him. ''You love it here, don't you.''

Surprise flickered over his face. ''I've only been in town a month, but yeah, I guess I do. I'd like Pleasant Ridge to become my home.'' The longing in his voice shocked her as much as did his next words. ''It would be my first.''

Belle blinked. ''That's impossible. Everyone has a home.''

''Not necessarily. I've had houses, apartments, condos, barracks, too. But a home…'' He shook his head. ''I've never felt that I belonged in any of the places that I've lived.''

''I'm sorry.''

He tipped his head. ''Not your fault. Where's home to you, Isabelle?''

In the past whenever she'd been asked that question, she had smiled brightly and made up the name of a town, then given the press a useless detail of her life so they'd forget the question.

Not that it would be hard to discover her place of birth. But so far no one had cared enough to go searching for the nonexistent towns she'd thrown out, or to plow through the hundreds of families by the name of Ash scattered across the country.

Eventually someone would, and then she'd have to deal with the ramifications of having her life dissected in the media. Still, she was tired of evading the truth, and she discovered she didn't have the energy or the inclination to lie to Klein.

''I was born in Virginia.''

"Ah, that explains it."

"What?"

"Sometimes you twist a word just so and make me think of places where there are warm winters and trees that flower. Then the next word out of your mouth comes from somewhere there's ice and snow and all the flowers are hardy, as well as the trees."

She smiled at his contrast of the South and the North. "I took speech lessons. Can't sound like a hick if you're going to get anywhere in my world."

"You plannin' on talking like a California lawyer while you're pretending to be a Tennessee sheriff?"

"That's the joke on me. All those lessons, all that money, and my first big break I gotta forget all about it."

"Maybe you should have just been yourself in the first place."

Belle stumbled, but quickly recovered her footing. Just when she'd begun to trust him, he made a comment like that.

"You have no idea of the responsibilities in my life," she said quietly.

He glanced at her, then away. "You could tell me."

She considered it. She very nearly spilled the entire depressing mess. And not about her past as Big Belle, not even the secret of being a high school dropout, certainly *not* her eating–exercising neurosis. There were some things a girl just did not discuss with a man she was attracted to, even if he did find her less interesting than the TV guide.

Instead, she very nearly told him about her father, the wheelchair, the operations—past and future—her mother's fears, her brothers' needs. All the pressures that kept her doing whatever she had to do to make enough money to keep her family afloat and her father alive.

"Hey, slow down. It's not a race."

Belle glanced at Klein, to discover she'd left him several steps behind. Thinking about her family, her responsibilities, how doggone messed up her head was, had made her push their stroll to a flat-out power walk.

"Sorry," she mumbled, and forced herself to slow down. The moment for sharing had passed. She'd just keep all her secrets to herself. She was used to it.

"That's better." He walked at her side again. "One thing I've learned, Isabelle—it's the journey that's important, not how fast you get there."

She wasn't going to contradict him, but the one thing she'd learned was that the journey was irrelevant. Fast and first was the only way she would get anywhere at all.

They reached Highway B and continued on out of Pleasant Ridge without pause. "Where's the journey taking us tonight?" she asked.

"I thought we'd stroll out to my place, have a drink, a snack even, then take Clint for a walk into town. He doesn't get out much."

"You don't have to come back here for me. I can make it on my own."

"I'm not doing it for you. I didn't get my walking quota in today and I'm feeling a mite stressed."

She lifted an eyebrow. Stressed? Klein? He was walking so slowly she wanted to grab his hand and tug him along. But she had a feeling that such behavior would only make him walk even slower. How could he possibly be in the shape he was in, when he strolled every damn place?

"Besides," he continued, "I might have let Virgil be in charge a while, but that doesn't mean I'm not going to check on him later."

"And anyone else he might have arrested while you were out?"

Klein slapped her on the back as if she were just one of the guys. "Now you're catching on."

IN KLEIN'S EXPERIENCE women liked to talk. Since he'd never been the chatty sort, he didn't mind listening.

Isabelle was different. She didn't offer anything. She responded to questions with the barest of answers. She didn't feel the need to fill the lengthening silence with useless words.

She was hiding something; he just wasn't sure what.

He had to admit, though, that he enjoyed their walk to his house. Usually he walked alone and preferred it that way. He did not have to entertain anyone, and he did not have to pace himself to the footsteps of others. But he had none of those concerns with Isabelle. She kept her mouth shut, and she kept on walking.

They turned into his yard and without conscious thought, Klein disguised his gun, then made it disappear, even though Clint was nowhere in sight.

"Where is he?" Isabelle's gaze swept the yard.

"Who knows. He likes to pretend he's a hunting dog and stalk around in the back field."

"Does he catch much?"

Klein sighed. "Not a thing. But don't mention that. It embarrasses him."

She laughed. "Embarrasses you, most like."

"Not me. I couldn't care less what he does, as long as he's happy. But Clint thinks he has to try."

"Do you really think that he thinks? That he understands what you're saying? That he can *be* embarrassed?"

"Yep. Now, have a seat. I'll be right back."

He left her smiling as if he'd said something incredibly cute. He hadn't been cute since 1968, and probably not even then.

She'd no doubt thought he was kidding when he'd said those things about Clint. But the dog had an uncommon ability to behave in a human fashion—sometimes more so than certain humans of Klein's acquaintanceship. And Clint's face could express a range of emotions that made Klein believe there was a lot more goin' on behind those eyes than contemplation of his favorite trees on the property.

Maybe he was giving Clint too much credit. Maybe all dogs were like that. Klein didn't know.

He hustled upstairs to his room and shucked his uniform. After a day in the sun, the standing, the lifting, the walking, he couldn't bear to wear the thing a moment longer. Instead, he threw on a pair of jeans and a worn Atlanta Falcons T-shirt. Barefoot, he descended into the kitchen.

His fridge was full. His mama hadn't raised no fool. A man of Klein's size needed to eat, and while he tried to eat right, every man had his Achilles' heel. His were cherry turnovers. He'd never met one he didn't like.

While he wouldn't turn down a beer and buttered popcorn, a Bloody Mary and Cheez Doodles, or ice cream smothered in Kahlúa, Klein had a feeling Isabelle's idea of cocktail hour would be somewhat different from his own.

So onto a tray he plopped a bottle of wine, some cheese, crackers, sliced apples and pears, two glasses and napkins, then headed for the porch.

Isabelle smiled at him. "What's this?"

"I promised you a drink and a snack."

"I'm not hungry."

He set the tray on a small table between two chairs and poured some sparkling white wine. "I always think that, too, until I start to eat. Anyway—" he held out the glass "—this wine is from Smith Winery in town. You'll want to try some."

Hesitantly she took the glass. "Research, right?"

"Exactly." He poured himself a serving, then held the glass aloft in a toast. "To you. You were something today, Isabelle."

He clinked his glass against hers and took a swig of the house specialty. He had to say one thing for the Smiths. They knew how to make a decent white wine.

He lowered his glass, and Isabelle still had not moved. "It's common to take a sip after a toast."

"To me?" she murmured. "But I didn't do anything."

He frowned. "Were you at the same accident I was? You did plenty, and I for one was impressed."

"I fell apart. I'm a complete wuss."

"You didn't fall apart when the going was tough—you fell apart later. That doesn't count."

"No?"

"Do you know how many big, tough soldiers lose it after a battle? How many cops end up shaking in their showers after facing a gun in the night? It's not what happens later that counts. It's what happens in the thick of things that's the measure of a man. Or a woman."

She seemed to be thinking about that. Good. He didn't give a shit whether she pretended to be Florence Nightingale, Marilyn Monroe or Andy Taylor, if she helped people.

"I guess I'll have to take your word for it. After all, you are the teacher." This time she clinked her glass against his, and she drank. "Mmm. Chai Smith makes this wine?"

Klein snorted. "Not with his own hands."

"I figured that out for myself."

They shared a smile. "His family owns the winery. You should stop by and see it. Interesting place."

"Mmm," she murmured again, absently this time as she stared at the horizon.

He extended the plate. "It goes better with a few of these."

"I'm fine."

He wanted to growl at the repeated response. Instead, he held the food under her nose. She rolled her eyes and took one of each offering, then turned her attention to the yard.

Klein set the plate on her side of the table, hoping she might continue to nibble. The memory of the pathetic offerings in her refrigerator gave him the uncommon urge to feed her. Despite his size and sex, he had a motherly soul. He just couldn't help himself.

"There's Clint."

He followed the direction of her finger to the tall grass at the edge of the yard. Slowly the dog approached, the grass parting in front of his long, red-brown body. His ears hung low; they wobbled to and fro. Klein shook his head as the words and tune of the old children's song went through his mind. They disappeared completely when a rabbit shot out of the grass and across the yard.

Clint let out a howl and leaped in pursuit. Klein knew what was coming. He groaned. "Don't watch."

Belle glanced at him in surprise. "You said he never catches anything."

"He won't."

Her brow furrowed, Isabelle focused on the high-speed chase occurring before their eyes.

Huge paws churning, Clint scrambled after the fleeing rabbit. He was close at first. He almost had a chance—or, at least, it appeared that way. Then the rabbit put on a burst of speed, flashed past the oak tree in the yard and disappeared beneath the house.

Clint stopped dead beneath the tree and looked up, panting, waiting, hoping. It was embarrassing.

Isabelle choked, cleared her throat to cover, but Klein could hear the laughter in her voice. "Does he think he treed a rabbit?"

"He thinks everything that runs is a squirrel." Klein sighed and shook his head. "He'll sit there all day waiting for something to come down that never went up in the first place. I've tried to explain to him that even if it is a squirrel, it won't come down while he's waiting, but he doesn't believe me."

"Well, I can see why he has a hard time catching anything." She glanced at Klein, then back at the dog. "And maybe that isn't the worst thing. It's not like you need him to bring home food for you to eat."

Something in her voice made him cut a glance her way. She was no longer smiling. Instead, she appeared pensive, as if remembering times gone by.

"True," he agreed. "But I worry about him. He doesn't seem overly bright."

She raised her gaze to his. "Appearances can be deceiving."

"So I've heard."

Klein whistled, and Clint's head whipped in his direction. After a longing look up the tree, he sighed and slunk over to join them on the porch. His snout sniffed the air and his sad gaze lit on the plate of snacks. Klein was gratified to see only two-thirds of the offerings remained.

"I don't think so, buddy."

Clint's shoulders sagged and he wandered off, desolate and starving.

Isabelle leaned back in the chair, holding the

wineglass loosely in one hand. For a moment he studied that hand. Slim fingers, long manicured nails; though he liked it, the polish would have to go. What self-respecting small-town sheriff wore hot-pink nail polish?

Her gaze now on the mountains, she appeared as relaxed as Klein had ever seen her. Well, that was what he'd been after. Getting her to slow down, smell the breeze, walk the dog. He just hadn't thought she'd take to it so well or so easily.

"You ready to head back to town?"

As if he'd shouted in her ear, she jumped, shot to her feet and began to gather the plate and the glasses. "Of course. You've got work. I was just—"

He touched her arm. Her skin literally vibrated; the muscles beneath quivered. Now *he* was reminded of times long past. For his mother, every day had brought a crisis, every minor annoyance a disaster; her entire life had been a running soap opera. Klein's duty had been to keep her calm, smooth the way, take care of every little thing. Because when he did, she loved him.

He sighed. Hyper people made him nuts. So why did they always surround him?

"Stop," he ordered.

Slowly she raised her gaze from his hand on her arm to his face. "Stop?"

Klein took the plate and glasses from her, removed several pieces of cheese, fruit and crackers and laid them in her empty hands. "Stop being so nervous. You're going to turn me into you, instead of the other way around."

She raised an eyebrow. "I don't see that happening."

From the way his heart was jumping, he did. "You need to quit hopping around like Clint's rabbits. No one's going to chase you up a tree while I'm around." She smiled. "Think small. Think slow. Think all the time in the world."

She took a deep breath, let it out, ate a cracker, swallowed. "I'll do my best, Klein, but I'm just not a small-thinkin', slow-movin' woman."

"I never would have guessed."

CHAPTER EIGHT

KLEIN HANDED BELLE Clint's leash as soon as they left his yard. Well, he had said she needed to walk the dog, and in truth she never had before. The dogs at home were either penned or set free to run in the mountains and bring home game for themselves or the family. Within five minutes she understood why such an activity was not considered exercise but a leisure activity.

Clint was more laid-back than Klein. Since the dog needed to smell every inch of the road all the way back to town—with occasional breaks to sniff, then drool on, Belle's shoes—she did a whole lot more standing than walking. And after the first half mile, she no longer gritted her teeth whenever he paused. He was having such a good time she didn't have the heart to tug him along at her usual pace.

As Klein had pointed out, *she* was supposed to slow down, not speed everyone else up. Belle couldn't help it; she was just a speedy kind of gal. In her world the motto was "you snooze, you lose." If she didn't get there first, someone else would. But suddenly, in order to succeed, she had to be what she'd spent years training herself to leave behind.

"How far to town?" she asked Klein, who was hanging even farther back than Clint.

He shrugged. "'Bout half an hour if I'm in a hurry."

"Hurry? You? Never."

He smiled. "I do. Sometimes. But I have to have a very good reason." He flicked a finger behind her. "You might want to roust Clint from the road. I expect that could be dangerous."

Belle turned around to discover that while they'd been chatting, Clint had fallen asleep on the center line of Highway B.

By the time they reached Pleasant Ridge, businesses had closed. Lights flickered to life both in town and in the distance. Long gray fingers of dusk spread over the mountains, then into the valley.

The three of them stopped right there on the sidewalk and together they watched the sun—a bright orange ball of flame circled by cobalt blue and wispy clouds of white—sink. Even Clint sighed.

Belle had thought days in Pleasant Ridge would be dull beyond redemption. She couldn't have been more wrong. Of course, not every day would be like this one. At least, she hoped not. But listening to Klein talk about people, places, the things that went on here, she could see that *dull* was not a word to describe the life of a small-town sheriff.

While Klein observed the vestiges of sunlight dribble into the horizon like a child's crayon drawing left to melt on the sky, Belle eyed his impressive chest and remembered all she had seen him do that day.

Besides the walking, he'd probably done fifty leg

squats as he bent to check on injured people. He'd lifted a good many, carried them, too, then twisted and turned to put them out of harm's way. She'd even seen him directing traffic, holding out his no-doubt-chiseled arms, pointing here, there, everywhere enough times to make Belle's arms ache just thinking about it. Gabe Klein's entire day was one long exercise class.

Which explained why muscles Belle couldn't recall even having ached as though she'd pounded on them with a rubber hammer. She was going to be even more sore in the morning. And she didn't care. She felt good. Sore, but good. She'd gotten her aches and pains by working, helping, doing, rather than running to get nowhere. Maybe there was something to be said about the exercise class of life.

Klein didn't seem to know she was watching him, or maybe he just didn't care, so she kept looking. The problem was, she couldn't look without wanting to touch. He had such nice skin, smooth and tanned, and his nose, while large, was straight and strong. She wanted to trail a finger down the bridge, smooth her thumbs over his cheekbones, run her palms all over his back. And that was just her hands. She wasn't even going to think about what she wanted to do to him with her mouth.

Belle's sigh was echoed by Clint's groan as he lay down on the sidewalk. Klein slid a glance at her. In his eyes was a wariness she couldn't quite fathom. "We'd best get a move on before he settles in for the night."

Without waiting for her answer, he meandered down the street.

KLEIN'S SKIN TINGLED. Why did she keep staring at him like that? Even now he could feel her gaze hot between his shoulder blades.

He'd been gawked at all his life; you'd think he'd be used to it by now. He'd thought he was. But Isabelle's staring got to him, made him think of things he hadn't cared about in years—like the size of his nose, the shape of his face, the shade and lack of his hair. All foolishness—things he could not control or aspects of him that did not matter. But tell it to a woman who looked like her.

Caught up in thoughts of Isabelle and all those foolish things that mattered to ''other'' people, Klein forgot to cross the street. He stopped dead as furious yapping erupted from the building to his left and a streak of black-and-brown fur cloaked in white shot from the doorway. Prepared for a lump with teeth to latch onto his leg, he tensed. But this time, T.B. raced past him in the direction of—

"Isabelle!"

He spun on his heel, already running, not sure what he'd do except scoop her off the ground and keep her safe from manic Mexican mutts. However, T.B. wasn't interested in her. He only had eyes for Clint.

Yap-yap-yap! Klein had never seen the animal so furious. Clint stared at the dog as though not quite sure what it was. Klein couldn't blame him. He'd never been quite sure, either.

Though T.B. talked a good game, his bark was too high-pitched to take seriously, and while the lace bonnet and equally lacy bloomers matched the bark, they didn't elicit the terror T.B. seemed to think followed wherever he roamed.

Before Klein reached them, Isabelle made a move to get in between the yapping dog and the silent one.

"No!" Klein snapped. T.B. might not look fierce, but Klein had enough shredded pants to prove that the little dog was deep-down crazy.

Klein glanced around for a bucket of water, some ice, a fire hose—anything to defuse the animals. He did not want to have to tell Mrs. Dubray that his huge hound dog had marked her cute, though insane, baby boy.

T.B. continued to yap. Clint leaned down and delicately sniffed the moving mouth. Then he sneezed—right in T.B.'s face. The little dog went silent.

"Oh-oh," Isabelle murmured.

Klein reached out, tugged her to his side and just behind him. In his mind he imagined something like a dogfight on Cartoon Network—animals rolling, spit spraying, fur flying. What happened was a whole lot different. Considering Clint and T.B., he shouldn't have been surprised.

The little dog vibrated with fury. A buzzing noise came from his throat. It took Klein a moment to realize T.B. was growling.

He glanced at Clint. Klein could almost see understanding spread over that hound dog face. The sniping, buzzing *thing* was a dog!

Clint collapsed to the pavement and rolled on his back, belly up, neck bared, complete submissiveness in every fluid bone of his chicken-hearted body.

"Oh man," Klein groaned. "He's gutless."

T.B. stopped growling, stared down his nose at the groveling hound dog and tipped his head in a regal manner made ridiculous by his bonnet. T.B. didn't care. He was a wolf in Chihuahua skin, while Clint was a wuss with a hound dog body.

As if to mark Clint's head as his territory, T.B. began to lift his leg. Klein could stand only so much. "Hey!" The dog looked at him. "Don't even think about it."

Klein took a step toward T.B., prepared to help him back home physically. After eyeing Klein's pants with interest, the dog trotted back toward the museum.

As soon as the little dog was gone, the big one rolled over and stared at Klein with his tongue hanging out. He appeared to be smiling. Considering Clint's face, this was quite an accomplishment.

"He has no idea," Klein said slowly. "Not a single clue that he's just rolled belly up to a dog one-twentieth his size."

"Did you want them to fight?"

"All he had to do was bark, growl, even stand his ground. Something. Anything. Now he'll *have* to fight, or keep crawling to that pipsqueak for the rest of his life."

"Maybe he doesn't mind crawling."

"How could he not mind?"

"Because he'd rather be a crawler than a fighter?"

Klein couldn't fathom that. He'd learned in

countless small towns in countless places that you had to stand up for yourself right off the bat or be a doormat forever. Klein had never made a good doormat. He was too big for the porch.

"I was hoping once he felt at home here, once he knew he was safe and I'd never let anyone hurt him, then he'd be braver, stronger."

Isabelle took Klein's hand. He started, but she just smiled and linked their fingers. "You were hoping his hound doggedness was more than skin deep?"

Klein blinked. "Yeah, I guess you could say that."

"Just because he looks like a hound dog and sounds like a hound dog doesn't make him a hound dog."

"What are you talking about?"

"He's just Clint—" She shrugged, but she didn't let go of his hand.

To be honest, Klein didn't really want her to.

"You can't make him what he isn't. You'll have to love him exactly as he is."

"Love him?" Klein glanced down, to find Clint happily licking his boots. *Oh man.*

"Isn't that what you do with pets? Love them, touch them, take care of them. Otherwise, why have them?"

Klein grunted. "Got me."

He walked away from Clint's devotion, and since Isabelle was still clinging to his hand, she came along. Clint followed. He had to. Isabelle was still clinging to him, too, by the leash.

He shouldn't let the idea of loving a dog bother

him so much. But there was the past to consider. Once Klein loved someone, all sorts of lousy things began to happen.

"Yoo-hoo! Sheriff!"

Klein froze. Wherever Miss Dubray walked, T.B. was soon to follow. However, the lady was nowhere in sight.

"Up there." Isabelle pointed to the second story.

Klein moved away from the building, nearer the curb, so he could see upstairs. Miss Dubray hung out the window of her apartment.

"Did T.B. eat your pants again?"

Isabelle choked. Klein tightened his grip on her fingers and kept his gaze on Miss Dubray. "No, ma'am."

"Oh, well, good. I heard him shouting and I just knew it had to be you."

She glanced at Isabelle, smiled, then turned her attention to Clint. The smile faded; her penciled-on eyebrows rose in a ladylike arch. "What is *that?*"

Klein sighed. "My dog."

"You have a dog, Sheriff? Well, no wonder T.B. has been attacking you. My baby can't abide other dogs. One sight, one scent, and he can't help himself—he attacks. He just has to be the king of the hill, lord of the manor." Miss Dubray giggled. "Top dog."

"Really?" Klein muttered. "I never would have known that."

Miss Dubray ignored him, turning her attention to Isabelle. "Now, this must be our new guest, Isabelle."

Women of Miss Dubray's advanced age never

bothered with *miss* and *mister* when addressing someone aeons younger than they were. Klein was surprised she called him *Sheriff* instead of *boy*.

"Yes, ma'am." Belle's voice had slowed, gone South in the space of a heartbeat.

Oh, she was very good.

"And you are?" she asked.

"Peg Dubray. Call me Peg."

Peg? Klein had never heard Miss Dubray's first name. *Ever.* Not that he'd been here so very long, but hey—how come Isabelle got to call her Peg?

"We've all heard how much help you were this afternoon."

Aha!

"Now, what I want to know is how a pretty little thing like you learned all that first aid?"

"My mama taught me."

Her mama? Klein glanced at Isabelle, but she was focused on Miss Dubray, and her face looked kind of sad, making him glad he still held her hand.

"Was your mama a nurse?"

"No, ma'am. We just…had need of a lot of first aid at our house."

"How lucky for us that you were around."

Klein wanted to hear more about first aid at Isabelle's house, but Miss Dubray had more questions for him. "Sheriff, what on earth was Jubel doing with a hunting rifle? Everyone knows he couldn't hit an aircraft carrier with that thing."

"He hit a bus. That's why he's in jail."

"He couldn't have meant to. You know that."

"He might not have meant to, but he did. That's

all I care about.'' Klein frowned. ''How did you hear about Jubel?''

''Me?'' Miss Dubray batted her eyelashes. ''Why, Sheriff, Virgil told me the entire story when he came by for his afternoon mint julep.''

''His what?'' Klein roared.

''Well, he didn't partake today. He had too much to do. But he had to come by and tell me why he wasn't coming by.''

Klein's head was starting to hurt. ''My deputy partakes of a mint julep every afternoon?''

''At three.''

''Why?''

''It's on the schedule.''

''What schedule?''

''His. He's been coming here for thirty years. We—''

''He can't drink on duty. He's the biggest rule stickler in three states. Why would he drink on duty?''

''Drink?''

She blinked as if confused. Though she was nearly as old as Virgil, Klein had never known Miss Dubray to lose track of a conversation before.

''Oh, yes, the *drink*.'' She winked. ''You needn't worry about the itsy bit of alcohol I might put in there.''

Klein had been born and raised in the South. He knew that a Southerner's idea of an itsy bit in relation to alcohol was a whole lot different from anyone else's.

''You especially don't have to worry about Virgil. Why, he's been partaking since he was—''

"I *don't* want to hear about it." Klein was gritting his teeth. It didn't help his headache.

"Now, now. Relax. Big man like you, all that stress today, out in the sun and the heat—you shouldn't get yourself excited. Go and have supper. Virgil's got everything under control. You just keep on holding Isabelle's hand."

He glanced down and saw that he was indeed still holding her hand—or rather, she was holding his. He'd forgotten all about it. How could that be? It wasn't as though holding hands was a natural state for Gabe Klein and Isabelle Ash. But it had felt right—or at least comfortable enough to forget about.

Klein snatched his hand out of hers. Now everyone would be blabbering that he and Isabelle Ash had been holding hands on Longstreet Avenue. *Hell.*

Miss Dubray made a tsking sound. "You *keep* holding her hand and strolling with the dog. That's what you need. Go have supper at Murphy's. Honestly, Sheriff, you work far too hard." She smiled, waved and disappeared inside.

"I'd like that."

"What?"

Isabelle inserted her hand back into his and held on when he tried to pull away again. "Supper."

"You would?"

"Don't sound so surprised. I eat on occasion."

"From the looks of you, occasionally is the only time you eat."

If she hadn't been holding his hand, he wouldn't have felt the sudden brittle tension in her fingers.

Klein hadn't gotten his detective's badge by being slow on the uptake. He'd insulted her somehow. Though in his experience with women—minor as that might be—telling one she was skinny was a compliment.

He began to walk down Longstreet Avenue, letting Isabelle hold his hand, walk his dog, while he tried to figure out where he'd screwed up. He couldn't, so he just apologized. "Sorry."

"For what?"

"Not sure. But I upset you by saying you hardly eat, and I'm sorry."

The glance she gave him was full of surprise. "You're very observant, Klein."

"My job."

"True." She swung their joined hands. "Well, call me silly, but I find it amazing that people think it's all right to comment on a thin person's eating habits. As if it's any of their business what I eat, when or even if. Yet if I was overweight, such comments would be considered rude."

Klein considered that. She was right. There was still something off about her defensiveness, but he could find no fault with her logic. "I see your point."

"Good. Now, where is this place?"

"You realize that the two of us holding hands and having supper will be news in this town."

"Isn't that what friends do?"

Klein couldn't recall holding hands and strolling with any of his other friends. Guys were funny that way. His friends who were women wanted to talk, or have him protect them from whatever it was that they needed a man like Klein as a friend for. They did not want to be seen in public holding hands with him. Odd that Isabelle didn't seem to mind.

"Friends have supper," he allowed. "But the hand holding—that's new to me."

"Me, too, but I like it." She tightened her fingers on his. "Don't you?"

Klein looked down into her hopeful, beautiful face. He should say no; he should take back his hand; he should drop her at home and not see her until tomorrow. But he just couldn't lie to eyes like those.

"Yes," he said.

"Then, let's give 'em something to talk about."

"You *want* people to gossip about you?"

"No, I want people to get used to seeing us together so they stop gossiping. The more they see me, the more they see you and me, the sooner they'll treat us like part of the furniture, and I can go about my business."

Was she serious? Did Isabelle really think she could ever be seen as commonplace anywhere on earth, but especially somewhere like Pleasant Ridge? Well, she'd have to learn the hard way.

"All right, but we'll have to stop at the station before supper."

"Work first, eat later?"

"Work first, everything later."

"I figured you'd say that."

"Then you're starting to get the hang of life as a small-town sheriff."

CHAPTER NINE

PERHAPS HAND HOLDING wasn't on the list of activities for friends. Belle wouldn't know. But since she was learning as she went, about a lot of things, she figured she could make up a few things, too. Besides, she *liked* holding Klein's hand. She wasn't going to give that up just because people might talk. People talked about her all the time. If she worried about it, she'd waste a whole lot of her life.

After leaving Peg Dubray and her crazy pooch behind, they stopped at the station, where Klein chewed out Virgil for his mint-julep habit.

"When you said you were taking a coffee break every afternoon at three, I thought you were having coffee. Not that you need coffee, mind you..."

Eyes on Clint, who was busy sniffing the garbage can, the deputy slipped his gun into a desk drawer. "You don't understand how things are done here, Chief."

"I understand mint juleps in the afternoon. Who else knows about this?"

"Me and Miss Dubray. The pup, I guess. It's not like we sit out front of the museum and do it."

"She said you've been going there every afternoon for thirty years."

"Give or take."

"You gonna stop?"

"No."

Klein sighed. "Well, try to keep it under wraps, then."

"I always have. Don't know why she had to tell you and the four-twenty-five about it, anyway."

"Her name's Isabelle, not four-twenty-five."

"Ach, I can't remember names no how."

"If you can remember all those numbers, why not a name?"

"You can't remember the numbers."

"I don't mind if he calls me four-twenty-five," Belle put in. "It's kind of cute."

"Cute?" both men said at the same time, each horrified.

"Yeah. Cute."

Virgil made a gagging noise. "Fine, I'll call her Isabelle."

Klein winked at her, and Belle resisted the urge to preen under his unspoken praise. If she wasn't careful she'd be following him around like Clint—she glanced at the hound dog—or lying at Klein's feet, staring at his face, waiting for one small pat on the head or mention of her name.

"Cass came by." Belle lifted her gaze to Virgil, who was smirking. "Something about her lawyer."

"Blah, blah, blah," Klein muttered.

Virgil's smirk became a smile. "Yeah, that's what I said. What did you do to her this time?"

"Ripped her film out of her camera." Klein shrugged. "Someone had to."

"Wish it could have been me," Virgil grumbled. "That girl is a P-E-S-T."

"Next time. Is everything else set here?"

"Been set since an hour after I got back."

"Paperwork?"

"Done."

"Lawyer?"

"Called."

"Arraignment?"

"Tomorrow."

"Family."

"Here and gone."

"Glad I missed it."

"Uh-huh. It wasn't pretty. Mama cryin'. Brothers cursin'. Daddy threatenin'."

"The usual, then."

"Pretty much."

"This time it's serious. Someone died."

"I was there, Chief. I saw. Jubel's locked up tight, and he ain't goin' anywhere." He glanced at Belle. "Saw you, too." He gave a sharp nod. "You done good."

Before she could thank him, a shout came from the jail cell and he scurried out of the room.

"High praise from Virgil, you know. He's never told me I done good."

"That's too bad. Because I'm sure you done good every single day."

Klein grunted. He appeared to be as adept at handling praise as she was. "Let's eat."

They headed for the door—all three of them. "Stay," Klein ordered.

Clint collapsed on the floor with a sigh of despair.

"Aw, can't he come?"

"No." Clint rolled over, grumbling. Klein yanked open the door and ushered Belle out.

Within minutes they were seated in a prime window booth at Murphy's. Seemed that everyone there had heard about Belle's heroics, too.

Serafina Murphy doubled as waitress and cashier, while her husband, Murph—Belle never caught his first name—did the cooking. The contrast between the big, bluff, redheaded Irishman and the petite, energetic, dark-eyed woman made Belle smile. As did the incongruity of a Murphy with an Italian accent.

"Ah, *sceriffo,* it is so good of you to bring her here. Sit. I will bring the specialty we have made just for you."

Before anyone could comment, Lucinda Jones bustled through the door, caught sight of Belle and made a beeline for their table.

"There you are." She beamed. "These are for you." She plopped a glass baking dish of brownies in front of Belle. "You just bring the pan back when you're done."

Done? The thought of taking an entire pan of brownies to her lonely apartment made a cold sweat start on the back of Belle's neck. She glanced at Klein, to discover him frowning at her. She probably looked as shaky as she felt.

Her gaze drawn back to the gift, her mouth watered at the prospect of thirteen-by-nine inches of chocolate just for her. With powdered sugar on top, no less. She was in deep trouble.

"It's not Monday," she protested.

"After what you did today, every day can be Monday for you."

"All I did was help the doctor. I didn't cure cancer or anything."

"Now, now. You're too modest. I heard tell you stitched up someone's head."

"No, I—"

"That's not right," said a man in the booth behind Klein. "She sewed someone's finger back on before the doc even got there."

"She brought a guy back to life with that CPA stuff."

"She pulled a kid from a burning car."

The litany continued. Belle sat there with her mouth open, not sure what to say. Not a single one of the offerings was true. She glanced at Klein helplessly, to find him staring at her with an "I told you so" twist to his lips.

The folks of Pleasant Ridge continued to argue about what she'd done that day. As they did so, they inched closer and closer, until there was a small crowd around their table.

Well, she'd just have to set everyone straight. As her mama always said, nip it in the bud—and more often than not her mama was right.

"Listen." Belle raised her hands, and the crowd quieted. "This is what happened." Then she proceeded to explain what she'd done to help in the aftermath of the accident.

In childhood, she'd played out fantasies in the quiet of her room; back then, she'd learned how to twist the truth, how to wait and wait and wait a little more, then hit her imaginary audience with a spark of humor when they least expected it. Today she used all she'd learned to make them forget the tragedy, at least for a little while.

"Out of my way." Serafina approached, steaming plates held high. "Lady with food."

She plopped two heaping helpings of lasagna in front of Klein and Belle, then placed a basket of garlic bread swimming in butter in the middle of the table. She slid toward Belle the huge pan of brownies that Belle had surreptitiously inched over to Klein's side. Belle's stomach rolled.

"On the house." Serafina beamed at her.

Belle tried to smile, but she couldn't quite do it. She glanced at Klein. He was no longer smiling, either. Instead, he stared at her speculatively. *Damn.* The man was far too smart and far too observant. If she wasn't careful he'd know everything without her telling him anything.

"Th-thank you," she managed to say.

"Say *grazie* by eating it. You will blow away in the next strong wind if we are not careful." Serafina patted Belle's shoulder and turned. *"Andare!"* She made a shooing motion until everyone moved away from their table.

Belle couldn't stop herself from staring at the mound of food and imagining it plastered to her hips. The bread she might as well just tape to her butt and be done with it.

"Eat what you can," Klein murmured. "I'll help with the rest."

He held the bread basket out to her, wiggled it a little. The butter at the bottom sloshed from side to side. The incredible smell, warm bread and garlic, hit her in the face. Hunger snarled deep inside, and she went dizzy with desire for something other than Klein's chest.

"One piece won't kill you," he said.

Little did he know.

"Around here," Klein continued, "gratitude is shown with food."

Belle let her gaze wander over their loaded table, then lifted one brow. "Is that so?"

"Sympathy, too. You ought to see the spread that's put on for a funeral."

"I think I'll pass."

"And sometimes food is a replacement for other things."

Belle's eyes met his. What did he know, or think he knew?

"For instance?" She kept her face as deadpan as Klein did on occasion. Maybe she had learned something after all.

"Confidence? Friendship?" He shook the basket again. "Success? Even love."

"Interesting theory."

"Isn't it?"

Intent on proving wrong whatever it was he thought he knew about her, Belle took a piece of bread and stuffed half into her mouth. She forgot all about proving anything as the taste exploded on her tongue—too wonderful to be believed. How long had it been since she'd eaten bread drenched in real butter?

Obviously longer than she'd thought. Her head spun. Enjoying herself too much to notice anything else, she jumped in her seat when a man asked, "What's this?"

Klein's aggravated sigh told her who had joined them even before she turned her head to discover the mayor—dressed as if he'd just played three sets of tennis but hadn't sweated a drop—beside their table.

Without invitation, he slid into Belle's side of the booth, bumping her hip with his. Too bad Klein hadn't sat next to her—so Smith couldn't. But she imagined that if she ever wanted to sit next to Klein again *she'd* have to manage the seating arrangements, rather than the other way around.

She swallowed the bread, and her mouth watered for more. Deliberately, she kept her gaze off the basket and turned her attention to cutting the lasagna into miniature pieces.

"This is supper," Klein growled in answer to the mayor's question. "I'm sure you've heard of it."

Smith ignored him, staring at the table incredulously before addressing Belle. "You eat like this?"

"Not every day." An understatement if ever there was one.

"I would think not."

The face he made at the table full of delicious food was insulting to say the least. How could he possibly be this annoying and still get elected? She'd known him only a day and already she wanted to avoid him for the rest of her life.

Belle slid a glance toward Serafina, who hovered behind the counter, pretending not to watch. The mayor's grimace had the tiny woman biting her lip. Belle grabbed her fork and dug into the lasagna.

"Mmm," she murmured several bites later. "You have no idea what you're missing."

Serafina's smile was a reward far greater than any accolade. Belle would worry tomorrow about the ramifications of the meal.

"I'm missing about eight thousand calories and too many grams of fat to count. Have you ever seen what cholesterol looks like in your blood?"

The lasagna churned in Belle's stomach. Maybe she'd worry right now.

"Shut up, Chai."

Klein's voice was mild, but Chai shut up. Oh, how Belle wished she could do that! She flashed Klein a grateful glance, which he answered with a flick of his finger toward the lasagna and a tilt of his head toward Serafina, who still watched expectantly.

Belle took another bite. Despite the heavy feeling in her stomach, the food tasted warm, inviting, comforting. She was reminded of a time when Mama could make everything better with a kiss and cookie.

"Shouldn't you be off duty by now, Mayor?" Klein asked.

"No rest for the weary."

His knee bumped against Belle's beneath the table. She froze with her fork halfway to her mouth, but his leg moved away as if the touch had been accidental, so she ate some more, which was a lot more fun than analyzing that knee bump.

Klein's sigh sounded more like a growl, and he gave up being polite. "What do you want?"

The mayor was undisturbed by the rudeness. No doubt he'd been confronted with it before. "I heard about the accident. About all you did to help."

He beamed at Belle. His hand patted her knee, then stayed there. She jumped.

Klein frowned. "Something the matter?" he asked.

Belle shook her head, shifted over, and the mayor's hand slid away, but not before he'd felt a whole lot more than her knee. Belle started eating again, so she wouldn't say something she'd regret.

How many men in how many places had thought they could touch her any way that they wanted to, just because of what she did for a living? Too many to count. You'd think she'd be used to it by now, but she wasn't. You'd think she'd have figured out a way to handle the insult, but she hadn't.

"Chai, spill what you came in here for, or get out. Isabelle has had a rough day."

"Isabelle, huh?" His friendly, down-home, good-old-boy voice took on the cultured coolness of a country club icon. "I heard you two were holding hands on Longstreet Avenue."

"My, my—" Klein drawled.

Belle stopped eating and met his gaze, which said "I told you so" again much louder than words.

"Folks have been busy."

"What the hell were you thinking?" the mayor demanded.

Klein's eyes narrowed, and Belle jumped in before he could. This was, after all, her fault. "I was thinking I needed my hand held after the day I had today. Holding hands isn't a federal offense. Or is it against the law in Pleasant Ridge?''

"Not that I've heard." Klein stared at the mayor with his arms crossed over his impressive chest. "But you'd better check with Virgil."

Belle began to laugh, but when the mayor glared, she turned the sound into a cough. Some of the spoiled little boy had leaked through the mask of the suave, golden man.

"Anything else you wanted, Chai?"

"I just wanted to see if Isabelle was all right." Klein rolled his eyes. "And... well...maybe you could give us a few minutes, Klein. Hmm? I don't need an audience."

Ah, hell, Belle thought. *He's going to ask me out.* Before she could send Klein a "don't you dare leave me with him!" message with her eyes, he exited the booth and strolled away.

The mayor faced her with a practiced smile. His fingers returned to her thigh. Belle glanced at Klein over Chai Smith's shoulder, but he was already talking to Serafina and he wasn't even looking at her. She was on her own. What else was new?

"I'd hoped to take you to supper on your first night here."

He was so close that his breath brushed her neck. Why when Klein's breath touched her did she feel hot, and when Chai Smith's did, did she feel nothing but cold? Perhaps because of the chilly beast that lurked behind the heat in the mayor's eyes.

Belle scooted a few inches away from the man, but her tailbone hit the end of the booth. Smith scooted after her with a smile. She should take his elegant fingers and twist them into a pretzel the way her brothers used to do to her. But she couldn't afford to piss him off.

So she smiled and put her fingers atop his—the best way she'd discovered to keep a man's hand from going any farther north.

His smile widened. "We could leave. Go somewhere much better than here."

Belle glanced at her plate, surprised to discover she'd eaten nearly all her dinner. "I'm not hungry. But if you'd like to discuss business, now would be a good time."

His face fell. "Business? Well, no, that's not what I had in mind."

She knew what he had in mind, and it wasn't going to happen. Not in this lifetime. But how did she say that and still keep him on her side?

By pretending, of course. She'd pretend she was as dim as he no doubt believed her to be.

"I thought I'd show you some of the finer places in this part of Tennessee." He squeezed her knee. "Just you and me."

She waited for the wink. She didn't have to wait long. Did women actually fall for this stuff? Belle resisted the urge to sigh. She knew that they did.

"How sweet." She patted his hand, a little harder than necessary, true, but he didn't notice. He probably wouldn't notice anything short of a sledgehammer over his head.

"I couldn't possibly." He frowned. "At least, not right now. Why, I'm just too busy to give a man like you the attention you deserve."

An Important Message from the Editors

Dear Reader,

Because you've chosen to read one of our fine romance novels, we'd like to say "thank you!" And, as a special way to thank you, we've selected two more of the books you love so well, plus an exciting Mystery Gift, to send you absolutely FREE!

Please enjoy them with our compliments...

Pam Powers

P.S. And because we value our customers, we've attached something extra inside...

Peel off seal and place inside...

How to validate your Editor's
FREE GIFT
"Thank You"

1. Peel off gift seal from front cover. Place it in space provided at right. This automatically entitles you to receive 2 FREE BOOKS and a fabulous mystery gift.

2. Send back this card and you'll get 2 brand-new Harlequin Superromance® novels. These books have a cover price of $4.99 each in the U.S. and $5.99 each in Canada, but they are yours to keep absolutely free.

3. There's no catch. You're under no obligation to buy anything. We charge nothing—ZERO—for your first shipment. And you don't have to make any minimum number of purchases—not even one!

4. The fact is, thousands of readers enjoy receiving their books by mail from the Harlequin Reader Service®. They enjoy the convenience of home delivery...they like getting the best new novels at discount prices BEFORE they're available in stores...and they love their *Heart to Heart* subscriber newsletter featuring author news, horoscopes, recipes, book reviews and much more!

5. We hope that after receiving your free books you'll want to remain a subscriber. But the choice is yours—to continue or cancel, any time at all! So why not take us up on our invitation, with no risk of any kind. You'll be glad you did!

6. Don't forget to detach your FREE BOOKMARK. And remember...just for validating your Editor's Free Gift Offer, we'll send you THREE gifts, *ABSOLUTELY FREE!*

GET A
FREE MYSTERY GIFT...

SURPRISE MYSTERY GIFT
*COULD BE YOURS **FREE** AS*
A SPECIAL "THANK YOU" FROM
THE EDITORS OF HARLEQUIN

Visit us online at
www.eHarlequin.com

"I don't need much time."

Probably not, she thought dryly.

"Now, you know I have to make this show a success. Otherwise, where will I be?" She lifted his hand from her knee and placed it back on his own. "Where will you be if everything we've planned falls down about our heads, huckety-buck?"

The reminder of his part in the deal seemed to reach the mayor. If she looked like a fool, he could very well look the same, and men like Chai Smith would do anything to avoid looking like a fool.

They never seemed to realize they could hardly avoid appearing what they already were.

SERAFINA GLANCED PAST Klein and muttered something in Italian that didn't sound like "honey." Then she sniffed, pointedly gave him a glare and flounced into the kitchen.

Klein leaned against the counter. He'd bet money that the mayor was fondling Isabelle beneath the table. Klein had to breathe deeply and focus on staying right where he was, because what he wanted to do was stalk over there, drag the mayor out of the booth and break any part of him that had touched any part of her.

But when he'd asked if anything was the matter, she'd shaken her head. Klein wasn't going to embarrass himself by stepping in when he wasn't needed. He'd been there and done that.

Still, he continued to watch them both, wondering what she was up to. She'd said the mayor was a molting vulture. From where he stood right now,

Isabelle seemed to have developed a deep fondness for molting vultures.

Her face was animated, and one hand emphasized her words while the other hid beneath the table, no doubt holding hands with this new friend, too.

Klein was gritting his teeth again, so he forced himself to stop. He knew better than to get emotionally involved with a beautiful woman. Heck, with any woman. He'd done so well for so long. Then Isabelle had come to town, and in the space of one day all his carefully laid plans, all his meticulously thought-out rules had gone into the trash.

He was lonely, but he would live. If a person could die of loneliness, Klein never would have made it past the age of eight.

Despite his good intentions, he found himself fascinated with the movements of her fingers and the shape of her mouth. Klein shifted against the countertop as an image of those clever fingers doing something else entirely sprang to life in his brain. If he didn't put a stop to this sudden obsession, he was going to get hurt, or at the very least be embarrassed. And he'd have no one to blame but himself.

Klein forced his thoughts from flashes of Isabelle in a towel, wet and warm from her shower, staring at him with what he'd sworn was invitation in her eyes, until he'd come to his senses...to the way she'd been only a little while ago.

Her tale of the afternoon accident had been different from Virgil's. From her point of view, the afternoon had been an adventure, though she had not styled herself a heroine. Instead, she'd added humor in just the right amount to make the tale bittersweet. She'd had everyone laughing if not smiling, including him. Isabelle had a wonderful imagination, a gift for words and an incredible sense of timing. Why hadn't she become a writer instead of an actress if she could concoct stories out of the air and keep people entertained with such ease?

One look at her face and he knew why. That face didn't belong in front of a computer; it belonged on the screen.

Because Klein was looking at her so closely, he saw her gaze lower to the nearly empty plate of lasagna. She blinked. He'd observed her methodically cutting the noodles into itty-bitty pieces and rearranging them on her plate, but since she'd been eating, too, he hadn't thought much of it.

Her eyes shifted to the brownies, and she turned away from the dessert so abruptly it was almost as if she was afraid of them. Which was too silly to be believed. So why did he believe it?

Focused on Isabelle and her odd behavior, Klein didn't notice Chai coming toward him until the man spoke.

"She's even more beautiful in person, isn't she." He sighed like a love-struck teenager.

"I wouldn't know, since I've only seen her in person."

Chai laughed. "That's your story and you're sticking to it, huh?"

Klein didn't bother to answer him. Of course, Chai had never needed any encouragement to keep right on talking. "What I'd like to see in person are those jugs." He smiled at Isabelle, who smiled back, unaware. "What a rack," he breathed.

Klein's hands curled into fists. Would the mayor be an idiot if he wasn't twenty-three and hormone challenged? Probably.

"Watch your mouth, Mr. Mayor."

Chai didn't even bother to glance his way. He was too busy staring at Isabelle, who slid from the booth and bent over the table to retrieve her pan of brownies.

"Would you look at her." The man actually licked his lips. "Honestly, Klein, don't tell me you haven't been staring at that all day and itching to put your hands on it."

Guilty as charged, but at least he wasn't talking about "that" in public or drooling over "it" in Murphy's Café. *Yet.*

"I asked her to go out with me," Chai murmured.

"What did she say?"

Klein held his breath. What would he do if Isabelle agreed to go out with the Mayor Wonder? Kill him? However appealing, things were no longer handled that way, even in Tennessee. He missed the good old days.

"She's too busy now. But later." Chai licked his lips again, as if Isabelle were a prime steak sizzling on his own personal barbecue grill. "Later she will. I just know it."

"She turned you down?"

The mayor flicked him a petulant look. "Because she's *busy.*"

Klein grunted as Isabelle spun about with the pan of brownies in her hands. Her gaze went directly to him. She smiled, and not just with her mouth. The expression went all the way to her pretty brown eyes. Klein's lips lifted in response.

"I've *got* to get her to go out with me."

The intensity in Chai's voice reached through Klein's foggy consciousness. Had the mayor become a charter member of a stalkers' association? From the expression on his face, Klein had to wonder.

Isabelle turned to speak with Serafina, and Klein fixed Chai with a glare. "Why do you *have* to?"

"Can you imagine Isabelle Ash and me? What a couple. I could go much further than Pleasant Ridge with Isabelle on my arm." He wiggled his eyebrows. "And in my bed."

"You've lost me." Too bad not literally.

"With her fame and face, my connections and looks, we could go straight to the top. You know, people miss glamour in the White House. They talk about Jackie all the time. They even elected an actor once."

"You think Isabelle could be president?"

Confusion settled over Chai's face momentarily before understanding dawned. He snorted. "Right, Klein. That'll be the day."

Besides being a pretty-boy moron, the mayor was a chauvinist. That oughta get him reelected.

"Does Daddy know you want out of town?"

Chai tensed. Klein smiled. Nope, Daddy didn't know.

"He won't mind if I leave to be a senator."

That remained to be seen, and Klein would love to see it. He'd just store Chai's secret political ambitions away for use on a rainy day.

"Can't you just see that face on CNN?" Chai breathed. "Staring at me with such pride and devotion. That body next to mine as she waves to all the people. Securing me every male vote."

The mayor was definitely adrift in fantasyland.

"What about her?" Klein asked.

"Her?" Chai repeated, as if the concept were a foreign one.

"Yes. Her. *Isabelle,*" he enunciated. "What if she doesn't want to be on CNN?"

Chai laughed. "Her life is television and print. CNN would be an incredible coup. Besides, what woman wouldn't want to be a senator's wife, instead of an underwear model? Do you think she'd be better off as a Mayberry-*Baywatch* hottie than a political asset?"

If that was what she wanted, yes. But Klein didn't bother to share with Chai a concept beyond his understanding. He was going to have to keep an eye on the mayor and make sure he didn't cross the line any more than he already had. Though, if Isabelle refused to complain, there wouldn't be much Klein could do. Legally, at any rate. Klein cracked his knuckles.

"Do you even like her?" Klein couldn't help but wonder aloud, even though he felt as if he were in the seventh grade. Next thing, he'd be asking Chai to ask her if she liked him!

"Like? Hell, I love her. What's not to love?" He

leered in Isabelle's direction again. Luckily she was still talking to Serafina and missed it.

''So you're interested in her face, her body and her fame?''

''What else is there?'' He flicked a glance at Klein. ''Oh, you mean her *personality* and her *mind*.'' His lips twitched. ''That, too.''

Chai began to leave, but unfortunately he came right back. ''She said she'd be too busy to give me the attention I deserved until the pilot was finished, and I can understand that. The next month is going to be important to us all. I'd be worried about other men poaching, but then she'll be with you. Her hand holding pal.''

Klein merely raised his eyebrows and waited for the mayor to get to the point.

''Keep the others away from her for me, Sheriff. I'm counting on you.'' He glanced at Isabelle one last time. ''Damn, we're going to have beautiful kids.''

Chai strolled out of Murphy's, and Klein watched him go as the past swirled all around him. The last time he'd watched over a beautiful woman for another man, he hadn't even known he'd been doing it. He'd been in love with Kay Lynne, and he'd believed she was in love with him. She'd wanted beautiful children, too. He would have given her anything. But some things lay beyond his control.

He'd grown up in the years since Kay Lynne had told him the truth about everything. He was not the kind of man who inspired deep, true, unconditional and forever love in women. He'd learned to accept that—to live with it, if not to like it.

Because while beauty might be skin deep, ugliness went a whole lot further. All the way to a man's soul, making him wish for everything, hope for nothing, and know in his heart that no matter who he might want, she would never want him in the same way.

CHAPTER TEN

BY THE TIME Belle had finished thanking Serafina for the wonderful meal and convinced the woman she did not need a doggie bag for the garlic bread and she really, really did not need a midnight snack of linguine, the mayor had finished chatting with Klein and disappeared.

Just what she'd been waiting for.

She extricated herself from Serafina's attention by promising to return and eat again on an unspecified day in the future, then hustled across the room toward Klein.

He lifted his head, and she could tell something had changed. Belle slowed her pace so quickly she nearly stumbled. Was he upset that the mayor had already heard about their holding hands? But Klein had warned her such a thing was bound to happen. She hadn't cared, and he hadn't seemed to. So what was the matter with him now?

"Did Virgil call?" she asked. "Is there an emergency? Do we have to go?"

"Not we. Me. *I* have to go. But I'll walk you home first."

"I'm supposed to be your shadow, remember?"

"Not for this. It's routine. Let's go." He opened

the door, waving absently when Serafina shouted "*Ciao!*"

The streets of Pleasant Ridge had become deserted. As Belle and Klein walked, the silver-blue light of the moon warred with the flickering, colorful images of televisions and the muted golds of lamplight. The spring chill in the air brushed Belle's shoulders, and momentarily she wished for a sweater, until a better idea for warmth came to mind.

She shifted the evil pan of brownies to her left hip and reached for Klein's hand with her free one. He eluded her by snatching the brownies from her grip and clutching them with both hands.

"I'll take those," he said unnecessarily, then set a brisk pace in the direction of the five-and-dime.

"Please do. Take them home. Take them to the station. Take them far away from me."

His answer was a long, slow frown. *Oops, too desperate.* Belle needed to be more careful of what she said and did around Gabe Klein, or soon she'd be interrogated about more than she cared to be.

"You don't have to walk me home," she blurted. "You're obviously in a hurry to get back to work, and it's not like the streets around here aren't safe for high-fashion models."

"You'd be surprised," he muttered.

"What?"

"Never mind. Just don't talk to strangers. Don't go out alone at night. Keep your doors locked. You know the drill."

"Doors locked? I thought that was an insult."

"Insult me. I can take it."

He might be able to take it, but what he couldn't seem to do was look at her. *Hmm.* "What did the mayor say to you?"

Klein tripped over a crack in the sidewalk, although when Belle turned around, she saw there *was* no crack in the sidewalk. When she glanced back at him, he kept on walking. She had to hurry to catch up. He didn't answer her question, so she kept talking.

"He asked me out."

"I heard."

Aha. From past experience she deduced the mayor had warned Klein away from her. But why would Klein listen?

Honestly. Men were such...men.

"I said no."

He didn't even look at her. "You said *later.*"

"That's what he heard." Belle shrugged. "To be honest, that's what I wanted him to hear. I can't afford to alienate the mayor. I don't need him causing trouble." She stared at Klein's stony profile. "But I can see that he already has."

They reached the back steps of her apartment, and she put her hand on Klein's wrist before he could run away. His pulse thudded beneath her fingertips, steady and sure like the man, and she couldn't help herself; she let her hand stay there because she liked touching him, and right now he was letting her.

"He told you to stay away from me, didn't he?"

"Not exactly."

"*What* exactly?"

"He told me to keep all the other men away."

Her mouth fell open. This was worse than she'd thought. "Of all the nerve! Who does he think he is?"

"Your future husband?"

"Has he always been delusional?"

At last Klein looked at her, and either it was a trick of the moon or she caught a flash of the humor she liked so much in the depths of his stunning blue eyes. "I'm not sure."

"Maybe you'd better keep *him* away from me."

"Funny, I was thinking the same thing."

"My hero."

Despite the teasing lilt in her voice, he stiffened and backed away, pulling his wrist from beneath her fingers, removing her latest weakness—a sudden craving for his warmth and strength—from her reach.

The humor was gone from his eyes, if it had ever been there at all. Instead, he gazed at her without expression, once again the stoic cop she so wanted to emulate.

"I'm no hero," he said softly.

"I don't agree."

"I'm just doing my job."

"You do a lot more than just the job. I haven't been here long, and I can already see that you go above and beyond, every minute of the day."

"*That's* the job."

"A lot of men wouldn't think so. They'd take the easy way out. They wouldn't bother to warn me that their boss is a stalker in training. That might cause too much trouble for them."

"I find that hard to believe."

"Believe it. You'd be surprised at how many people believe that because of how I look or how I earn my living, I deserve whatever hassles might come my way."

He scowled. "They're idiots."

"You'll get no argument from me. But I'd still be on my own."

"You won't be on your own here."

"I know." She stared up at the bright, shiny moon and took a deep breath of fresh, cool night air. Funny, but Pleasant Ridge smelled just like home. "As handsome as the mayor is, as suave as he thinks he is, there's one thing that determines I'll never be in his presence for longer than I absolutely have to be."

His shoes scraped the pavement as he moved near her once more. "What's that?"

"He makes me feel like less." She lowered her gaze from the sky to his face. "But you..." She inched closer, too. "You make me feel like more."

Grateful for that, she went up on tiptoe and pressed her mouth to his cheek. She'd planned on just a quick, friendly, thank-you kiss. But the proximity to that chest, his heat, the scent of his skin in her nostrils, the taste of him on her lips made her freeze as a need for so much more washed over her. Her mouth lingered, brushing his jaw on the way back down.

Then she was staring at his suntanned neck, the smooth hollow of his throat, the pulse that beat hard and fast just beneath his ear. If she dragged her teeth over that pulse, would he come upstairs and make her forget the mayor, the accident, even the lasagna for an hour or two?

"Isabelle."

His voice, gentle and soft, trilled along her skin like a breeze. Hope fluttered in her heart, even as desire flared in her belly. Cool against hot, they mixed somewhere in between, and she swayed toward him. He shifted and raised one palm to cup her bare shoulder. The chill of the night dissipated as the heat of him called to the need in her.

Would he gather her close, hold her tight? Anticipation made her shiver. She caught her breath and tilted her head so she could see his face.

Concern etched his brow; kindness flickered in his eyes. "You have to get some rest."

The truth came to her as clear as the stars in the sky above. His hand was not caressing but comforting, not pulling her nearer but keeping her steady. In his gaze she saw no reflection of her desire, no interest in her at all.

Belle's cheeks heated, and she backed away. His fingers did not cling; they released her with ease. He was being her friend as she'd asked him to be— nothing more.

She'd kissed him, her mouth trailing along his skin, heart thudding, pulse skipping, desire spiking, and he'd stood there, one hand holding her at bay, the other holding the pan of brownies, no doubt waiting for her to finish drooling on him. Belle and Clint had more in common than she cared to admit.

Talk about feeling like less instead of more. Her lack of control where Gabriel Klein was concerned could become a problem if she let it. But if there was one thing Isabelle Ash knew, it was how to regain control—of both her mind and her body.

"You're right." Her voice sounded indifferent to what had just happened, though she was anything but. "I am tired."

"You should be. Here—" He held out the brownies.

There was no way she was taking those upstairs, where they could call her name all night long.

"You keep them." Belle fled, pounding up the steps without a backward glance.

"But—"

"Good night." She opened the door.

"Tomorrow at noon," he called. "The station."

Her answer was an absentminded wave before she shut and locked the door behind her. No time to chat. Belle had a date with her neurosis.

KLEIN STARED AT THE DOOR for a long time after Belle slammed and locked it. There was a tickle in his brain that usually signified the answer to a pressing question, if only he could focus.

Unfortunately, he had no idea what the question was, and he couldn't focus worth a damn right now on anything other than her lips against his jaw and her breath along his neck.

He gripped the pan of brownies and fought the urge to run upstairs, pound on the door, grab her and kiss her until her body throbbed the way his did.

Klein cursed and turned away. If it wasn't for his rich fantasy life, he'd have no life at all.

He skirted the five-and-dime, emerging on Longstreet Avenue. He should go directly back to the station, give Virgil the brownies, then take Clint home. But he made the mistake of glancing up, and then he was no longer moving but staring.

Her lights were on. He could see her shadow moving back and forth behind the curtains. She wasn't sleeping. What *was* she doing?

He had no idea, but since he was an inquisitive man, he leaned against the lamppost and watched awhile.

You make me feel like more, she'd said.

Those words had him as curious as the odd movements that continued unabated in the upstairs apartment.

He had learned early on that allowing other people to affect how he felt about himself was asking to feel pretty bad for a whole lot of his life. He'd been about to tell her that when she'd kissed him, and he'd lost any trace of a brain.

Her mouth was soft, her breath sweet. He'd been unable to keep himself from touching her skin. Thank God for Lucinda's brownies, which had kept one of his hands off Isabelle. If he hadn't been holding them he might have grabbed her with both massive paws and scared her to death.

As it was, she must have sensed how he burned for more, because she'd held very still and stared at his neck, no doubt terrified to meet his eyes and give him ready access to her lips. By the time she had, he'd regained his control.

Klein was adept at hiding what he felt. Being laughed at enough times would do that for a man. The kiss had been about gratitude; he'd known that all along. But tell it to his body. Ever since Kay Lynne had betrayed him, beautiful women had turned Klein cold. Why, then, did Isabelle make him hot?

Because when he looked at her, he didn't see Isabelle Ash anymore; he saw Izzy—the vulnerable, uncertain girl who lurked in her eyes—and he wanted to help her, protect her, heal her.

Klein frowned. Heal her? Where had he gotten the idea she needed to be healed?

He focused again on her window, contemplated the shadow that continued to move this way and that. *Vulnerable* and *uncertain* did not describe Isabelle Ash. She never could have gotten where she was in her business by being either. But Klein knew what vulnerability and uncertainty looked like. He saw them often enough in the mirror.

Which was no doubt why he felt the need to heal her. Because deep down he wanted to be healed, too.

Klein snorted. There was nothing wrong with him, just as there was nothing wrong with her, and the sooner he stopped trying to be her hero, the better off he would be. Delusions of knighthood always got him into trouble.

He'd just begun to stroll toward the station, when his walkie-talkie sent out a burst of static that almost made him drop the brownies. Cradling them against his hip, he answered the call.

"Chief, you better get in here. We got trouble."

"What now?"

The sound of crying—wailing, actually—came

through the walkie-talkie along with Virgil's voice. "Just come. Quick."

"On my way."

As he returned the walkie-talkie to his belt, Isabelle's window slid open. He glanced up to see if she was watching him, but she was still moving back and forth behind the curtains.

The beat of drums, fast and furious, followed him down the street. He still couldn't figure out what she was doing up there, and he no longer had the time to wonder. Duty called.

AN HOUR AND A HALF of aerobics did amazing things for Belle's state of mind and body. The leaden weight of the lasagna in her belly, while not gone, had diminished, and the pulsing, pounding beat of desire in her blood had ceded to the pounding of her pulse.

Her ability to exert control over her body in another way had overridden the lack of control she felt over her body whenever she was near Gabe Klein. In years past she might have resorted to the customary bulimic tricks. But she was better now.

Simply put, she'd exercised until she was lightheaded enough not to care about much and sweaty enough to feel as if she'd done something worthwhile. The old runner's high worked just as well when it was a dancer's high, instead.

Of course, being Belle, she wanted to keep going. Was tempted to start the CD all over again and exercise until she dropped. Tempted, but not insane.

She'd learned over the years that the inner mechanism that told most people when enough was enough didn't work quite as well for her. Her logic was often skewed. If eating vegetables was healthy, then eating *only* vegetables was better. If running a mile was good, well then, running twenty had to be damn near orgasmic.

So even though the voice in her head was saying, *If you feel great now, imagine how you'd feel if you did the same thing twice,* she knew better than to listen to it.

Instead, she took a tepid shower, put on a nightgown, pulled her bed out of the wall and crawled in. Then she lay there wide-awake, remembering the taste of Klein's skin and aching for the touch of his hands.

CHAPTER ELEVEN

MEANWHILE, back at the station, disaster awaited the unwary sheriff.

The voice in Klein's head, which sounded suspiciously like the narrator from a *George of the Jungle* cartoon, signaled imminent exhaustion. Too bad he didn't have the time.

"I don't know where my baby went," Miss Dubray wailed for the tenth time in the past hour. "That's what I want you to find out."

"What was he wearing at the time of his disappearance, ma'am?"

Klein shot Virgil a dirty look, but the deputy was focused on the sniffling woman in their visitor's chair.

"Um, let me think." She dabbed her eyes with a linen-and-lace handkerchief. "The last time I saw him he had on his sailor suit. With the blue captain's hat." She smiled at Virgil through her tears. "Does that help?"

"Yep. Now I know why he ran off."

Her mouth trembled and she glanced at Klein, who barely managed to keep from cursing. As usual, Virgil's victim-side manner left a lot to be desired.

"Virgil, quick, go see if you can find him around town."

"If I were him, I'd be in Knoxville by now. Naked."

A choked sob came from Miss Dubray. Clint, who had been sniffing her shoes unmercifully ever since Klein returned, and probably before that, too, lifted his head and howled.

Klein's patience snapped. "Quiet!"

Miss Dubray jumped and clamped her mouth shut. Virgil grumbled and slammed out the door. Clint dropped his head between his paws for an instant, then stretched his neck out until his nose touched Miss Dubray's toe.

Klein rubbed his eyes. What he really wanted to do was go home and get some sleep. Maybe dream some more about Isabelle. A man had to have a hobby. But he was going to be stuck here, or maybe out there in the dark, searching for an AWOL Chihuahua all night long. Sometimes duty sucked.

He dropped his hand. "Does T.B. have a license?"

"No, Sheriff, he's too young to drive."

For a moment, Klein just stared, waiting for her to smile or even wink. When she didn't, merely contemplated him with damp eyes and a serious expression, he resisted the urge to bang his head against the desk. He went on to the next question.

"How about a tag with his name and your number?"

Her brow creased. "But everyone in Pleasant Ridge knows him. Why would he need that?"

"In case—"

Klein snapped his own mouth shut. There was no reason to get Miss Dubray any more upset than she already was, by mentioning that T.B. could have wandered out of town where no one knew him. Because out of town there were all sorts of things that wouldn't be reading his tag. They'd be spitting it out after they ate him.

"Why don't you just go on home and get some rest. We'll bring T.B. by as soon as we find him."

"Oh, no. I couldn't sleep. Not without T.B. right next to me."

Clint grumbled and stood up, fixing Klein with a reproachful stare. Klein never let him sleep on the bed.

"Well, you can at least go home and try to relax." Klein came around the desk and helped Miss Dubray to her feet. "I'm sure Virgil will find T.B. directly, and I'll send them both to your place."

She put her hand over his. "Do you really think so, Sheriff?"

He could feel her trembling, so he smiled and then he lied. "Sure I do."

BY MORNING they'd searched every inch of Pleasant Ridge. There was no sign of T.B.

Miss Dubray returned at dawn. That she wore a dressing gown and slippers instead of her usual day dress, heels and pearls, revealed her state more clearly than did the paleness of her face and the dark circles beneath her eyes. She looked as if she'd slept as little as Klein and Virgil had.

Clint, however, had had no such compunctions. He snored with his head on Miss Dubray's ankles, drooling onto the floor. She didn't seem to mind, so Klein let him be.

He and Virgil stood by the coffeepot, out of Miss Dubray's hearing, filling their cups with more coffee that they did not need.

Virgil had just returned from delivering Jubel to the courthouse, where the man would be arraigned as soon as court convened. Which left the members of the Pleasant Ridge police force free to tackle other problems.

"If T.B. was in town," Virgil murmured, "someone would have called in a 10-91 by now. With him, maybe a 10-91A. But as long as it isn't a 10-91C or D, we've got to keep searching."

Klein was too tired to decipher the codes. "Again. In English."

"You need to study, Chief."

"What for, when I have you?"

The deputy's sigh was long-suffering, but he complied. "Someone would have called in a stray animal, or with him maybe a vicious animal. But as long as they didn't call in an injured animal or a dead one, we should keep looking."

"Why didn't you say so?"

"I did." Virgil added sugar to his coffee.

Klein resisted the urge to snatch the sugar and the coffee away from him. The old man was practically bouncing on his heels, he was so ready to rumble.

"Should we take the squad car? Maybe head out toward the mountains?" Virgil asked.

"I guess that's the logical choice. You get the car. I'll tell Miss Dubray where we're going."

Virgil started for the exit, then stopped abruptly. His shoulders sagged and he turned around. "No. I'd better tell her."

Klein frowned. What difference did it make who told her?

Before he could ask, the door opened and they all held their breath. But Isabelle entered, with no T.B. in sight. A collective sigh of disappointment whispered around the room.

"Well, you don't all have to jump up and down, but you could be a little happier to see me."

Klein glanced at his watch. It was barely seven a.m. "You're about five hours early."

Isabelle shrugged. "Couldn't sleep."

"Join the club."

His voice was hoarse from a night spent calling "Tid Bit! Here, boy!" He coughed, and the sound woke up Clint, who caught sight of Isabelle. The dog came to his feet with a welcoming *woof* and hurried toward her with all the joy he was capable of—which wasn't much—taking a good long whiff of her designer running shoes.

Once Clint met someone, he never forgot the face, or perhaps shoe. The dog sat at Isabelle's side, her friend for life just because he knew her, and she absently rubbed his ears as her gaze wandered over Klein from head to toe.

He could imagine what he looked like—bloodshot eyes, pale skin, dark shadow of a beard. He probably smelled even better, after living in the same uniform since... He couldn't quite recall.

"You were up all night, weren't you."

"What was your first clue?"

To her credit, she didn't even blink at his sarcasm, which only made him feel smaller for resorting to it. "Sorry," he mumbled. "It's been a long shift—or three."

Isabelle waved away his apology, her eyes going to Miss Dubray, who still sat poker stiff in the visitor's chair by his desk, then flicking to Virgil, who still hovered halfway between the door and Miss Dubray. Concern washed over her face, and she returned her attention to Klein.

"What happened?"

"T.B. is missing."

"The Chihuahua?"

Klein shrugged.

"You've been up all night searching for a stray dog?" Her voice was incredulous. "Both of you? After all that happened yesterday?"

"He was lost yesterday. I certainly couldn't wait and hunt for him next week when it was more convenient for me."

"That's not what I meant. But—"

"He's not just a dog," Miss Dubray whispered. "He's my baby. The only one I'll ever have."

Klein spread his hands wide. How could anyone argue with that? He certainly couldn't, and from the expression on Isabelle's face she couldn't, either.

"Let me help," she said.

He nodded. Another pair of eyes wouldn't hurt. "We were just about to—"

"Chief!" Virgil interrupted. "Could you and—" he waved a bony hand in Isabelle's direction "—get the car?"

Klein shrugged. "Sure."

He crossed the room, and Isabelle opened the door. Clint trotted outside; Klein let him go. He'd drop off the dog at home on their way out of town.

He turned back to ask Virgil to leave his pistol in the desk, and froze with his mouth half open. The deputy stood next to Miss Dubray, staring down at her bent head as she dabbed her eyes with a similar, though fresh, handkerchief. The softness of the man's expression was completely foreign to Klein.

"Hey," Virgil murmured, and went down on one knee next to her chair.

Klein had never heard that tone of voice from Virgil before—gentle, almost caring—and while he *should* leave, all he could do was listen.

"We're goin' to look outside of town now. You go on home."

"I know you don't like him."

"No one does."

Klein winced. Couldn't Virgil lie just once? Probably not.

"But that doesn't mean I ain't gonna find him if I can."

Miss Dubray drew in a deep breath that hitched several times. Virgil patted her knee and stood.

"I'll be over for my mint julep, same's always."

Miss Dubray stiffened. "How can you think of mint juleps at a time like this?"

Virgil's face crumpled in confusion. "Every day at three you give me my mint julep. We've been doing it for thirty years now. Why would today be different?"

"Because today my baby is missing."

"But—"

"Don't 'but' me." She stood and poked the deputy in the chest. "There'll be no sex until you find him."

Now Klein's mouth fell all the way open. Sex? *Them?* What the—?

Isabelle grabbed his arm and tugged him outside, closing the door quietly behind them. Then she collapsed against him, and she was shaking so badly Klein had no choice but to hold her up.

Concern had him forgetting for an instant what he'd just overheard. He rubbed Isabelle's back, instantly fascinated with the long line of her spine and the play of the muscles along her shoulders. Man, he had it bad if all he could think of was her body while she was crying in his arms.

"Shh," he murmured. "What is it? What's the matter?"

She lifted her head. She *wasn't* crying but laughing—until tears ran down her face. "They— they—" she pointed at the station "they're—"

"I know," he interrupted. He really didn't want to talk about that.

"Mint julep." *Snort.* "Thirty years." *Giggle.* "I can't stand it."

"That makes two of us."

She glanced into his face with surprise. Her laughter not yet under control, she pulled away from him and sat on the station steps. Clint, who had been looking back and forth between them, tongue lolling as if he were laughing, too, took the opportunity to slobber on Isabelle's shoes.

A few moments of deep breathing and Isabelle

could speak, though her eyes still chortled. "What's the matter? It's kind of sweet, once you get over the shock."

"I'll never get over the shock. I think I'm scarred for life."

"Now, now. It's not the end of the world."

"The end of the world as I know it. It was bad enough when I thought my deputy was drinking every day at three, but now to find out that he was—"

Klein couldn't finish the sentence.

"Having a quickie."

Klein groaned.

"A little afternoon delight?"

"Don't." His throat got tight.

"Slap and tickle?"

"Please." He coughed.

"Wham, bam, thank you—?"

He couldn't help it. He started to laugh, and then he couldn't stop. He had to sit down on the steps next to Isabelle because he could no longer stand up.

After a few seconds she put her arm around his shoulders and tugged him close, almost like a hug, except she did not release him—and he didn't want her to.

Klein hadn't felt such a lightness of heart or freedom of being in far too long—perhaps ever. He'd always been too aware that he was often laughed at, and therefore laughing for him was minimal—especially around women.

He liked to see the humor in life, but far too often no one saw it along with him. His job was serious.

His friends and acquaintances were, too. But he'd never had a friend or an acquaintance like Isabelle. How could he feel as if he'd known her forever when he'd never seen her before Wednesday?

His laughter slowed. Her arm slid off his shoulders, but when he turned to look at her, she was still grinning.

Her smile disappeared as the door opened behind them, and they both jumped to their feet to face Miss Dubray and Virgil.

The elderly lady marched out of the station. At least she wasn't crying anymore. She nodded at Klein and stomped off in the direction of the museum.

Klein glanced at Virgil, who appeared as happy as Clint on a bad day.

"Let's go," the old man grumbled. "We're wastin' daylight."

He hustled toward the squad car, which was parked a few storefronts away.

"He doesn't know that we heard," Klein said.

"No."

"And I don't want him to."

"Why not?"

"Because then I might have to hear all about it."

"Come now, the details of..." She paused, thought, then smirked. "A little roll in the hay never hurt anyone."

"My mother said listening to such things would make me go blind."

"I doubt that."

"You doubt I'd go blind?"

"I doubt your mother would say it."

"You don't know my mother."

Out of the corner of his eye he saw her glance at him, then away. *Damn.* He must have let some telltale emotion slip into his voice when he spoke of his mother. And he was usually so careful, too. But Isabelle seemed to see things in him that others did not.

Virgil honked the horn, and relieved, Klein began to walk toward the squad car. However, Isabelle followed, and she brought along her questions.

"You have a problem with your mother?"

"I didn't say that."

"You don't say much."

"It's one of my charms."

"You'd think, wouldn't you?"

"You don't think I'm charming?"

"I think you're spectacular, but—"

He stopped dead. "What did you say?"

"She said you're spectacular, Klein. But don't let it go to your head."

Both of them jumped. Klein didn't even have to turn around, so he didn't. "What do you want, Cass?"

"My film restored to its original condition—" She stepped around Isabelle, who watched her with a wary expression, most likely because of the ever-present camera strung around Cass's neck.

"But since I can't have that, I'll take an answer to my question."

Klein tensed. Cass had a way with questions and a habit of seeing what she wasn't meant to see. He'd always thought she'd make a better reporter for one of those grocery store sleaze papers than she did for the *Pleasant Ridge Gazette*—which, now that he thought about it, had taken on the tone of one of those papers since Cass had been in charge. Perhaps that was why circulation had increased. A sad testament to the curiosity of mankind—and Pleasant Ridge.

But instead of a mortifying query, she pulled a swatch of blue from her pocket and twirled it around one finger. "Anyone recognize this sailor suit?"

"Where did you find that?"

He reached for T.B.'s outfit, but Cass jerked it out of his grasp. The momentum from her twirling swept it right off the end of her finger, and the blue cloth hit Clint in the head, then fell to the ground.

He lowered his nose, sniffed the material and sneezed—once, twice, three times. Everyone ignored him.

"Where, Cass?"

"At the edge of town. Highway B."

The highway. Klein's heart turned over, then dropped into his belly. "Was there anything else nearby?"

"No. Just the baby outfit from hell. So what's up?"

Klein glanced at Isabelle. He could tell she was thinking the same thing he was, even before she said, "We'd better go take a look."

THEY ALL PILED into the squad car—Virgil and Klein in the front; Cass, Belle and Clint in the back. Belle tried to keep her distance from Cass and her camera by shouldering Clint into the middle. But as soon as the car started moving, he climbed right over her and stuck his head out the window. She had little choice but to get out of the way or be danced on by four happy feet.

Except, moving away from the window and avoiding Clint's waving behind put her so close to Cass that she could see the freckles on the woman's nose.

Klein mumbled into his radio, and Virgil produced a cell phone from somewhere and did the same thing. Cass gave Belle a sidelong glance.

"Klein *is* pretty spectacular."

Belle resisted the urge to snarl.

"He's a good pal. A faithful friend."

"Get yourself a dog," said Belle.

"Well, *meow*." Cass stared at Belle contemplatively.

Danger, danger. The warning in Belle's head sounded suspiciously like the robot from *Lost in Space*. Regardless, it was a warning she should heed. If Cass Tyler had any inkling of what Belle truly felt for Gabe Klein, Belle would never get the woman out of her face.

So Belle stared right back until Cass shifted, obviously as uncomfortable at being close to Belle as Belle was at being close to her.

"Listen, I heard what you did yesterday."

Belle stifled a sigh of relief. Cass was still thinking about the accident. Thank God. Maybe her secret was safe.

Which secret would that be, girl?

The robot was gone and her mama's voice had come back. *Swell.*

Take your pick, Mama, I got secrets to spare.

"Everyone in town thinks you're a heroine," Cass said.

"If you're looking for heroics—" Belle pointed at the front seat "—look that way."

Cass nodded. "As you said, Klein's spectacular. But I wanted to apologize. I would never have stuck a camera in your face if I thought it would make you go off like you did."

Belle frowned. Was Cass serious in her apology? Or was she merely trying to get a lead on Belle's problem? What a story that would be: Supermodel Afraid of Having Picture Taken: Fresh, Young Actress Loses Big Chance Because of Camera Phobia.

Cass continued to watch Belle, patiently waiting for an explanation, no doubt. She'd be waiting a long while. Belle had never confided in anyone. She wasn't about to start blabbing now, especially to a woman like Cass.

Of course, Belle should know better than to judge a person by her occupation. But in this case, she'd just have to be prejudiced. Better safe than sorry.

Klein ended his conversation at the same time Virgil ended his cell transmission.

"Highway patrol reports no Chihuahua, dead or alive," Virgil stated.

"That's good news."

"How you figure?"

"Not dead is good news, isn't it?"

"I guess," Virgil grumbled.

Obviously the deputy didn't care for T.B. With the revelations Belle had overhead that morning, she had to wonder if his dislike stemmed from jealousy more than anything else.

"Right here," Cass blurted. "Stop."

Virgil turned off the road and onto the shoulder just past the sign that read: Pleasant Ridge. Population—1,064.

They all got out of the car. Behind them was the town; in front of them, the mountains. In between, nothing but highway flanked by farms and fields.

"He could be anywhere," Belle murmured.

The sound of Clint's violent sneezes captured their attention. His nose buried in the blue sailor suit Klein held in one hand, he sneezed, sneezed, then sneezed again.

"Stop that," Klein ordered, and stuffed the material into his back pocket. He gazed across the rolling hills. The only thing that moved was the breeze through the trees and some cows, or maybe horses, in the distance. "Where could T.B. be?" he murmured.

Clint howled as if in answer, jumped up, snatched the suit from Klein's pants and took off through a ditch filled with spring runoff.

They were all so shocked that they just stood there watching him. Until the whirring of Cass's camera as she fired shot after shot woke them from their stupor.

"Get back here!" Klein ordered.

Clint continued to lope up the other side of the ditch. He paused to shake off the water, then turned and wagged his tail. He barked once, which caused the sailor suit to fall to the ground. Unconcerned, he plucked it up in his teeth again and glanced at the four people standing across the wide ditch.

"Do you think he wants us to follow him?" Virgil ventured.

The bloodhound put his nose to the ground and made a beeline for the nearest field.

Klein cursed. "We're going to have to follow him now." He turned to Belle and Cass. "You two stay here."

He headed into the ditch with Virgil on his heels.

Belle and Cass glanced at each other. Belle raised her eyebrows. "Follow that dog?"

"I'm right behind you."

CHAPTER TWELVE

KLEIN DIDN'T BOTHER to tell the women to go back. He doubted Cass had ever listened to anyone in her life, and he was beginning to think Belle wasn't much better. Besides, they weren't doing anything dangerous. Knowing Clint, he was probably leading them on the trail of a rabbit—directly up the nearest tree.

But the dog was behaving differently from usual. For one thing, when small game was involved, Clint stalked and then chased, like a clumsy dumb cat with a mouse. Right now he actually seemed to be following a trail the way a bloodhound should. He'd even gone through water and picked up the scent on the other side—a trait distinctive to his breed. But what scent did he have?

Nose to the ground, butt wagging in the air, Clint, with his red fur was a sharp contrast to the bright-green, knee-high weeds and tangled yellow, white and purple wildflowers. Every once in a while he would stop and glance back to make sure they were behind. When he saw that they were, his tail would swish and he would prance, as if he couldn't believe they were following him. Klein couldn't believe it, either.

Suddenly the dog sprinted ahead. His ears

streamed back in the wind; his huge paws spit torn grass and flowers in every direction. Klein's heart leaped. What if Clint was after something dangerous and deadly, instead of fuzzy and furry?

Though copperheads were common in this part of Tennessee, the majority were probably still hibernating. The snakes preferred rocks over trees and grass, but Klein wasn't going to bet Clint's life that a belly-crawling fang face would follow the rules. He began to run.

"He's headed for those trees," Virgil shouted, keeping pace with Klein easily. He was no doubt in better shape than Klein himself in a year-by-year comparison.

Clint disappeared into a line of red oaks. Though he hadn't known he could, Klein ran faster. What if the dog kept going past the trees and into the mountains?

Klein had only been in Tennessee a month, but he knew bigger, meaner animals than Clint lived in those hills. Of course, *any* animal was meaner than Clint, but that wasn't the point. If the dog got lost up there, they wouldn't find him in one piece—if they found him at all. He shivered despite the heat of the sun on his head and the sweat running down his back.

But when they burst from the sunlight into the shadow of the spring leaves, Clint patiently awaited them beneath a tree, his gaze turned not upward but down on a small cave-like hole at the base.

The women caught up. From the sound of Cass's labored breathing, she didn't jog much. He glanced at them. She was bent over, hands on her knees, head drooping to her chest, but she didn't appear to need CPR. Yet. Isabelle wasn't even winded. He wasn't surprised.

"Squirrel or rabbit?" she asked.

Her question surprised a short laugh from him, and she grinned.

A snarl erupted from the dark hole beneath the tree, and Clint whimpered. Klein cursed and hurried over, pulling Clint out of the way. All he needed was for his dog to have holed a bobcat, though those animals usually prowled at night and didn't come this close to where people lived if they could help it.

"Look—" Virgil pointed to the ground.

Blood spattered the surrounding area. Not a lot, but enough to deduce something had been hurt.

The sound of a camera shutter whirring revealed that Cass had recovered. Isabelle started and glared at the other woman, but when she saw Cass was taking pictures of the tree, the blood and Clint, she relaxed, though not by much.

Another vicious snarl came from beneath the tree, and Klein realized the sight of blood and Isabelle's jumpiness had made him loosen his hold on Clint. The dog had leaned his long neck toward the hole, sniffing madly.

He didn't appear frightened by whatever slavered and growled in the dark. In fact, he dropped the blue sailor suit, sneezed, then began to bark and wiggle with more glee than Klein had ever seen from him.

"I'll be damned," Virgil muttered, as T.B. emerged, blinking in the dappled sunlight.

Klein was so shocked he let Clint go. The bloodhound took the opportunity to fall on the ground and roll belly up. T.B. didn't even spare him a glance. Instead, he trotted over to the sailor suit and lifted his leg.

"I told you he ran away because of that thing," Virgil observed.

"How did he get it off?" Cass asked.

"How did he get out here?" Isabelle wondered.

"Whose blood is all over the ground?" Klein added.

"Not his."

Klein shifted his attention from the dog to the deputy. "How do you know?"

Virgil waited for T.B. to finish his comment on sailor suits for Chihuahuas, then picked him up and turned the animal this way and that. From the look on the little dog's face, he had similar plans for Virgil that he'd had for the suit.

Satisfied, the deputy set T.B. back on the ground. "Not a mark on him. He got the better of something out here."

T.B. trotted over to Clint, who still groveled. One sharp bark and the big dog flipped upright. T.B. tossed his head into the air, turned his back on Clint, lay down and closed his eyes. Clint crawled on his belly until his nose touched T.B.'s tail.

"I wonder what that something was." Cass moved closer to the Chihuahua and raised her camera. "And if it chased him in there." She took several shots of T.B. "Or if he kicked it out when he went in."

"Knowin' him, not only did he kick somethin'

out, but he drove it far, far away.'' Virgil stuffed the ruined sailor suit into an evidence bag he pulled from his uniform pocket. Klein was continually amazed at the amount of paraphernalia Virgil managed to secrete in his uniform.

"We'd better get T.B. back to town before Miss Dubray becomes despondent," Klein said.

"She'll be so grateful." Virgil's smile was distant. "We'll be able to get him back long before it's time for my mint julep break."

Isabelle choked. Klein had a hard time not doing the same. For a moment they stared at each other and shared the joke. A seventy-year-old lothario with the face of Barney Fife and a geriatric sex goddess. Talk about appearances being deceptive.

Cass's camera fired, breaking their moment of camaraderie, but when he shot a glance her way, she was watching the dogs.

Virgil didn't notice—the humor or the camera—his mind no doubt occupied with all the forms that gratitude could take.

THE REST OF THE MORNING passed without incident. Cass disappeared as soon as they returned to town, mumbling about deadlines and animal interest stories. Virgil returned T.B. to Miss Dubray, then called in a 10-8X.

"What is that?" Klein grumbled, and yanked out his code book.

Seconds later he cursed, though there was no real heat in the words. He thumbed his walkie-talkie. "Virgil, 10-8X is in service with female. I don't think you're funny."

"Funny? No, I didn't mean—"

The old man sounded distracted. Belle could imagine by what. She could tell Klein was imagining, too, and it was making him crazy.

"Wait, Chief. Make that—"

A giggle interrupted him, and his walkie-talkie cut out. Klein put his head down on the desk. Belle resisted the urge to walk over and rub the back of his neck. He was so tired.

He'd spent yesterday morning aiding people who were hurt, the afternoon and early evening calming her, the darkest hours out searching for someone's pet when any other man would have put off the task until morning. Belle had been tempted by his physical merits; now she was captured by the inner wonder of Gabriel Klein.

The walkie-talkie came to life. "Make that 10-7B. Out of service, personal."

"Too much information," Klein mumbled.

The hero of the day lay sprawled at his master's feet, sound asleep. Even when Belle stood and moved to sit on the desk next to Klein, Clint didn't even open one eye.

"I think he's down for the count," she observed.

Klein lifted his head and glanced at the dog. "Bein' a hound dog is hard."

"Must be."

"Especially when you aren't one."

"That looks like a hound dog to me."

"On the outside. Inside beats the heart of a true French poodle."

Uneasy, Belle slid a glance at Clint, but he

snored on, oblivious. ''Don't let him hear you say that.''

Klein gave her a slow smile that did funny things to Belle's insides. She'd never seen him smile like that before—lazy, sexy, inviting—as if he'd just asked her to go home with him for a little mint julep.

Belle's eyes widened, and a giggle bubbled in her throat.

''What's so funny?''

She shook her head, afraid that if she opened her mouth the laughter would burst out—or worse, the truth. She wanted him. Even more now than she had before.

The lust wasn't going away. In fact, it was getting stronger the longer she was with him. The more she knew about Klein, the more she liked him. The more she saw of his body, the more she wanted to run her hands all over it. She must be wearier than he was, and that was saying quite a bit.

When they'd returned to the station, there'd been a message that Jubel was remanded to county court since the accident had taken place on the highway. Klein had muttered, ''That gets him out of my jail,'' then asked her to man the phones while he took a shower.

He'd returned dressed in a fresh uniform, which he must have kept at work for just such an emergency. He'd also shaved the two-day-old shadow, revealing a face pale and exhausted.

Yet he hadn't gone home. He'd sat down at his desk, and he'd been sitting there ever since, slugging coffee and working his way through the pan of Lucinda's brownies. Just the thought of the amount of caffeine and sugar in his system made Isabelle's pulse skitter and her stomach gurgle in sympathy.

"Hungry?" He rubbed his neck absently.

"Not really."

"Have you eaten today?"

She experienced the annoyance that usually came on the heels of such a question. "What are you, a cop?"

He laughed. "That's me, the food police." He broke off with a hiss of pain.

"What's the matter?"

"Nothing. Just my neck. Old football injury."

Belle wasn't sure if he was serious. She didn't particularly care. She could no longer keep herself from touching him.

She slid from the desk and moved around his chair. At the first touch of her fingers, he jerked away. But she wouldn't let him go. Hands on his shoulders, she eased him back in the chair.

"Relax," she murmured. "You're way too tense."

"What are you, a massage therapist?"

"I could pretend to be, if you'd like."

She ran her thumbs down the tight cords of his neck, smoothed her palms across the width of his shoulders, skimmed her fingers over the muscles of his arms. His skin fluttered beneath her hands. He was warm and strong and good. She wanted to keep touching him forever. She wanted to touch him and more.

But he held himself stiff and still, as if he wanted

to run but was too polite to do so. He was no doubt mortified she was touching him like this, but he was too much of a nice guy to push her away. That would be like him. He put on a tough front, yet she'd seen over the past few days just how gentle he could be.

She should stop. She was being foolish. He'd shown her time and time again that he wanted nothing more from her than friendship. In truth, he hadn't *wanted* that; she'd forced it on him. She didn't know how to make friends, didn't know how to have one or how to be one. But she was pretty certain friends didn't feel about other friends the way she felt about Gabriel Klein.

So instead of touching him the way she desired, she merely imagined rubbing her cheek along his short, dark hair. The movement would press her breasts against the solid wall of his back. She'd unbutton his shirt, slip her hands inside, memorize the muscles of his chest in the way she was learning the contours of his back right now, under the guise of massage therapy. Then she'd press her lips to where her hands had roamed. Would he taste as good as he smelled—clean, fresh and hot?

Belle glanced down, watched her hands trace his shoulders. Her fingers slipped beneath his collar, slid along the sides of his neck, smoothed over the rolling spike of his collarbone. He hadn't completely buttoned the new shirt after his shower, and she could see the bright-white cotton of a T-shirt. But what kind of T-shirt? If she sneaked her hands beneath the uniform, would she be able to feel his arms bare against her palms, or would she have to run her fingertips beneath the crisp cotton sleeves to know his warmth?

The phone rang, shrill and loud. He jumped and so did she. They both laughed.

Belle leaned down, reaching for the phone, one hand still on his shoulder. He reached for it, too, and the phone stopped ringing.

"Hmm," he murmured, and turned his head.

Their noses bumped. His blue eyes opened wider. His breath brushed her mouth.

"I wonder who that was," she whispered, and then she was kissing him.

Beyond gentleness, starved for the taste of his mouth, she feasted. Warm, sweet and wet, she would drown in him gladly. Consumed by desire, she cradled his face, holding him close, hoping he would not run away.

He swiveled his chair, and suddenly she stood between his legs, supported by his hands at her waist, their heat scalding through her blouse. Where it had come untucked from her pants, flesh on flesh made her moan. She wanted to grab his hands, rub his callused palms along her stomach, her ribs, higher. Beg him to stroke her, tease her, take her.

She put her tongue in his mouth and tasted him, then shuddered when he tasted her. Her hands moved without her consent, touching his arms, kneading his shoulders, learning the texture of his skin.

And the phone rang again.

He stiffened, tearing his lips from hers. He yanked his hands away as if she were on fire. The expression on his face made her heart stutter. He was horrified.

She backed away, lifting one hand to her mouth, touching where he had touched, trying to feel again the magic. But it was gone.

Pity in his eyes, sadness cast over his face. "Isabelle, I—"

She didn't want to hear him say, *I don't feel that way about you.* She couldn't bear to have him tell her, *I can't see you anymore.* So she ran.

The phone continued to ring. As she escaped onto Longstreet Avenue she heard him curse, then he answered it.

EVEN AS HIS BODY SHOUTED for him to chase her down and drag her back into his arms, duty made him grab the phone. But nothing could make him happy about it.

"What?" he barked.

"Klein?"

Still frowning at the door through which Isabelle had disappeared, he scowled when he recognized the voice. "Chai."

"How are things, Sheriff?"

Klein looked at the phone, then put it back to his ear. "Not bad. How are things on your end?"

"Cut the crap, Klein. How is Isabelle? Did you run into any poachers today?"

For a minute, Klein thought the mayor actually meant poachers out in the woods. Then he remembered their conversation at Murphy's. A sudden image came to him of lips on lips, tongue sliding along tongue, hands spanning a soft but firm waist.

Any poachers? God, he felt like one. And not because he thought Chai had any claim to her, but because he was supposed to be her friend and he'd taken advantage. No wonder she had run from him with a hunted expression in her eyes. Guilt loomed heavy, thick, smothering.

"Hey! Klein? You still there?"

"Yeah."

"Did any man get near her today?

"Me. And Virgil."

"Good. Good. Keep it that way."

Klein should be insulted that Chai didn't think he was any threat. But he'd been insulted so many times before that he didn't bother to waste the energy caring right now.

"She took off jogging," Chai said. "I suppose she'll be safe enough. Although it would be better if you went with her."

"I never run for fun."

The mayor kept yapping as if Klein hadn't even opened his mouth. "I'd go. But I've got to get back to the office for a meeting. And to be honest, she'd run me into the ground. Don't you think she overdoes it sometimes?"

Something Chai had said hit Klein funny. "Wait a second. Where are you now?"

"On Longstreet Avenue."

Cell phone, Klein thought.

"*Why* are you on Longstreet Avenue?"

"Watching Isabelle, of course. You aren't."

Anger pulsed at the base of Klein's throat. He could just see Isabelle headed out for a jog, hoping for some peace and quiet, unaware that she was being ogled by someone she should be able to trust, after she'd been mauled by a friend.

Again he wanted to get up and go after her, make sure she was safe from everyone and everything. Except, he was one of the things she needed to be protected from. Maybe he'd just hunt down the mayor and shake him until he rattled.

Klein recognized the danger in what he wanted. He was getting too close to her, but he couldn't seem to stop himself.

"Mr. Mayor, you're skating perilously near stalking."

"Me?" Chai laughed. "But I'm the mayor."

"I don't care if you're the pope. Stay away from her."

"I'm the mayor," he repeated. "I have to go near her sometime."

"Only if you have a damn good reason. Imagine how embarrassing it would be to find yourself behind bars on a stalking charge."

"You couldn't."

"Could. And if that isn't enough, think about Daddy's reaction to the news that you're planning a Senate run behind his back."

"You wouldn't."

"Would. Go back to your office, Chai. Stay there."

Klein hung up. He stared at the door and he thought about Isabelle.

He suspected situations like this followed her everywhere she went. Guys who figured she should be thrilled to have their attention. Men who wanted her for nothing more than the way she looked.

Somehow, Klein thought that was as bad as women who didn't want him for the same reason. He and Isabelle had a lot more in common than an obscure sense of humor.

Clint yipped in his sleep, paws spinning as he chased another rabbit up the tree. "Get him, boy," Klein murmured, and the dog quieted.

Klein glanced at his watch. It was time he headed home, but first he'd take a little side trip past Isabelle's. Make sure the mayor wasn't lurking in the alley; then, if he could figure out what to say, Klein would apologize when she returned from her jogging expedition.

He pushed the button on his walkie-talkie. "Virgil, get back to the station, please."

"Code one, Chief?"

Klein scratched his head and searched his weary brain for what that meant. "No, not at your convenience. Finish up your mint julep and get back here code three."

The walkie-talkie was dropped and the resulting bang woke Clint, who woofed and peered around the room, shaking.

"Relax." Klein smoothed a hand over his head. "Nothing to be scared of anymore."

"Chief? Chief! Code three emergency. The squad car is with you. I can't come with red lights and the siren."

Klein muttered a few curses. "No, I meant urgent, no red light and siren."

"That's a code two." Virgil's voice was accusing.

"Sorry."

"You know, Chief, if you're not going to keep on top of the codes, maybe we better just forget about them."

"Isn't that what I told you the first week I was here?"

"I didn't think you were serious."

"I am. Get your butt over here."

"Ten-four."

Klein scowled at the walkie-talkie, but Virgil was gone.

CHAPTER THIRTEEN

BELLE TRUDGED up the steps to her apartment. She didn't feel any better. For the first time in a long time, jogging wasn't enough.

The skittery sensation in her belly and the creeping unease along the back of her neck were still there. As if someone watched and waited for her to make a mistake, to let a secret out.

She glanced over her shoulder; no one was there. She shook her head, lifted her shirt and wiped the sweat from her face. Paranoia was nothing new. She lived with it every day. But she usually did a better job of controlling it.

It was cooler inside her apartment than it was outside, in the spring sunshine. She'd kept her curtains drawn all day, but now she opened them and glanced out at Longstreet Avenue.

People milled about. It was late afternoon on Main Street, U.S.A. Of course there were people, but they weren't watching her.

Even if they were, so what? She was used to being watched, being photographed, being dissected inch by inch and ounce by ounce. But sometimes she wondered if an observant person could see the cringing fat girl who still hid behind the assured, glamorous Isabelle Ash.

Lucky for Belle there weren't very many observant people in her line of work. They might be creative artists, but in the end they saw only what they wanted to see.

Belle stood in front of the mirror, turned this way, turned that. Common sense told her that nothing was wrong with her a shower wouldn't fix, but she saw something else entirely. More often than not, whenever she looked into a mirror, Big Belle stared back. Because Isabelle Ash was now and always would be a fat girl shoved into a skinny woman's body.

She moved away from the mirror. Why did she do this to herself? She was better. She *was*. There was no reason to wonder if she had any laxatives in her cosmetics bag or if she should go on a juice-only fast until the whirling madness went away.

Actually, there was a reason. Because she didn't want juice; she wanted mashed potatoes, spaghetti, bread or the brownies Klein had been eating. And she knew why.

Belle had not realized the depth of her loneliness until Klein had stopped touching her, and she ached to be touched again—by him. As in childhood, rejection made her crave comfort, and the only comfort she'd had back then was food.

Though her family had been poor, her mama's large garden and her father's knack for hunting had assured that there was always enough food. However, there never had been enough to fill the ache inside Belle. Eventually she'd trained herself to exercise instead of eat whenever she felt out of control of her feelings and her life.

Belle powered up her portable CD unit and let the music take her away.

VIRGIL HADN'T SHOWN UP for half an hour. Of course, Klein *had* told him to finish his mint julep. But half an hour?

The pulse of bass made Clint shy as they ducked into the alley next to the five-and-dime. Isabelle was doing it again. Whatever *it* was.

"Just music, big guy. Nothing to worry about."

Clint didn't appear to believe him. He stuck his tail between his legs and walked so close to Klein that he nearly tripped him.

"I don't even want to imagine what you're going to be like on the Fourth of July."

Clint grumbled and pressed closer. Obviously he didn't want to imagine it, either.

Klein had planned to knock on Isabelle's door and discuss what had happened at the station earlier. He would promise never to do it again—make some excuse for why he'd done it at all. But when he glanced at her window, instead of the shadows he'd seen last night, there she was—and then he could not move.

Because she was dancing—fast and wild, free and fair, as if her very life depended on the dance.

Though her braid appeared like a rope of gold twirling through the air, her arms graceful, her torso lithe as she dipped to the beat, he discovered that the dance itself did not concern him as much as the fact *that* she danced.

Chai had informed him she was jogging. Now she was dancing. Why?

He inched closer, up the steps halfway, and saw that her red tank top was drenched with sweat and stuck to her chest in a fashion that would be intriguing if all sorts of puzzle pieces weren't clicking together in his overly busy brain.

Klein turned from the sight, retraced his steps and emerged onto Longstreet Avenue with Clint in tow. All the way home, he thought and he thought, so that by the time he reached his house and then the office off his bedroom, where he kept all his electronics, he had a pretty good idea what he was looking for when he began to surf the Internet.

He wasn't surprised when he found it. What did surprise him was that he hadn't figured things out sooner. Now that he knew, what should he do?

He was still wondering that when he parked his pickup in front of the station. Darkness had settled over Pleasant Ridge like a cool piece of navy blue velvet. Virgil had gone home. All calls had been transferred to Klein's cell phone, which he wore on his belt. He hoped no one needed him before morning, because he was just about played out. However, he had felt a pressing need to talk to Isabelle before he collapsed for the night.

Klein passed the museum. T.B. started yapping on the other side of the door as if his mortal enemy were near. Some things never changed.

In front of the five-and-dime, he glanced up. Her lights were on, the curtains drawn once more. She passed in front of the window, and the flow of her silhouette captivated him. She reached up and pulled her braid loose, shook her head. His body leaped in response, and he looked away. He had no business desiring her now. He had no business desiring her at all. But he did.

Determined, Klein marched through the alley to the back steps, climbed them and knocked. Seconds later, she opened the door.

The desire he'd beaten down came roaring back. Her hair reached to her waist, growing lighter the longer it became. With the braid unfastened, the gold tresses flowed like a river. He wanted to bury his face in the strands, have them cascade over his skin, fill his hands with their softness, wrap a length around his wrist and—

"Hi."

The shyness in her voice reminded him of what had happened the last time they'd been together. The taste of her returned to his mouth; his palms itched to touch her again.

"Hi." His voice was hoarse with desire, and he coughed, pretending it wasn't.

She'd changed her clothes and now wore emerald-green sweatpants, jaggedly cut at midthigh. Her sapphire-blue T-shirt had been cut, as well, just below her breasts. Her feet were bare; she wasn't wearing a bra. The scent of pink soap and honeysuckle shampoo made him dizzy. In a haze of sensory overload, he forgot what he'd come there for.

Most folks didn't think a guy of his size and profession could care about colors or textures, shapes, sizes or scents. But the essence of life fascinated him, and right now the essence of life was her.

"Come on in." She tossed a sheaf of papers onto the table, then picked up a glass of sparkling red liquid. At first he thought it was wine, until he caught a whiff of raspberries.

"Juice?" She tilted her glass in question.

He could only shake his head.

She frowned. "What's wrong?"

He shook his head again, terrified that if he opened his mouth, he'd beg to touch her—or beg her to touch him.

She drained the glass, set it down with a *click,* then swayed and caught herself against the table.

He was across the short distance, putting his hands on her shoulders before he remembered he should not touch her.

"Are you all right?"

"I'm just tired. You should be, too. Why aren't you in bed?"

His gaze slid to the bed beneath the window. He could imagine her in the tousled sheets. Worse, he could imagine himself there with her.

Klein yanked his hands from her shoulders. But before he could move away, she grabbed them between hers. "I'm sorry," she whispered. "I don't want our friendship ruined because I kissed you."

She actually believed that *she* had kissed *him!* Klein kept forgetting how young she was. When he looked into Isabelle's eyes he did not see a twenty-five-year-old girl but a mature woman who had seen more than she cared to. A woman very much like him.

He shook his head. "No, Isabelle, I—"

"Foolish of me—" she continued right over his protest "—but I couldn't stop myself. I've wanted to touch you since you walked in the station and let me out of that cell.''

All Klein's protests died in his throat, and he stared at her, amazed. She let him go, and began pacing between the bathroom and the kitchen table.

''I've been dreaming of your chest.'' She waved in that general direction. ''I can't stop thinking about kissing your nose.''

He touched his huge snout, mystified.

''I've never been drawn to a man physically the way I am to you, and I'm not handling it well. I know what lust is, and I should be able to control it.''

Physical? Lust? For him? Klein glanced behind him, but he was still the only man in the room. Maybe he'd fallen asleep at home and he wasn't really here.

Confused, he could only stare at her. Was she saying what he thought she was saying?

Isabelle covered her face with her hands. ''I must be more light-headed than I thought, to be telling you all this.

Light-headed? He had a flash of her holding on to the table for balance. Maybe she hadn't been drinking just juice after all.

Klein moved close enough to catch her if she fell. ''Are you all right?'' he repeated.

''I don't know what I am anymore. Confused. Embarrassed. Afraid.''

He inched back. He was big—huge, in fact—strong, scary looking, too. He'd been trained in violence, committed it on occasion—though not lately—but for her to say she was afraid of him hurt more than Klein could have imagined.

"But, Izzy, you don't have to be afraid of me."

She dropped her hands and stared at him with wide eyes. "Afraid of you? How could anyone be afraid of you?" She shook her head as if she could not fathom it. "I'm afraid that wanting you so badly I can't think straight will take away the one thing I've always wished for and never had."

"What?"

"A friend," she whispered.

He frowned. "I can't believe you've never had a friend."

"Believe it."

She shut her eyes. With her dark lashes lying long against her cheeks, he could see how pale she was. She swayed alarmingly. He took two large steps and caught her in his arms.

"What is *wrong* with you?"

"I'm tired, Gabe. Don't worry. Just tired."

She'd called him Gabe. Usually that annoyed him. Right now he was anything but annoyed.

"Can I lean on you a minute?"

She already was, her cheek against his chest, her arms around his waist.

"Of course. Isn't that what friends do? Lean?"

"Is it?"

"So I hear."

"Then, we're still friends? You forgive me for kissing you?"

She sounded like a child who wanted to make amends for a mistake. He couldn't help himself; he kissed the top of her head. "There's nothing to forgive."

"You're so sweet."

Klein stifled a snort. One thing he'd never been called was *sweet*.

"I admit I was attracted at first because of how you looked, but then I discovered that your inside was even better than your outside. But don't worry, I'll get over it."

He should leave well enough alone. Let her get over it, as she said. Just hold her as long as she needed him to and then release her forever. But she felt too good in his arms, too right, and Klein knew that holding her wasn't going to be enough.

"I hope not."

She went still in his arms. "What did you say?"

"I hope you don't get over it."

Slowly she raised her head and gazed into his face. "But why?"

God help him, he wanted the relationship she'd just described—purely physical because each desired the other.

Women had slept with him for one reason or another, but none because they were attracted to him physically. Of course, once he'd slept with them they came back. He'd decided years ago that if he couldn't be handsome he'd at least be exceptional.

Yet here was a beautiful woman saying she wanted his body; she craved the sight of his face. It was every ugly man's fantasy.

A disturbing thought insinuated itself into his mind. Isabelle might be pretending. But what reason could she have for that? What possible advantage could come from her sleeping with him? He was already helping her, protecting her from poachers and the mayor; he had nothing to give her but what she said she wanted.

Himself.

"I know you don't find me attractive."

Now he snorted. "I'm neither blind nor stupid."

"But you were so sarcastic, even rude. Whenever I got close to you, you shoved me away."

"Defense mechanism."

"I don't understand."

He hesitated, but since she was being honest—he thought—he would show her the same courtesy. "I wanted to kiss you the first moment I saw you, and that's something a man like me should never want."

"A man like you." She shook her head. "Who told you you were ugly? Who made you believe it, too?"

Memories flickered, distracting him so that when she touched his face, he jerked back. She followed. As she traced the line of his jaw with her thumb, the angle of his cheekbones with her fingertips, he found it impossible to believe that the desire and admiration in her eyes was a lie.

"Izzy?" He did what he'd been dying to, filling his hands with her hair and tilting her head just so.

Her eyes half closed, her mouth half open, she breathed, "Mmm?"

"Just to get things straight. At the station today?"

She nodded.

"You didn't kiss me. I kissed you."

When she smiled, he did it again.

BELLE HAD FOOLISHLY exercised too much and eaten too little. The dizzy rush of deprivation imitated power. The false sense of inner strength was as addictive as drugs.

Her head had been spinning even before Klein walked into her apartment. She'd been reading the script for her show, which had been crammed into her mailbox sometime that day. The show *was Baywatch* meets Mayberry and she wasn't sure what she was going to do about it. She wanted to cry.

So when he'd strode into her room she hadn't exactly been at the top of her game. She'd blabbed her newest secret because of her oldest. If she wasn't careful, he'd get every last one of them out of her. All he had to do was ask.

His mouth on hers was firm and warm; the hands tangled in her hair were gentle. She enjoyed kissing, probably because she never got enough of it. Men usually wanted to see for themselves what they'd seen enough of already and touch what they'd only been dreaming of. They always moved on to stage two long before she was ready.

But Klein made love to her mouth slowly, reverently, as if he had an eternity just to kiss her, as if he enjoyed the melding of lips and tongue and teeth as much as she did.

When he lifted his head, she sighed, disappointed, but before she could lead him to the bed, he buried his face in her hair, then sweetly kissed her neck, her jaw, the corner of her eye.

His hands wrapped around her waist, and she

waited for them to surge upward, cup her breasts, feel their weight. Instead, he kept his hands right where they were, thumbs tracing the quivering muscles of her belly.

The juice she'd drunk began to work. As her head cleared, she chastised herself for comparing past to present. How many times already had Gabe Klein demonstrated he was unlike other men?

Enough for her to trust that he wasn't.

As if to prove her every thought true, his mouth returned to hers and time lost its hold on them. His lips nibbled and caressed, nipped and suckled. The man could certainly kiss. He practiced innovations of old favorites, even as he invented seductive novelties with her as a willing partner.

She unbuttoned his uniform shirt, discovered the white cotton beneath it. Her fingertips fluttered over his chest, his belly, rubbing the T-shirt against the ridge of muscles, the strength of bone. When she shoved the shirt from his shoulders it hung trapped by his heavy utility belt. Her palms slid up his arms, until the sleeves of his T-shirt tickled her hands and answered her earlier question about the nature of his underwear.

Her lips curved against his, and she yanked the shirt free of his belt, then did what she'd been wanting to do from the beginning. She touched her hands to his skin.

His indrawn breath tightened the muscles of his stomach. She ran her fingers up his rib cage, tangled them in the soft hair across his chest. Then she tore her mouth from his.

''Off,'' she muttered, and pulled up his T-shirt.

He obliged, tugging the garment over his head. And then he stood before her in khaki trousers, his utility belt filled with sexy cop tools, his chest even more beautiful than she had imagined.

Copper skin enhanced by crisp black curls glistened in the lamplight. She trailed her fingers across his chest, over the spike of his nipples, then through the path of hair that disappeared into his pants.

She hooked her fingers in the belt and tugged. "Off," she repeated.

He grinned, and she had to smile, too. She felt as though she could demand anything of him that she desired. How was it possible that she had known him less than a week?

He unbuckled the belt, removed his gun from the holster and the clip from the gun. Then he put the gun on top of the refrigerator and everything else on the table.

"Safety first," she murmured, and lifted her mouth toward his.

He swore.

"Excuse me?"

"Safety." He ran his hand through his short hair. Leaned down and grabbed his T-shirt. "I'll be right back."

"Like hell." She took a fistful of his shirt and tugged. He wouldn't let go. "You're not going anywhere."

"I have to. I don't have anything, Izzy."

"You've got everything, from where I'm standing."

He laughed. She loved making him laugh. He didn't do it often enough.

"I was talking about safety. I need to go buy some at the five-and-dime." He cursed again. "Or not. If I buy condoms downstairs, I won't be able to come back up here afterward. Although by morning, everyone in town will know that the sheriff bought condoms, and they'll be speculating why."

He sighed. "Sorry. Most guys keep safety in their wallets, but I always figured if I did it would fall out when I was paying for my groceries. Maybe it's for the best. This is probably a mistake."

"No." She yanked on his T-shirt, and this time he wasn't holding on, so the thing flew across the room.

"Isabelle, be reasonable. No condom, no sex. I might not be a new millennium Casanova, but I know that much."

Funny that he could know that much, yet not even consider that she might have a condom or two. She was almost embarrassed to say so, except that the reason she had them was she'd never used them. She hoped the things didn't disintegrate with age. Besides, if she didn't admit to condom possession, he was going to take that incredible chest and innovative mouth out of her apartment, and knowing Gabe Klein, she'd never get him undressed again.

"Don't move." She ran into the bathroom, grabbed her cosmetic bag and returned. He was bending over to retrieve his T-shirt. "Freeze," she ordered. "Drop it!"

He did, then turned to her with an amused tilt to his lips. "Cop talk, Izzy? Did you want me to keep the handcuffs close?"

She ignored his jokes as she pawed through the

jumble of tubes and bottles, then upended the thing with a growl. "I own every shade of lipstick I might need for any occasion. There's *got* to be a condom in here somewhere. Aha!" She snatched two packets from the depths of the mess. "I knew it."

She raised her head. He still held his T-shirt loosely in one hand. The way he looked at her made Belle uneasy. Did he think she had a case of condoms stashed somewhere so she could take a lover in every city where she stopped? It was a common opinion, one she usually shrugged off because she knew the truth. But she didn't want *him* to think that.

"My jokester brothers gave me these the last time I went home. I—I had to hide them from my mama. In there—" She waved vaguely at the empty cosmetic bag.

"I don't care where you got them." He dropped his shirt, and she let out the breath she hadn't known she held. "I'm just glad you found them."

He crossed the room. Her mouth watered in anticipation as she watched. For a man his size, he moved with uncommon grace, comfortable in his skin, in a way that she could never be in hers. When he reached her he held out his hand. She placed the packets in the center, and he pocketed both.

"Now—" he skimmed his palm down the side of her face, and she rubbed against him like a cat "—where were we? Oh, yeah, I was just about to do this."

He dropped to his knees and pressed his mouth to the skin between her shirt and her shorts. The arousal that had faded during her mad search and their conversation came thundering back. His tongue circled her belly button, and the shudder that racked her body made her knees tremble. He steadied her with his hands on her hips, then drew a taste of her skin into his mouth and suckled.

Her fingers on his shoulders clenched. His skin was hot and smooth; she touched his back, caressed his hair, then held his mouth right where it was.

His hands lowered, cupping her rear, sliding down her thighs, then his fingers explored the tendons of her calves and his thumbs stroked higher and higher until he traced the quivering skin just beneath the ragged hem of her cutoffs. She held her breath, waited for him to go higher still, but he didn't. Instead, he pressed one last openmouthed kiss to her belly and stood.

Without a word, he took her hand and led her to the bed, then lifted his fingers to his zipper.

He saw her watching and hesitated. "Should I wait?"

"No." She placed her hands over his. "Let me."

Surprise, then pleasure, lit his eyes. "Whatever you want, Izzy."

"You," she said. "I want you."

"And I'm right here."

Emboldened by his assurance, she caressed him through his trousers, ran her finger over his tip. He went still, but a glance at his face revealed he enjoyed the way she touched him; he didn't want her to stop. So she made quick work of his zipper, then slipped her hand inside.

He was hot and smooth, pulsing against her

palm. She looked up once more, and his mouth took hers. No longer gentle, she didn't mind. She stroked him with her hand as his tongue mimicked the movement within her mouth.

Moments later he lifted his head and stilled her caress. "I need to lie down before I fall down."

His voice was breathless; his hand atop hers trembled. The idea of making this strong man need, of making such a serene man yearn, aroused her.

She shoved his trousers and his briefs from his hips. To stand there fully clothed while she removed every last stitch that he wore felt strange. Strange, but at the same time empowering and seductive.

He didn't care that he was naked and she was not. He didn't tug at her clothes; he didn't yank her onto the bed. Instead, he lay down and let her look at him.

For days she'd been nearly senseless with desire at the mere thought of what was beneath his uniform. Now, seeing him, she knew that her imagination had not done him justice. Even his feet were perfect—long and slim and pale—and his hands... From the first she'd adored his hands—callused from work, yet tender when they touched her, they were the hands of a man, and he knew what to do with them.

"You're going to give me a complex if you keep staring at me like that," he murmured.

She raised her gaze and caught a flicker of uncertainty in the depths of his sky blue-eyes.

"You're the most beautiful man I've ever seen," she whispered.

He gave a short bark of laughter, then held open his arms.

She sank into them gladly. Having his arms around her was almost as good as having her hands all over him. She hadn't realized how much she needed a hug until he'd started hugging her. She hoped he would hug her a lot—every chance that he got.

His palm kneaded the soft skin at her waist. His fingers played with her rib cage. His breath tickled across her neck as his mouth warmed the skin just below her ear. He appeared inordinately fascinated with the bones beneath her skin.

She shifted, restless, needing him to touch her where her body tingled and begged. Surely his hand would move upward soon. He had not touched her breasts once, and in her experience that was very unusual. Ordinarily men's fascination with her breasts bored her. Right now, all she could think was that he was never going to touch them, and if he didn't she might explode.

"Do you want me to take off my clothes?" she asked.

"Only if you want to."

She'd found his patience comforting, but the tension in her belly, her breasts, her being, was past soothing. She sat up and yanked her T-shirt over her head. She had no idea where it landed, because her gaze returned to his face.

She expected him to be staring, even ogling, the impressive size of her breasts, but was surprised to discover he was watching her face, as well. Would she ever learn that he did nothing the way she expected him to?

Her fingers lowered to her cutoffs, but his hands were there before her, easing the sweatpants over her hips, sliding them down her thighs and dropping them over the edge of the bed and onto the floor. Her white, cotton granny underwear sagged. His lips twitched, and he drew a fingertip across her belly. She arched into his touch.

"I take it you don't get too many free samples at work."

"Ever had a wedgie?" she managed, even as her body shrieked for him to lower his fingertips to the place where she wanted them the most.

"One or two."

"If you took a peek at the underwear in those catalogs, you'd know I've had one for five years."

His smirk turned into a full-blown grin, and she couldn't help but grin, too. How could she feel at the edge of reason one minute, then be laughing with him the next? Because in his arms she felt everything was all right—whatever she said, whatever she did, whoever she was.

The last thought sobered her. She needed to be a part of this man who made her feel special and distinct, and she wanted him to be a part of her.

Taking his hand, she placed it on one breast. "Touch me, Gabe. Look at me. Please."

Even then, he pressed a kiss to her temple first before he leaned back and lowered his gaze. The brush of his eyes was a near physical thing; heat spread over her body.

"You're a very pretty girl, Isabelle."

For some reason his words disappointed her, or maybe it was his use of her professional name and not the ''Izzy'' she'd begun to crave.

Then he lifted his gaze, and she was captured by the intensity on his face. ''But the most beautiful thing about you is that you're aware how very little *pretty* means in the scheme of life.'' He pressed his palm against her heart. ''It's what's in here that counts.'' He lowered his head to kiss the skin that his hand had covered. With his breath warm on her breast he murmured, ''The longer I know you, the more I see that you're even more exquisite inside than out.''

He was wrong. Inside she was a whirling, dark storm of lunacy—weak and confused and stupid. Ugly beyond redemption.

She meant to tell him; she really did. She even opened her mouth. But all that came out was a moan when his lips closed over her breast.

He might not have been interested in them before, but he made up for it now, driving her to a clinging, shaking peak with his mouth alone.

All thought lost, sensation took its place. Gentleness abandoned, madness overcame the two of them. He touched her everywhere, in every way. Drove her up, then held her as she fell, and drove her right back again.

When at last he made use of a condom, she was already limp and hoarse, but when he filled her and kissed her once more as he'd kissed her already a hundred times before, she arched to take him deeper, felt him touch her inside where it counted, and called his name as she followed him home.

CHAPTER FOURTEEN

KLEIN LAY with Isabelle sprawled over his chest as the moon slanted silver across the bed. While he couldn't believe he'd just done what he'd done, he also couldn't regret it, even though he had no doubt this would end badly.

He couldn't let himself become emotionally attached to her. He was asking to have his heart ripped out again. Isabelle was special and different, but she wasn't going to stay, and she certainly wasn't going to ask him to go with her when she left, even if he could. There was no future for them, and he couldn't delude himself into believing there was, as he'd deluded himself once before.

Tonight might be the only night they would have, and perhaps that was for the best—though he didn't know how he would be able to keep from touching her, wanting her, needing her every minute of every day they had left.

He sighed, and she lifted her head. Her loose and tangled hair drifted across his belly, tickling as well as arousing him. He stared at the ceiling and counted backward from forty.

She pressed her mouth to his stomach, rubbed her face in the curling black hair that dusted his skin. "Mmm," she murmured, the sound of her voice and the drift of her breath making him lose count at about twenty-nine.

"Izzy," he groaned. "There's only one condom left. Hadn't we better pace ourselves?"

She licked his belly button, then blew on the moist trail.

Twenty-nine, twenty-nine, twenty-nine, he thought.

She tossed her hair over her bare shoulder and winked at him. "Tonight maybe. But tomorrow one of us will have to go to another town and buy more safety."

His heart stuttered, and he forgot to count. "Because?"

"Because one more time isn't going to be enough for me." She paused, and uncertainty flickered over her face. "Will it be for you?"

Her skin slid along his as she took a deep breath, then waited for his answer. How could a woman like Isabelle have so little confidence?

"After what just happened, *enough* is no longer in my vocabulary." He held open his arms.

The relief in her smile, the way she came to him with no hesitation made his belly roll up toward his heart. There was something about Isabelle that called to the caretaker in Klein. The way she cuddled against him like a child made him want to hold her whenever vulnerability shadowed her eyes.

He'd come here to confront her with what he'd discovered. But suddenly he wanted her to confide in him, to trust him with a secret, even two.

"Did you know that Serafina makes the best homemade pizza in the state?" he asked.

"I didn't. But then, how many Italians live in Tennessee?"

"You'd be surprised." He kissed her hair and disentangled himself from her arms.

The uncertainty returned to her eyes. "Where are you going?"

"To order pizza. Murph will bring it over."

"Oh. Sure. If you're hungry, go ahead."

He raised a brow. "Aren't you hungry?"

"Not for food."

"Lame line, Izzy." He sat down on the bed and ran his fingers through her hair. He couldn't stop touching her even if he wanted to. "Do you mind that I call you Izzy? Everyone can't call you Isabelle. It's a mouthful."

"My family calls me Belle. The world calls me Isabelle." She turned her head and pressed her mouth to his knuckles. "I like it when you call me Izzy. No one else ever has."

He kissed her, long and thoroughly, then stroked her shoulder for a while. He'd never get enough of the sweet, scented softness of her skin.

"Aren't you going to phone Serafina?" she asked.

"Nah. If you aren't hungry, I don't need anything. I can eat when I get home."

"You should eat. Go ahead and order."

"I can't sit here and stuff my face while you watch."

"I suppose I can manage a piece."

He was shamelessly manipulating her. Klein knew it, yet he did it anyway. After what he'd read on the Internet that afternoon, he was afraid. Afraid if he told her he knew her secret she'd deny it, admit it, leave him or make him leave. But what scared him the most was that he wanted to help her more than he'd ever wanted to help anyone, and he had no idea how.

"Great," he allowed, and picked up the phone.

While he dialed, then waited for Serafina to get her order pad, he watched Isabelle get dressed. He was fascinated by the way she moved, the precision with which she picked up his far-flung clothes and smoothed them as she laid them on the bed. Serafina yelled, *"Sceriffo!"* twice before he remembered what he wanted to order.

When he hung up, Isabelle was staring out the window, braiding her hair. "All set?" she asked without turning around.

"Yeah."

The need to go to her was as overwhelming as his need to help her, so he crossed the room and together they contemplated the moon. She leaned back against his chest and pulled his arms around her, crossing his hands over her belly. Something deep inside him shifted, and his throat went thick. He glanced around the apartment.

Tousled sheets, kitchen table spread with papers, his clothes folded and waiting for him on the bed.

Just like his white picket fence and wraparound porch, his funky kitchen, sad-eyed dog and well-stocked library, this apartment made him feel at ease. Maybe he was beginning to fit into Pleasant Ridge at last.

"Gabe?"

"Hmm?"

"You don't mind me calling you that, do you?" She echoed his question.

Amazingly he didn't. "Most people call me Klein. A few call me Gabe. Only my mother calls me Gabriel."

"Let me guess, whenever she's mad at you."

"No, all the time. It's embarrassing for a guy of my size to have the name of an angel."

"When I first heard your name, I didn't think it fit you any better than Isabelle fit me. But now I know better." She turned in his arms, slipped her hands around his waist as easily as if she'd been doing it all her life. "I can't think of anyone more deserving of an angel's name. But I'll call you Gabe anyway."

She went on tiptoe and pressed a kiss to his jaw, then she laid her head on his chest. Funny, but now she seemed to be holding him, and he hadn't even known that he needed it.

They'd begun this relationship based on attraction, but if he wasn't very careful he'd end up in love with her, and Klein knew very well what would happen then.

He'd be the one to get hurt.

SHE WAS ACTUALLY EATING pizza after eight o'clock at night. Sacrilege in the bulimia handbook. But Belle couldn't work up any angst over it at the moment. She was too happy.

The loneliness that had been her constant companion all her life faded when she was with Gabe. She forgot so many things when she looked into his eyes. She remembered what it felt like to touch him, to be a part of him and have him be a part of her. The wonder of him made all the problems and secrets in her life recede. Though she had no doubt they would thunder back to the surface soon enough.

"You were worried that sex would ruin our friendship?" He took a fifth slice of pizza and cocked a brow. "Does it feel ruined?"

With the scent of him still on her skin she had a hard time focusing on friendship. But as she considered his question, Belle realized she felt comfortable, at ease, at home for the first time since she'd left home—and it was because of Gabe.

"No," she admitted. "In fact—"

"It's enhanced," he finished, sounding as shocked as she was. "I always thought I made a better friend than a lover."

"Then, you must be quite a friend."

He caught her meaning immediately. "Thank you."

He tossed his crust into the box. It fell in the middle of the other four crusts, which were all that was left of a cheese-and-pepperoni. Belle had eaten three slices of her own—crusts and all.

"Didn't anyone ever tell you that crusts give you curly hair?"

"What would I do with curly hair?"

She glanced at his crew cut and smirked. "Good point."

"I could grow it out until I have a ponytail. Get an earring, a tattoo."

"Oh, yeah, I can see it. Very you. I might have

some pooka beads around here. Would you like to wear them?''

''Why don't you? With nothing else.''

Her body heated. His slightest look, the merest touch of his hands, a foolish innuendo, and she wanted him again.

''What's this?'' He held up the script she'd been reading earlier.

''My script. Read it and weep. I wanted to.''

He skimmed the first page, his forehead twisting into a frown. The second page had him scowling. After the third, he slammed the script on the table and growled. ''I don't think so.''

''Weren't you the one who told me *Baywatch* meets Mayberry? Well, you were right.''

''Bully for me. That's a disgrace, Izzy. You're better than that.''

Though his defense warmed her, still she had to ask. ''How would you know?''

''What?'' He glanced up from the script.

''That I'm better than that. Maybe *that's* all I am. All I'll ever be.''

''You believe all you've got to give the world is a few jiggles of those breasts and a choice view of your ass?''

''It's worked pretty well so far.''

''I thought you wanted more.''

''I do. But how am I going to get it if all anyone sees is…?'' She stabbed a finger at the script.

''By fighting for it. By proving you're more, instead of letting them make you into less.''

''How?''

"By *being* Sheriff Janet Hayes the way you imagine her to be."

Hope spread through Belle, driving out the lingering despair that had weighted her heart since she'd opened the package and read the first page of the script. "You think I can?"

"I know you can. But that script has got to go."

"Well, there are some parts that could work, if they'd nip a little here and tuck a little there."

His smile was like sunshine across a mountain peak covered with snow. "You gonna rewrite that script, Isabelle?"

"Rewrite?" She blinked. "Me?"

"You see anyone else?"

"But—but I can't."

"Who said?"

You don't have to worry about spellin' no more, Belle. The ABCs won't matter once they get a gander at your face and body. Stick with your strengths, girl. And they ain't in that pretty head of yours.

"I'm not a very good speller," she admitted.

"Is that all? Neither is half the world."

Belle *wanted* to do what Klein suggested, but she was afraid. Afraid she'd be no good. Afraid everyone would laugh at her—again. Afraid she'd just prove beyond a shadow of a doubt that the only thing she had to give was something that mattered not at all.

"When you can't spell, you appear ignorant."

"If you don't even try, then you are." He shoved the script to her side of the table. "Write down your ideas, then I'll tell you what I think."

She hesitated, and he reached across the table to cover her hand with his. She lifted her gaze from the damned script to his beloved face. "You can trust me, Izzy."

As she stared into his eyes she had an odd feeling he was asking for more than a first look at her writing skills. She was tempted, not for the first time, to spill the whole sorry mess of her life. But she was afraid of that, too.

What man would want all that baggage? If he knew she was crazy as well as ignorant, ugly beneath the beautiful, defective in a way there was no fixing, would he ever touch her again?

She couldn't take that chance. He made her feel too special, and she needed that right now. She needed him.

So she smiled and turned her hand around to clasp his. Then she gave him one thing, so he wouldn't search for all the others.

"Got a pencil?"

KLEIN CLEANED THE KITCHEN while Izzy scribbled madly on the script from hell. When he'd read what they expected her to do on television he'd wanted to rip the thing into bits and then start them on fire. Could those morons possibly be unaware of the gem they had in her?

He finished putting everything away and sat on the couch. Isabelle continued to work as if alone in the room. She either didn't notice, or didn't mind, his staring. And why would she? Being stared at was part of her job. For some reason, that annoyed him more today than it had in the past. He didn't want anyone staring at her but him, and that kind of thinking could get him into trouble.

"There." She dropped the pencil and pushed back from the table. Her face held a note of wonder, as if she couldn't quite believe she'd done it.

"Finished?

"With the first scene." She took the few steps between the table and the living area, then offered the script to him.

He took it and patted the couch at his side. She folded herself onto the seat, cuddling against him as though having done it for most of her life. His arm curled around her in the same way.

A flash from outside made Klein glance out the half-open window. Must be a storm coming, though he hadn't heard of it on the news. Well, he didn't plan to go out for several hours, anyway, and Clint had a doggie door at home. Klein began to read.

Several chuckles and quite a few outright guffaws later, he was done. He placed the papers in his lap and glanced at Isabelle. Apprehension darkened her brown eyes nearly to black.

"It's good," he said. "Very, very good."

"Really?"

"You heard me laugh. I wasn't kidding. You've got a sense of comedic timing that the idiots who wrote this would sell their souls to have."

Isabelle's smile was joyous, but it faltered almost immediately. "Now what do I do?"

"Now you finish this script and you learn it this way, because when the director sees what you've done here, if he's any kind of director he'll know the show has to be performed as you've written it."

She sighed. "Klein, I wish I had your confidence."

So did he. "Lesson number five." He held up one hand, fingers spread wide. "Confidence is pretending you know exactly what you're doing, even when you don't."

"You're saying you don't know how to be a Tennessee sheriff?"

"I didn't when I started."

"You faked it?"

"Sometimes."

"Is the mayor aware of this?"

"The mayor couldn't tell his butt from a hole in the ground."

She laughed. "Can I quote you on that?"

"In the script. Not in the newspaper."

She froze. Her eyes became dark pools of shock in the stark white of her face. "The newspaper," she murmured. "Oh, no."

"Relax, Izzy, I was just teasing."

"No, you don't understand." She jumped up and began to pace in front of the couch. "We have to keep this a secret."

"This? You mean the fact that you're rewriting the script?"

"No." She waved her hand, dismissing that. "You and me. Us. This."

He frowned, confused and suddenly wary. Not that he'd wanted to announce their liaison to Pleasant Ridge—he wasn't that dumb—but her agitation made him nervous. "Why?"

"Because if the tabloids get a hold of it—" She

broke off and groaned. "It would be so embarrassing."

Klein stiffened. He always expected the worst. That way he was rarely disappointed or surprised. So why was he both right now?

"I can imagine. How would it look for the beauty to belong to a beast?"

She glared at him. "That's not what I meant. Although I could see them making up something just like that. The public would adore it. You wouldn't believe the things they say, what they dig up, what they twist and turn until it's not even close to the truth. I don't want you to have to go through that, Gabe."

He was having a hard time following the conversation. "You're worried about me?"

"Of course." She shrugged almost sheepishly. "And I admit I don't need the attention, the scrutiny, the hassle right now. If I'm going to do this show my way, I'm going to have hassle enough without constant questions about my sex life."

Sex life, not love life. Why did her choice of words bother him? He'd been the one to jump at the chance for a purely physical relationship. Even though, deep down, he still didn't believe she wasn't embarrassed to proclaim him as a lover to the world, nevertheless, he didn't want cameras in his face, either.

"It shouldn't be too hard to keep this a secret," he allowed. "After all, I'm supposed to be teaching you. We're required to be together."

"Not in bed."

"No, that's just my requirement."

A startled laugh erupted from her lips, and he was glad. She appeared so pale, so fragile, so worried, he'd half expected her to need holding up again.

She sat back down on the couch and threaded her fingers through his. He loved it when she did that.

"Well, we *have* been seen holding hands already. If that didn't escalate into a torrid love affair on the Pleasant Ridge grapevine by now, we should be safe," she said.

"True enough."

And it obviously *hadn't* escalated, or the mayor would have been whining instead of asking Klein to watch over her. Perhaps she'd been right about their being seen together enough that people began to ignore them.

"Speaking of safe..." She kissed his jaw, then frowned and glanced at the window behind him. "Was that lightning?"

"Mmm." He pressed his mouth to the warm, scented skin where her shoulder met her neck. "Seems to go off every time I touch you."

"Then, touch me some more, Sheriff. We could use the rain."

CHAPTER FIFTEEN

LIFE SETTLED into a pattern. Klein was with Isabelle day and night. They spent time at her apartment and his house. Together they remodeled his avocado bathroom. She painted ivy on his picket fence and planted more flowers.

Isabelle accompanied him on all his calls. She asked questions constantly, took copious notes and rewrote the script for the pilot in a week. It was brilliant, so Klein suggested she write an original script for the second episode. She took to the idea so fast that he could tell she was enjoying her new pastime nearly as much as he was enjoying his.

He'd had to return to an out-of-the-way drugstore twice in order to replenish their safety supply. Both times he'd felt someone watching him. But no one knew him there, and he hadn't worn his uniform.

Klein shook his head. All the sneaking around was making him jumpy. Though necessary, creeping into Isabelle's apartment after dark, or seeing her leave his house before dawn smacked of guilt and he didn't like it. But he did like her, and he wasn't willing to give up what they had.

Isabelle had been right about one thing. No one in Pleasant Ridge seemed to notice or care that the two of them were always together. In a town that thrived on gossip as its main source of entertainment, he should probably be insulted that nobody suspected anything was going on between the sheriff and the supermodel. But he wasn't.

The only shadow over his yippy-skippy happiness was Isabelle's refusal to share any part of herself other than her body. He tried to talk to her about her family, her past, her childhood. She turned the conversation to other things with the ease of a practiced politician.

But he had not found her weak and dizzy again. They ate meals together and she *ate* them. Once in a while he caught her frowning at her plate, pushing her food around or cutting it into itty-bitty pieces, but everyone had foibles.

She walked with him day in and day out, and she was so busy observing his job and writing her script that he hadn't caught her running since the night they'd first been together. Maybe he'd been wrong about her, but he didn't think so.

Klein turned his attention to the reports that covered incidents of the previous week. Thankfully nothing as serious as the feudal accident had occurred. Their days had been filled with the usual.

Joey Farquardt put a hole in Serafina's garbage can with a slingshot. Slingshot confiscated.

Jesse Wright was late to work one morning and tried to make up time by driving his truck down Longstreet Avenue at fifty miles an hour. He argued that it was still dark out and no one was there to see—except Klein. Speeding ticket issued.

T.B.'s night in the open, and his subsequent rescue, did little to improve his disposition. The new sailor suit Miss Dubray whipped up on her Singer hadn't helped. T.B. attacked the pants of a tourist from Knoxville who had driven in to see the Shiloh exhibit. Pants paid for by Miss Dubray, disturbing the peace citation issued to the Chihuahua.

Of course, there were other more serious issues. Runaway teen picked up hitchhiking on Highway B. Given lecture on the evils of the world and taken directly back home. A bag of marijuana discovered in a middle school locker. *Sheesh*—middle school! Drugs traced to the kid's pot-head parents. Arrest made; Social Services notified.

Then there was yesterday's domestic disturbance at the Trumpens'. Such disturbances were every cop's worst nightmare, and Klein refused to have Isabelle anywhere near something so volatile. So she hadn't seen him slam Mr. Trumpen against the wall a few times—just until the man promised that the missus would no longer run into any doors. Because if she did there'd be another, less pleasant, visit from the sheriff.

God, Klein loved his job.

He was helping people; he was accomplishing something worthwhile. Pleasant Ridge had begun to feel like home, which was what he'd always dreamed of.

Now Klein glanced at Isabelle, who had commandeered Virgil's desk and was scribbling again. Had he dreamed of her, too? No, he'd never dared to dream of a woman who could make him forget all his insecurities, a woman who could make him feel beautiful whenever she touched him or even looked at him. He wanted to cross the room and kiss her neck until she melted into his arms. But that was a job for tonight.

"What are you doing?" he asked.

She glanced up, eyes unfocused, expression vague. She got like that when she was writing, although today she was more distracted than usual. This morning her phone had rung before the sun was up, and even though he'd been half asleep, he'd heard her whispering to whomever had called. But when he'd asked who it was, she'd shaken her head and refused to answer, which only reminded Klein that she still held parts of her life secret from him. He didn't like it, but he wasn't sure what to do about it.

"I was working on a scene with T.B. and Clint," she answered. "You think we could use them in the show?"

He snorted. "T.B. *will* hurt someone. You'd better get a stand-in."

"And Clint?"

He shrugged. "You can try, but he might fall asleep."

She laughed and returned to her work.

The door of the station opened. Chai stepped in, accompanied by a man near Klein's age, with the same salt-and-pepper hair, although his was pulled into a ponytail and covered by a beret. In Klein's experience hats on men with ponytails usually indicated male pattern baldness.

Klein recognized the thought for what it was— envy. Not that he wanted a ponytail or a beret, but the guy was another pretty face. Was the whole world full of them?

"Sheriff," Chai began. "This is—"

"Isabelle, my angel!"

The man breezed past Chai. Klein would have enjoyed the expression on the mayor's face if the ponytail man, who was kissing Isabelle on the mouth and sliding his hands around her waist, hadn't distracted him.

He took a step forward, and then he remembered he was her secret lover, not her husband. Hell, he wasn't even her boyfriend. He had no right interfering unless she asked him to. And she wasn't asking; she was kissing the guy back.

"California." Chai stood next to him. He looked as happy as Klein felt. "They're very friendly there."

"So I hear. Who is he?"

"Daniel Dimato. The director. He just arrived, along with the rest of his crew and cast."

"You don't sound happy. I thought this was going to do wonders for Pleasant Ridge."

Chai straightened and wiped the pout off his face. "It will. When this is over, I'm going to remodel Longstreet Avenue. People will come from all over just to see it."

"Oh, that should be fun."

"Do I detect sarcasm, Sheriff?"

"I doubt it."

As Isabelle was beckoning him to join her, Klein left the mayor stewing over the comment.

"Daniel Dimato," Isabelle said, "I want you to meet Sheriff Gabe Klein. He's been such a help to me."

"Sheriff—" Dimato held out his hand.

Klein glanced down and was surprised to discover the insignia of the U.S. Marines tattooed on the man's forearm. His grip was firm and his gaze met Klein's squarely. "*Semper fi,* man."

"You were a marine?"

"Don't sound so surprised. If we all became cops when we got out, the U.S. of A. would be overrun by the establishment."

Klein scowled. The guy spoke as if he had lived through the sixties. But unless Klein missed his guess, Dimato had been born too late to do much but goo and ga through the end of the decade.

"Relax, Sheriff. I'm kidding." He glanced at Isabelle. "He does laugh, right?"

"He laughs a lot, and he's funnier than you, Danny. In fact, you two probably have a lot in common."

Klein and Dimato looked at each other. "Us?" they said at the same time.

Isabelle chuckled. "Yes, you."

"I could have been a marine," Chai interjected.

"What happened?" Dimato asked. "Did Daddy say no?"

Klein blinked. Dimato caught on quick. But then, marines had to.

"I had responsibilities at home," Chai said; however, his face had gone pink. "And right now, as well. Good luck, Mr. Dimato."

Chai made a quick exit.

Dimato turned to Klein. "Can you imagine him in the corps?"

"Yeah, I can," Klein said. When Dimato gave

him an incredulous stare, he quirked a brow. "I can imagine how much fun he would be to watch."

Dimato grinned and slapped Klein on the back. "Me, too."

In another world—one where Dimato didn't call Isabelle "my angel"—Klein might have liked the guy.

"Chief? Hey, Chief!" Virgil's voice burst through the walkie-talkie. "The town has run amuck."

"Amuck?" Dimato murmured. "Who is that guy?"

Klein ignored him. Virgil was often hyper, and even more often an alarmist, but Klein didn't like the panic he heard in the old man's voice.

"Whataya got?"

"You name it—2-88 for certain. Several 4-15s. More 6-47s than I can count. There's a 10-33 on the next street over and a 10-34 next to the museum. We're going to need 11-84 at the corner of Longstreet and Lee. That's a code twenty, Chief." The walkie-talkie cut out.

"What in hell did he just say?" Dimato asked.

"I'm not sure." Klein's head was whirling. "Vagrancy? Maybe a stray horse? Littering?"

"No, that's a 4-25," Isabelle offered.

"How would you know?" Dimato appeared as confused as Klein.

"I got arrested for littering the first day I came to town."

"What?"

"Forget about it, Danny." She gave Klein a smile. "I didn't mind."

Dimato gave Isabelle a sharp, suspicious look that Klein didn't care for. But he didn't have time to put anyone's mind at ease.

"I've got to go," he said. "Code twenty is assist officer, urgent. I think."

"I'll come with you." Isabelle took a single step toward the door.

Dimato held up a hand. "No can do, sweet cakes. You need to get to wardrobe. Then I want you to do a run-through with me on the script."

Klein hesitated halfway to the door. His eyes met Isabelle's. Hers were wide and uncertain. He made a right-on gesture with his fist and forearm. Her answer was a weak thumbs-up, but she straightened her shoulders and faced Dimato.

"Danny, about the script…"

Unreasonably proud of her, Klein slipped out the door.

"WHAT ABOUT THE SCRIPT?" Danny asked. "You got your copy, didn't you?"

"I did."

"And?"

She took a deep breath and plunged in. "It stinks, Danny."

Belle had met Daniel Dimato in the autumn of her nineteenth year. He'd directed the first music video she'd been in. He'd taken her out to dinner, told her she had talent, then tried to seduce her.

She didn't hold it against him. Just as he obviously didn't hold her refusal against her. At first Belle had been embarrassed whenever she ran into him. But after the first couple of uncomfortable encounters, he'd taken her aside and said, "Sweet cakes, if everyone in our business stopped talking to everyone they'd tried and failed to nail, no business would get done at all."

He had a point. In the years since, they'd carried on a mutually satisfactory working arrangement. They had a rapport. Belle hoped that was still true after she finished speaking her mind.

"Stinks, how?" Danny sat at Klein's desk and thumped his snakeskin boots on top of the blotter.

"I was promised a different kind of show than this script indicates."

"How so?"

He seemed genuinely puzzled, and her unease increased. "The script as written makes me out to be a bumbling bimbo babe."

"It's funny."

"Not to me."

He frowned and sat up. His boots clicked as they met with the floor. "What did you think this show was going to be like with you in the lead, Isabelle?"

"I thought—" She broke off, swallowed and tried again. "I was told by the producers that the show would be the new *Picket Fences*. Serious *and* funny. Intelligent humor. Not adolescent."

He shook his head. "They must have wanted you pretty bad." He looked her up and down, then winked. "And I can't say that I blame them. But they lied."

"Lied," she echoed, feeling the world slip out of control all around her.

"Like rugs. Does it mention in your contract anything about the show's tone?"

She shook her head, and he shrugged. "You're the jiggle, sweet cakes. Exquisite, classy, top of the line—but jiggle all the same. Why would you think any different?"

"Why?" She sighed. "I have no idea."

"Right." He brushed his hands together, dismissing her concerns like dust. "Now, hustle on over to Ruby. She's set up in one of the empty shops on Main Street."

"Longstreet Avenue," Belle corrected listlessly.

"Whatever. The one next to that funky Civil War Museum. Is this place as full of rednecks as it looks?"

That snapped Belle out of her apathy quickly enough. "You better watch your mouth around here, Danny boy." She let her down-home Virginia drawl thicken. "Or you'll find yourself in more trouble than you care to."

He blinked at her, shock spreading over his features. "That's perfect. How did you do that?"

"Got me. All I know how to do is jiggle."

She escaped from the station. On the street chaos reigned. A town of just over a thousand did not handle the sudden addition of over a hundred easily. She didn't see Gabe in the crowd anywhere. He was no doubt handling a 10-lord-knows-what in another location.

Besides, she didn't want to see him now. She didn't want to explain that she'd failed. That no one but Gabe Klein saw her as anything more than what she was.

Only a few weeks in his company and she'd come to believe it, too. Amazing how easily a woman who needed to feel better about herself could become delusional. But Belle had learned long ago to listen to her mama. She just hadn't lately—and therein lay her mistake.

She wasn't smart, but she *was* pretty—on the outside. She'd make do with what she had. There were worse things. Although the thought of performing that script the original way made her stomach roll and pitch.

She walked past Lucinda's. Maybe the roll and pitch was hunger. Just her luck, today was brownie day.

Ten minutes later Belle reached wardrobe. She'd slammed one brownie while still in the store, finished the second on the street in two bites. She was making her way through the third when Ruby stepped out of the back.

Belle swallowed. She'd worked with Ruby before. The woman could have passed for an army nurse. Maybe Danny had stolen her from the marines. But Ruby knew how to sew, an increasingly lost art in this day and age. She also knew how to browbeat models and actresses so that they could fit into whatever she'd designed, in time to face the cameras.

With a snarl, she snatched the brownie from Belle's hand and tossed it into the trash. Then she spun on her heel and marched back the way she had come. Belle followed.

"There—" Ruby snatched a length of khaki material from a rolling coatrack and shoved it into Belle's hands. "Put it on."

Belle glanced around for a dressing room. There wasn't one. "Uh—"

"Since when are you shy? Off." She waved at Isabelle's clothes. "On." She pointed at the costume.

Two weeks in Pleasant Ridge and Belle had reverted to the innate modesty that it had taken her nearly a year of concentrated effort to suppress. In her day-to-day life, stripping to her skivvies and beyond in front of the wardrobe mistress and unknown others was no big deal. Or at least, it wasn't supposed to be. So Belle gritted her teeth and did what she was told—but she didn't like it.

The material Ruby had used for her sheriff's uniform was not the crisp cotton blend of Klein's but rather the stretchy, confining spandex of a swimsuit or biking shorts. The pants clung to her like a second skin, and the shirt was cut so low that her cleavage was the first thing anyone would notice. But the most disturbing thing about the costume was that she couldn't get the pants zipped.

"What have you been doing?" Ruby demanded. "Sitting on your butt and eating brownies for breakfast, lunch and dinner?"

Belle ignored that. "Your measurements must be wrong."

"I don't do wrong. The costume was made to the measurements you sent me." She pulled a tag off the hanger and shoved it at Belle. "See?"

Ruby was right, which made Belle even more nervous. How could she possibly have put on enough weight in two weeks to pop out of her uniform? Of course, with a uniform like this, a single pound was a disaster.

"Take it off before you rip it in two."

Belle didn't think there was any danger of that, but she yanked the uniform off, anyhow. She hated spandex.

"Do you want to measure me before I get dressed?"

"What for?"

"To fix the uniform."

"What needs fixing is you. Here." Ruby handed her a box of pills. "Use these for the next few days. By the time we shoot, you'll be ready."

With a heavy feeling in her belly that was more than just brownies, Belle contemplated the package. *Diuretics*.

She could already feel the dryness in her mouth that would follow several doses of the anti–water-retention aid. But she'd be able to dump a few pounds quickly, and in her crazy world that was what counted.

The disgusted expression on Ruby's face made old insecurities revive. The woman had looked at Belle and found her lacking. Belle had failed at the simple task of fitting into a costume. How was she going to manage anything if she couldn't even manage that?

She wished she had the luxury of throwing a snit fit, threatening to walk if she didn't get her way— on the uniform and the script—but she didn't.

Just this morning her mama had called. Her father needed another operation, and he needed it quickly. Belle was scheduled to get paid as soon as they began to shoot the pilot. If she got fired, her family would suffer, and *that* she could not allow. So she'd better fit into that disgrace of a sheriff's uniform and she'd better do it quick.

The dream had been nice for a while, but it had been only a dream. Reality had intruded and wasn't going to go away.

Belle shoved on her clothes, pocketed the pills and headed for home.

KLEIN HAD DRAGGED THE mayor out of his office and put him to work on crowd control. Well, he hadn't actually dragged the mayor, but he'd imagined it. Several times in several different ways. The fantasy kept him from going crazy during the long afternoon in a town gone mad.

Long about suppertime things slowed down. All the California visitors had settled into their temporary homes. The hotel-motel was full. Every spare apartment was rented. Even unused storefronts had been snapped up. All the parking spaces on Longstreet Avenue were taken, and in a field beyond town they'd parked trailer after trailer and motor home. Pleasant Ridge resembled a tourist mecca, and he hated it.

Klein groaned and rubbed the small of his back as he climbed the stairs to Isabelle's apartment. He'd been on his feet all day and what he wanted was a glass of wine, a hug and then a kiss. Not necessarily in that order.

He used the key Isabelle had given him after their first night and slipped into the darkened apartment.

The place was so quiet; maybe she hadn't returned yet.

In the back of his mind all day had hovered a question: Had Dimato liked her script as much as Klein had? The guy seemed to have a few brain cells. If Dimato didn't recognize her brilliance, Klein would be surprised.

A muffled shuffle from the bathroom made him glance up just as Isabelle came into the room. She raised her head and then she stiffened, eyes darting to the kitchen table, the countertop, then back to him. The fear on her face made him nervous.

"What is it? You look like hell."

Her skin was pale, her hair sweaty and tangled; her hands shook when she reached up to rub her eyes.

"I'll be all right."

He crossed the room and pulled her into his arms. Her skin was clammy, and she shivered.

"You're sick." He led her over to the couch, and she sat down at his urging like a child. "What's the matter?"

Her eyes flitted to the table again. Klein strode over and picked up a packet of pills.

"No!" she cried.

But it was too late. Anger bubbled in his belly as he read the label.

He'd wanted to give her a chance to confide in him, to trust him, but the time for patience was past. Klein tossed the pills on the floor and ground them under the heel of his boot. Then he grabbed the laxatives off the counter and did the same thing with those.

He lifted his gaze to hers. "Anything else around here I need to know about?"

She shook her head, wide-eyed.

"Good. Now we're going to talk."

CHAPTER SIXTEEN

HE KNEW THE TRUTH that no one else had ever discovered. He knew just how ugly she was beneath her skin. Now he'd never touch her again. Belle waited for Klein to sneer at her weakness and walk out the door.

But he didn't.

Instead, he sat down next to her on the couch and drew her against his side, just as he always did.

"Talk to me."

"I—I can't."

"Why not?"

"I've never told anyone."

"So many secrets, Izzy. Why do you think you have to keep everything locked inside?"

She stared at him with her mouth hanging open. He'd called her Izzy. As if nothing had happened. As if everything was still the same. As if he hadn't just discovered the monster inside her.

"What set you off?"

How could he sound so calm when her head, her stomach, her heart whirled in weary confusion?

"Set what off?"

"Anorexia, bulimia. One or the other—I'd say the latter, since you don't look so thin you make my teeth ache."

Hearing the words made her cringe. What if the entire world found out? What would happen to her then?

"I don't want to talk about it."

"Obviously, since you never have. But maybe you should, hmm?"

He smoothed her damp hair away from her face and kissed her brow. She wanted to turn herself over to his care, to let him make everything all right. But she'd been self-sufficient for so long, and now nothing would ever be all right again if she lost him.

"How can you touch me now that you know?"

"I've known all along."

She stiffened. "You have not!"

"All right, maybe not from the first. But I started to suspect when Lucinda brought you the brownies, and you kept staring at them as if they were poison."

"That's not a crime."

"Then there was the jogging and the dancing. The whole control issue."

"So?"

"The tossing out of a perfectly good cherry turnover."

She rolled her eyes.

"Cutting your food into itty-bitty pieces. One night you ate lasagna and garlic bread. The next day you didn't touch a thing. I'm not blind or stupid. Binge and purge, Izzy." He shrugged at her surprise. "I looked up eating disorders on the Internet."

"When?"

"The afternoon before we first slept together. Why do you think I came over here in the first place? I wanted to talk about it, but I got a little distracted. And then—" he shrugged "—I wanted you tell me on your own. To share it with me by your choice and not mine."

He had known and still he had slept with her? He'd known, yet he'd continued to come to her again and again, day after day? She just couldn't fathom that.

"I don't believe you."

"Here—" He pulled out his wallet, tugged several sheets of folded paper free and tossed them into her lap.

She picked them up. Internet information, run off on a printer, dated the afternoon in question.

She raised her gaze to his. "I still can't understand why you'd touch me if you discovered this."

"And I can't understand what one has to do with the other."

She groped for the words to explain what she felt. The duality that lived within her. The darkness she could never quite conquer. The truth she hid and never shared with a soul.

"Isabelle is perfect and beautiful. But if you understood what lived beneath…that I'm Belle in here—" she thumped her chest "—and I'm ugly beyond redemption—"

He touched one finger to her chin and turned her face toward his. "You're Izzy to me. Funny and smart."

She winced. Secrets and lies—she didn't think

she'd ever be able to share them all. Not even with him.

"Smart," he repeated. "Talented. Gentle. Giving. Kind. From the skin all the way into your heart."

"And you're delusional."

"I've been called worse."

"So have I."

"Who told you you weren't beautiful?" he murmured. "Who made you believe it, too?"

He used her own words against her, and made her want to tell him everything she'd hidden for so long.

"I'm not beautiful. Not inside where it counts. Inside I'm lost and lonely and dumb. And when I look in the mirror, I'll always be—be—"

She faltered, and he took her hand in his. "What?"

"Fat. Just because I lost weight and grew into my face doesn't make me any less the fat little girl who never had a friend."

"Ah, I wondered about that."

How could he be so nonchalant? "Don't you hear what I'm saying? I was fat. Huge, in fact. No one liked me. Then I dropped out of school. No wonder I can't spell."

"And didn't you hear what I've been saying? Spelling is overrated, and being fat isn't the end of the world."

"Obviously you've never been a teenage fat girl."

"True enough. But that's behind you. Why do you let the past affect the present?"

"Because for me the past lives in here." She touched her heart. "And in here." She raised her hand to her head.

"You need to make it stop."

"Easy for you to say."

"No. No, it isn't. I haven't let the past die, either. I still let memories hurt me, and I've lived my life so I can't be hurt the same way again. Until I met you, anyway."

"I don't understand."

"We're not done talking about you," he warned as he pulled her close. "But maybe it'll help you to understand why I was such a jerk in the beginning. Why I understand how a person's past can leak into their present and flood their future."

"I know why you behaved the way you did. You were forced to help me. You have better things to do than teach a ditzy underwear model your job."

"If you keep calling yourself names, I'm gonna get mad." He sighed. "I have...or make that I *had* an aversion to beautiful women."

"What?" She leaned back so she could see his face. He wasn't kidding.

"I know. What kind of man am I? But you see..." He struggled with the words.

She wanted to help him, but she wasn't sure how.

"My mother is a very beautiful woman. It killed her to have a son like me."

"Strong, proud, brave, a marine?"

"Shh." He hugged her, then held her a moment. "She's not here. You don't have to defend me."

But Belle wanted to. Just as he defended her— even *to* her.

"I never knew my father," he continued. "My mother kept trying to replace him—five times now."

"She's had six husbands?"

He shrugged. "She was a woman who needed to be taken care of. Between men, she leaned on me, and those were good times, when it was just the two of us. But they never lasted long. There was always another man around the corner. I embarrassed her. How could someone as beautiful as her have a son who resembled...well, a hound dog."

Belle's eyes narrowed. Without knowing it, her hands had clenched. She wanted to meet Gabe's mother—in a dark alley, just the two of them.

"I can see why beautiful women annoy you."

"I'm not done yet."

"There's more?" she muttered.

He took a deep breath as if bracing himself for the rest. Instinctively, Belle slipped her arms around his waist and held on.

"Her name was Kay Lynne. She was seventeen. The prettiest girl in school. A cheerleader, class president, homecoming princess."

Belle growled. She didn't like Kay Lynne already.

"Down girl." He passed a hand over the top of her head, and she quieted. "When she asked me to take her to the dance, I knew it was a joke. But she kept following me around. Sitting with me at lunch. Calling me. After a few weeks..." He shrugged. "I was eighteen. Never had a girlfriend, and she wouldn't leave me alone. So I took her to the dance, then we started dating."

"What's wrong with that?"

"She was the prettiest girl in school. I was the biggest guy."

Belle frowned. She was missing something here. "So?"

"Boys bothered her constantly. Once she started dating me, they backed off—because I made them."

"Okay. I still don't see where this is going."

"Neither did I."

He paused, and Belle knew he'd never told anyone what he was about to tell her. It would probably hurt him to say the words as much as it would hurt her to hear them.

"I never saw it coming. I was in love with her. Foolishly, blindly, stupidly crazy for her. And she was laughing at me all the time."

She inched out of his arms so she could see his face. But he was staring into the past and not at her.

"We went to the prom. She didn't come back from the ladies' room for quite a while, so I went searching for her. She was with a group of friends, standing just outside the door on a balcony. I heard every word."

"What did she say?" Belle whispered, and slid her hand into his.

"One of the girls asked her if she was serious about me, because I was definitely serious about her. Kay Lynne laughed. Of course she wasn't serious. After all, she wanted children, and could anyone imagine what my children would look like."

Anger flashed through Belle with a heat and intensity that surprised her. She wanted to meet Kay Lynne in a dark alley, too.

"She was a vicious, selfish, vapid little girl, Gabe. Forget her."

"There's more."

Hell.

"The entire relationship was a setup. Kay Lynne had a boyfriend away at college. He'd suggested she pick out the biggest, dumbest geek in school and give him a thrill. That way none of the other guys would bother her. He wouldn't have to be jealous, and I'd do anything she asked of me because I'd be so damn grateful just to have her. Then when he came home from school for the summer, she could dump me and never look back."

"I'm sorry."

"It was my own fault. I should have known no one like her would ever want someone like me."

"She threw away the most beautiful thing she could ever have hoped to have."

He shook off her praise as he always did. "That's my story. Let's hear the rest of yours."

They were back to her, and suddenly she couldn't sit still. So Belle extricated her hand from his and stood. "What else do you want to know?"

"Why would a woman with your health issues choose a career dependent on appearance?"

"I didn't choose the career—the career chose me."

"You should do something else. Something less stressful."

"What we should do and what we can do are often two very different things."

"You can do anything you want to do."

"No, I can't. I never got past the eleventh grade. All I've got is what you see."

"You sell yourself short."

"No, I face the truth."

"The truth being that you have to risk your health, your very life for your job? That's bullshit, Izzy. Quit. Nothing's worth such a risk."

"There you're wrong."

"You need to see your face on television so badly?"

Agitated, she began to pace. "I admit I want this show to do well because it'll be a step up. No more posing in skimpy spandex on a beach in the sunny winter. No more taping low-cut outfits to my skin so I don't fall out of them when I walk. No more wedgies for weeks on end until I can't remember what it's like not to have one. So sue me. I want something else for me, too."

"Too?"

No moss on Gabe Klein. He picked up on every little word that she said. Well, she'd told him everything else; why not tell him the rest?

"My family need money."

"Give them some."

"I give them most of it. And that's still not enough."

His gaze sharpened. "Why?"

She could imagine what he was thinking—drugs, gambling, other overindulgences of the rich and famous. But, as in most cases, the truth was far from glamorous.

"My father was a farmer. We didn't have much,

but we made ends meet. Until one Saturday when he was clearing an old tree and a widow maker crushed his legs.

"He lived, but he couldn't work." She went silent as she remembered her father's pain and her mother's tears. "Those words don't describe how our lives were torn apart. My father was always a happy man, full of energy. He loved the outdoors. He was big, bluff, tanned...and then he was in a wheelchair—sickly pale and too quiet."

She began to pace again. "My mother, brothers and I tried to keep the farm going, but in the end all we could do was hang on and go deeper into debt. My mother didn't have any schooling past sixteen when she had me, and my three brothers were too young to get jobs. We'd never had enough money for insurance, and now my father needed extensive medical care, special help—the house even had to be altered."

"So you learned first aid and CPR."

She gave a wan smile. "Among other things."

"How old were you?"

"Sixteen. I'd had a late growth spurt, and it was just like that ugly duckling story. I didn't become a swan overnight, but near 'nuf. I still had some baby fat, and one day I was listening to some of the girls talk at school. It was cool to eat like mad, then throw up."

She shrugged at the disbelief on his face. "Teenage girls are the craziest people on the planet. Believe me. They'd pass around tips about laxatives, speed, water pills, fasting. Weird diets like eggs, bananas and hot dogs only. High protein, low carb. You name it, they knew about it.''

"You have to be kidding."

"I wish I were. I tried out a few of their ideas, lost some more weight, and people started to remark that they'd always thought I'd have a pretty face if I could just find some self-control and lose the weight—"

"Morons," Klein muttered.

"Because I'd lost weight, I started to feel special for the first time in my life—"

"Being special doesn't have one damn thing to do with your weight!"

"Really? Tell it to the world, Klein." He scowled and opened his mouth to argue. "Let me finish. You did." His mouth snapped shut. "I read up on eating disorders. Biographies and interviews of ballet dancers, actresses, just plain folks. Instead of being horrified, I was intrigued. Books, magazines—they were full of brand-new ideas. I made up my own variations—coffee for breakfast, milk for lunch, an apple for dinner, with water to take off the edge of hunger in between. But try doing that for a week. I'd be so hungry I'd lose control and eat too much." Her head spun just remembering that time in her life. "But I knew how to fix that.

"Then I discovered exercise. If I jogged every day, I could actually eat almost normally and still lose weight. Talk about a head rush."

Klein was staring at her as if she were another person entirely. Maybe now he'd understand the truth about her. Maybe now he'd turn his back and walk away.

Instead, he narrowed his eyes. "What did your mother say?"

"As I recall—congratulations. I had turned up thin and beautiful when she wasn't paying attention. I'd become an asset, and she wasn't going to question how I'd gotten that way. Not when I could save them all. And since I'd dreamed of saving them, I didn't mind. When I was seventeen, there was a beauty contest in Richmond."

"And you won."

She nodded. "The prize was a modeling contract. More money than any of us had ever dreamed of. But I had to quit school. Our debts were high, but I paid them off. I saved the house and the farm, got my father some psychiatric help. But the surgeries and the setbacks kept coming. My mother had to take care of my father, and my brothers needed to stay in school."

"Why?"

Her eyes widened. "They certainly aren't going to be able to become lingerie models. Call it silly, but men who don't finish high school don't do as well these days as they used to. I can help them, and I will."

"You're trapped."

She blinked. He'd put words to the secret feelings inside her. She was trapped by love and responsibility. There was no way out. But that same love and responsibility made her argue the truth.

"I'm not trapped. I'm blessed. I was given a gift

so I can take care of the ones I love. It was like a miracle. Just when we needed help the most.''

''That's your mother talking.''

She scowled. ''I can't quit, and I certainly can't make a fuss about this job and get fired.''

''Fuss? Why would you need to make a fuss?'' His eyes narrowed. ''What haven't you told me?''

''You asked what set me off tonight.'' She quickly filled him in on the afternoon's excitement, then spread her hands wide. ''Take your pick.''

He shook his head. ''Quit this job, Izzy. You can get another.''

''Eventually. But not right now. I need the money I was promised for doing this show. The circulation in my father's left leg has gone bad. Something has to be done immediately, or he'll lose it.''

''And there you are, trapped again. You'll do this show, however they want it, even if doing it their way ends any chance you might have of becoming more. Am I right?''

She saw her father's tired, pained face and her mother's desperate eyes. She heard her brothers' voices, deepening from childhood to manhood, thanking her for a chance.

''Yes,'' she answered. ''I'll do anything I have to do for the people I care about.''

''So will I.''

Before she could ask what that meant, he got up and walked out the door. She'd been expecting him to leave since the moment he walked in. So why was she surprised when he did?

KLEIN'S HEAD SPUN at all Isabelle had told him. He'd read about eating disorders, but reading didn't bring home how devastating they could be to the person afflicted, or to those who cared about them.

Anorexics could become so thin they permanently injured vital organs, even lost the ability to bear children, and this was if they didn't die before they admitted they were ill.

Bulimics had other problems—not as severe, but nothing to be blasé about. In fact, bulimics often went undiagnosed and untreated longer because they weren't obscenely thin, and they were able to function near to normal.

What with the pressures of Isabelle's job and her family, Klein could understand the resurgence of her illness. He wanted to help her, to make everything right, to take all her problems and solve them himself, but he couldn't. One other thing he'd read: the only way for an anorexic or bulimic to get better was to want to.

He couldn't solve her family troubles, either. He'd give her everything he had, but he was a cop. He didn't make much money. All that he'd saved he'd put into the farmhouse, trying to make it into a home. Even if he had every cent back, it wouldn't be a drop in the bucket compared with what she needed. But there was one thing he could do—one thing he was very good at.

Klein returned to the station and tore through his desk until he found his address book. Two minutes later Garrett Stark answered the phone in Savannah.

"What can I do for you, Detective Klein?"

"It's 'sheriff' now. But never mind that. I'm calling for a personal favor."

"Anything."

Klein raised his eyebrows. "Anything?"

"Of course. I know we didn't hit it off at first. But then I thought you were a scheming lothario, after Livy."

Klein nearly choked at the image of himself as a lothario. Was everyone delusional? "That's all right, I thought you were lowlife scum."

"I was." Stark laughed. "Now that we're done exchanging compliments, you were a good friend to my family when I didn't even know I had one. Anything you want that I can give you, consider it yours."

Klein was used to being everyone else's friend, helping whenever help was needed. He had so rarely needed it, had even more rarely asked for it. He wasn't quite sure how to handle being guaranteed anything right off the bat.

"Uh, your agent."

"Andrew? What did he do? Scare someone to death again?"

"No, it's not like that. I need an agent to handle a television script."

"You've got a television script? Since when do you write?"

"Not me. A friend. Would your agent handle that or know someone who might?"

"Call him." Garrett rattled off his agent's number. "If anyone can help you, that someone is Andrew Lawton."

"FAX MACHINE?"

Klein also discovered that Lawton didn't spare breath or time for such niceties as verbs. He was required to puzzle out the meaning for himself.

"Uh, yes, I have one."

"First five pages. Now."

Klein did as Lawton demanded, sliding the first five pages from the script into the fax machine and transmitting them, now, to the number Lawton had snapped out.

When the machine stopped whirring, all he could hear over the phone was Lawton's breathing and the rustle of paper.

"Brilliant," Lawton murmured after several moments. "Who did this? You?"

"No. Her name is Isabelle Ash."

"The model?"

Klein rolled his eyes. Was he the only man on the planet who hadn't known her? "Yes."

"Based on what I've seen here, I'll take her on as a client."

"You do this sort of thing, too?"

"Sure. When Garrett started getting offers for film versions of his books, I started dealing with Hollywood. I enjoyed it, so I set up an office there. Split my time between the coasts. Made myself into a multimedia agent. More interesting that way. Tell Isabelle to call me, or if there's an offer pending, have whoever call me. Same number."

And he was gone. Klein picked up the script and went to find Daniel Dimato.

It wasn't hard. There was only one hotel, and Dimato was in the best room. He opened the door minus his beret. Klein had been right about the male pattern baldness.

"Sheriff." Dimato's smile appeared genuine. "What can I do for you?"

"Read this." Klein tossed the script at him. To Dimato's credit, he caught it with one hand.

The man glanced at the title page. "The script? I don't understand."

"You will. Read the first scene." Klein stepped into the room, shut the door and leaned against it. Then he crossed his arms across his chest. "I'll wait."

Dimato frowned. "Now, just a minute—"

"What are you going to do?" Klein smirked. "Call a cop? Go ahead and read it. You'll thank me."

Dimato shrugged and read. Klein relaxed. One thing he was very good at was intimidation.

BELLE HAD JUST GOTTEN OUT of the shower and dressed in a fresh, loose pair of shorts and T-shirt, when someone knocked on the door. She saw Gabe through the window and wondered why he hadn't just walked in, but then again, maybe he'd come to return her key.

Tears sparked her eyes. What did she expect? That he'd want to saddle himself with a nutcase like her?

Rubbing the tears away, she gathered what was left of her pride and opened the door. Only to stumble back when Danny rushed into the room.

"Sweet cakes, you are brilliant. Wonderful. I never would have thought you had it in you."

She frowned and glanced at Gabe, who was staring at Danny too.

Danny grabbed her and kissed her on both cheeks. ''My angel. Why didn't you tell me you'd been working on the script? When you said it stunk, I thought that was rhetorical, baby. I didn't realize you had better things in mind.''

She shook her head to clear it. Gabe had not left her—for good, anyway; he'd gone and talked to Danny, securing her the chance she'd wanted so desperately.

''You read the script?''

''Sure did. And I took a look at the second one, too. I'll be going out on a limb here, but I know a hit when I read one. Can you do it, Isabelle? Can you be Janet Hayes the way you wrote her?''

She glanced at Klein again. He was no longer frowning at Danny but staring at her. In his eyes she saw the certainty she'd always wanted to see in her own. He gave her a right-on sign with his fist again, and she knew she had to try.

''I can be Janet that way a heck of a lot easier than I can be her the way she was written.''

''Excellent. We'll try it tomorrow.''

Danny started for the door. Klein held out a piece of paper as he passed. ''What's this?''

''Her agent's phone number.''

''I already did the deal with her agent.''

''This is her script agent.''

Danny goggled. ''She has one?''

Belle shut her gaping mouth. ''I have one?''

Klein nodded, staring at Danny, patiently continuing to hold out the phone number. "She does now."

Danny took the paper, glanced at the name and number. "Lawton? You're kidding. He's one of the biggest agents in New York." He glanced at Belle. "How'd you get him?"

She shrugged as Klein answered. "Because she's good, Dimato. From the top of her brilliant brain to the tip of her beautiful toes, and she's only going to get better."

Looking into his eyes, Belle started to believe it.

CHAPTER SEVENTEEN

"HOW DID YOU make him agree?" Belle asked as soon as Dimato left the apartment.

"I didn't *make* him do anything. He read your work. He loved it. So did Lawton. You're an amazingly talented and bright young woman. Why can't you see past your own face?"

"Because no one else can?"

He sighed, crossed the room, then drew her into his arms. Since Belle had feared she'd never be held by him again, the pleasure was twofold.

"Forget about everyone else. How you see yourself is more important than how others see you. Look at T.B. He thinks he's a pit bull. And to be honest, I think he is, too. He scares the crap out of me."

She laughed. "Nothing scares you, Gabe Klein."

"Except for you," he murmured against her hair.

"Me? Why would I scare you?"

"Because I'm afraid you're going to really hurt yourself one of these days if you continue to do what you've been doing."

The bulimia. She should have known he'd get back to that.

Belle extricated herself from his arms and went to the front window, where she opened the curtains.

From there she could see the shape of indigo mountains against a purple sky.

"I'll be all right," she said. "In fact, I'm better already. I know how to handle myself."

"You should see a doctor."

"Doctor?" She spun around to discover him right behind her. "No. The media will catch wind of it, and that will ruin my chance here."

"Why would a doctor tell anyone anything?"

"It wouldn't have to be the doctor. Just anyone who saw me anywhere near an office, clinic, hospital or treatment center. And you can bet they'd make up something far worse than the truth."

"So tell the truth." He put his hands on her shoulders and stared into her face. "Then it can't hurt you anymore."

How little he understood the realities of her world. "If they think I'm sick, I'll lose this job, and I've already told you how much I need it."

"But you *are* sick, Izzy. And the quicker you admit that, the better off you'll be."

The gentleness in his voice did not take away the sting of his words. "You think I'm crazy, don't you."

"I think you need help. There's nothing wrong with needing help once in a while."

To Belle, needing help had always meant failure, lack of control over her world. She'd seen what lack of control could do—how it could ruin lives and separate families.

Panic fluttered in her belly. She had to make him see that she wasn't out of control. There was no problem here, no problem with her, no need for help.

"I just had a little setback. I've been better for a long time now, and I will be again. Please." She slid into his arms. "Don't tell anyone. I'll be okay. You'll see. I promise."

When his arms closed around her, and his sigh raised and lowered his chest beneath her cheek, she relaxed against him.

"All right," he agreed, but he didn't sound happy about it.

She leaned back so she could see his face. He didn't *look* too happy, either, and that tore at her heart. But she could cheer him up.

"You know what I'd like right now?" she asked.

"Pizza?" he said hopefully.

"How about a little mint julep?"

He snorted, choked, and then he did just what she'd hoped for. He laughed—deep, long and loud. Pulling her back into his arms, he hugged her tight.

"Izzy, you make me happier than I can ever remember being."

Her throat went thick and her eyes went hot. "Kiss me," she whispered before she blurted out her newest and deepest secret. She loved him, and she had no idea what she was going to do about that. "Kiss me, then take me to bed."

His lips touched hers before the last word was out of her mouth. Gabe's kisses were like none she'd ever had. Gentle and firm, tentative yet complete, they made her feel...so happy. His hands skimmed her waist, moved up beneath her T-shirt, warmed the weight of her breast as his tongue tangoed with hers.

Beyond her closed eyelids, bright lights of arousal flared. Klein lifted his mouth and glanced out the window. "Damn lightning."

She tugged his face back to hers. "Forget the lightning," she murmured, even as it flared again. Then she set him to work on the second half of her request.

DANNY TOOK ONE LOOK at Belle in the sexiest sheriff's uniform in the world and said it had to go. The skimpy, clinging costume did not match the image of the new Janet Hayes.

From that moment onward, Belle's life continued to change.

While she was in makeup, explaining that no, she didn't want her nails painted bloodred...in fact, she wanted them filed to a nub, she had a phone call from Andrew Lawton. The amount of money he'd gotten for the scripts she'd already written was enough to cover her oldest younger brother's college tuition next year.

When she stepped in front of the cameras for the first time, her heart fluttered and her stomach rebelled, but she caught sight of Klein lounging on the other side of the street. One wink and a righton from him and everything they'd shared through the night came back, as did his words of confidence in her and the still-secret, but no less beautiful, love she'd discovered for him.

Once the hoopla was over and she had some time to herself, she would tell him all that she felt, and then she would pray he might someday feel the same way about her. Asking a man like Gabriel Klein to share her manic lifestyle would require a leap of faith that Belle didn't yet have the courage for.

But because of him, she could do this job. He'd believed in her and made her believe. So Belle stepped into the role of Janet Hayes and made it hers. When she finished the first scene, the crew actually clapped—and Danny did, too.

She'd just sat down when Klein plopped a granola bar and a carton of milk into her lap. "Bottoms up," he told her. "You were wonderful." Then he disappeared into the crowd again.

Belle drank the milk but saved the granola bar. Her stomach was whirling too much to put anything more than liquid into it.

The day passed quickly. She did the first scene again, then moved on to some others. The work was going well, but by afternoon her confidence wavered.

Klein came by several times pushing food—an apple, a sandwich, a pear. He was worse than a dealer, and she felt more trapped than a junkie.

Because for Belle, food was her weakness—not pot, not coke, not blues, whites or reds—and her strength lay in refusing it.

KLEIN'S DAY had been busier than usual, but nothing he couldn't handle. He'd warned Virgil not to arrest anyone for anything less than a felony for at least a few days. They didn't have adequate jail cells to house minor offenders.

Chai was in his element, chatting it up with the television types. But that kept him out of Klein's hair. An asset if ever there was one.

The townsfolk didn't seem to mind the additional people and excitement. In fact, they appeared to revel in it. The cash registers in Pleasant Ridge were jumping and everyone was smiling.

Klein had taught Isabelle all he knew about being a small-town sheriff, but he'd learned something, too. His job wasn't just to protect and defend the people but to save the place through any means available—and that appeared to be Isabelle's television show.

He stood in the center of the buzzing, broiling town and just looked at the place. At the moment, Klein's world seemed pretty darn bright. He should have known he was in for a sucker punch.

As he returned to the station, whispers followed, a few people pointed. He began to feel squirrelly and paranoid. Then someone laughed. That did it.

He whirled on the yuckster—a teenage kid amid other teenage kids lounging outside Lucinda's after school. "What's so funny?" Klein demanded.

Every face froze; all eyes widened. The kids pointed to a newspaper spread out over the picnic table. A glance at the front page revealed the paper was one of those sleazy tabloids they sold next to the gum and candy bars at Wright Grocery Store.

"You kids shouldn't be reading that tripe," he advised. "It'll rot your mind."

"So it isn't true?" The boy who had laughed stared at Klein with an amused expression.

"What?"

The kid picked up the paper and turned it so Klein could read the headline: Beauty and the Beast.

His blood went cold even before he saw the picture below the words. Isabelle and him, locked together in the open window of her apartment. His hand up her shirt, their mouths inches apart.

He grabbed the paper out of the boy's hand and fled toward the station.

"If it isn't true, how did they get that picture?" the kid yelled after him. "Computer compilation?"

The laughter of the crowd ended when Klein slammed the door behind him. He skimmed the caption beneath the picture:

A source close to Isabelle Ash claims that she and the sheriff have been involved for weeks. In the guise of teacher and student, they've studied each other. And Belle is learning more from her beast than what it takes to be a Tennessee sheriff. Turn to page 5 for more photos.

Shit! Klein scrambled for page five and discovered pictures of them kissing on her porch, cuddling on the couch, holding hands on the street, having dinner at Serafina's. Everywhere, doing just about everything. He was surprised there wasn't a picture of them in bed.

Knowing that someone had been following them, watching them, cataloging their every mood made him more than mad. If this was what Isabelle's life was like, no wonder she didn't want anyone to know he was in it.

Isabelle. Klein hastily folded the paper back together as he recalled her warning him about just this problem. Unease prickled the back of his neck. He looked at the front page once more.

A source close to Isabelle? Who? She said she had no friends but him, and he certainly hadn't told anyone.

Although he *had* been the one to bring up the cutesy concept of beauty and the beast. Now here it was on the front page for everyone to see.

Coincidence? He wasn't sure, but he was getting a very bad feeling, and the only way to find the truth was to find Isabelle.

Ignoring the continued smirks, snickers and winks, Klein hurried down Longstreet Avenue.

DANNY SLAMMED into her dressing room while Belle was changing clothes.

"This must be important," she murmured, and finished buttoning her blouse.

"What's with you and Klein?" he demanded.

She raised her eyebrows and glanced at him in the mirror as she braided her hair. "He's helping me."

"I'll say." He tossed a newspaper onto the vanity beneath the mirror. "This is a publicity coup of the highest order, sweet cakes. Was it his idea, or was it yours?"

A trickle of premonition traced her spine. Belle dropped her hands and picked up the paper. One glance at the headline, then the picture, and she sat heavily in her chair.

Danny didn't notice. He was too excited at the prospect of all the free publicity. "Everyone is going to love you, Isabelle. Guys already adore you because of—" He flipped a hand at her face and chest.

Her heart sank at the proof that no matter what she did, she would always be seen as a beautiful object.

"Now every ugly man will believe in the fairy tale. That someone with a face like this—" he tapped Klein's nose with his finger "—can get a woman like you. Every woman is going to eat up this beauty-and-the-beast crap like there's no tomorrow. And the angle of the love story between teacher and student is brilliant."

Belle started to laugh, and then she couldn't stop. She put her forehead on her knees. How could anyone believe the relationship between herself and Gabe was a publicity stunt? Even in the photo she saw the love in her eyes. Couldn't everyone?

"What's so funny?" Danny asked.

"Yes," another voice said, "what's so funny?"

Belle raised her head, to find Gabe standing in the doorway. From the look on his face, he'd heard everything. From the paper in his hands, he'd seen everything, too, and he didn't feel like laughing about it.

She went light-headed with dread. He couldn't believe everything they'd shared was a lie. Could he?

ISABELLE PALED at the sight of him in the door-way—an admission of guilt if Klein had ever seen one. And he *had* seen one. How could the same thing happen to the same guy twice in one lifetime?

Probably because he'd been asking for it. What fantasy was he living in that a woman like Isabelle might want him? The same fantasy that he'd lived in when he'd believed Kay Lynne could love him.

Well, at least he hadn't made that mistake twice. This had been about sex, not love. Funny, but it hurt just as badly all the same.

"Go away, Danny," Isabelle said, though she continued to stare at Klein.

"Hey, Sheriff!" Oblivious as ever, Dimato shook Gabe's hand. "No offense or anything. I appreciate your helping us out. But then, I imagine it wasn't any hardship for you." He winked and punched Klein in the arm as he left.

The room was silent, Isabelle's face stricken. "Tell me you don't believe the bullshit Danny was spouting."

"What he was saying makes a lot more sense than what I've been believing for the past two weeks."

"You can't think that I'd let you touch me, that I'd cry in your arms and tell you all my secrets for publicity?"

He stepped farther into the room. "I've been racking my brain, trying to figure out what you saw in me. Almost believing that maybe, just maybe, you were the woman who could see past my face. It made sense. You wanted to be seen as more. You'd understand that I did, too. But all the time you were playing me—for publicity, for sex, for information.''

''That's ridiculous! This picture was from the other night. Someone got lucky. Why is that my fault?''

''Obviously you haven't had time to view what everyone else has.''

Klein opened his newspaper and plopped it on the one she'd been looking at. Isabelle frowned at the pictures of the two of them almost from the moment she'd walked into town, then she raised a very convincing, very puzzled gaze to his.

''Someone's been following us.''

She sounded as confused as he was. But she was an actress, and he had to stick to the facts as he knew them or risk what remained of his self-respect. He'd built it painstakingly over the years—ignoring the slurs, suppressing the heartache, living alone and lonely. Aware that his job, helping others, was all he would ever have. And that was enough; that was what he was good at.

Then Isabelle had come to town, and she'd made him believe for an instant that beauty of the soul meant something to her. He'd let her into his life, and he'd begun to dream. He should have remembered dreams were only for the beautiful people.

''Why would anyone follow us? How could they possibly conceive that they'd see something like this? Everyone in Pleasant Ridge thinks we're pals. Which is just what you wanted them to think.'' He threw up his hands. ''Hell, I even gave you the headline—Beauty and the Beast. There wasn't anyone else in the room but us when I said that, Isabelle.''

She winced. *Guilty!* his mind shouted, even as his heart bled.

''I'd never do this,'' she insisted. ''If you believe it, then you don't know me.''

''Does anyone? Do you even know yourself? You're Florence Nightingale, Janet Hayes, Supermodel Susie, Beauty and her Beast.''

''I thought I was Izzy,'' she whispered.

''So did I.''

CHAPTER EIGHTEEN

HE WAS BREAKING her heart, and he didn't even realize he held it in the palm of his hand. But if he could believe she'd use him, discard him, sell him for a sound bite, then he would never believe that she loved him.

"You've been waiting all along for me to hurt you, just like she did."

His face closed. He went as still as the mountains in winter and just as cold.

"That's why you're acting like an idiot and throwing away the best thing you ever had."

His eyes narrowed; a bit of fire leaped to life within them. "You think I should be grateful that a woman like you slept with me?"

Her sadness melted into fury. "I think you should shut up before I hurt you."

"You already have."

"Gabe, every pretty woman in the world isn't like Kay Lynne. Won't tear out your heart and stomp on it for the world to see."

He lifted one of the newspapers. "Really?"

There was no talking to him. He expected to be hurt; he saw betrayal even when it wasn't there. He wasn't going to believe her. Tears threatened, and she had to get away. She could no longer look at him and love him and know that he would never, ever be hers.

Belle walked to the door, then paused. "You might have been expecting me to tear out your heart, Gabe, but I certainly wasn't expecting it of you."

ISABELLE HAUNTED HIM. In his sleep, Klein reached for her. Every night he ached for her. He'd hear her laughter at breakfast, remember her voice during lunch, catch a hint of her scent in the dusky hour just before supper. Clint sat on the porch every night, staring at Highway B and sighing when it remained empty hour after hour.

Klein avoided the set, sent Virgil to deal with Dimato and the others, and kept to himself on the other side of town. Nothing helped. She'd ripped out his heart and stomped on it, but all he could think about was going back for more.

He refused to speak with the clamoring reporters. Of course Dimato tried to keep the fantasy alive— but without any comments from the beauty or the beast, or any new pictures, eventually they went away.

The mayor was seriously pissed off when he discovered that Klein had been poaching. He couldn't fathom that Isabelle had turned him down to sneak around with Klein, and he'd finally concluded that something must be wrong with her mind. Therefore she would not make a good senator's wife. Imagine the scandal if those sordid pictures came to light during an election. Klein was extremely proud of

himself when he didn't tear the mayor limb from
limb.

Of course, he couldn't work up much emotion
for anything lately. He drifted through his days
without anger, happiness or passion. His house had
become just a house, and Pleasant Ridge was just
another place to live.

Klein sat on his porch one twilight evening in
mid May watching the mountains, just Clint and
him, when Virgil came tearing into his driveway.

The old man slammed the squad car door and
tromped up the steps. The only thing Klein could
imagine that would bring the deputy to his house
on the run was a missing person. For that they'd
need Clint's help.

Cass's animal-interest story on Clint and T.B.
had sparked phone calls asking for the hound dog's
help. Clint had proved surprisingly adept at rescue
work. He'd even been used in recovering a few of
the television folks who had wandered off the tourist trails in the mountains.

But to Clint's welcoming bellow, Virgil snapped,
"Quiet, you."

Clint did so with a *yip.*

"I wish that worked with the Mex pup," Virgil
grumbled. "Even though Miss Dubray stopped
dressin' him up, he's still the meanest cuss this side
of the Tennessee River."

"I think that's just his nature."

"I think you're right."

"So what's the rush?" Klein asked.

"We got trouble."

Klein started to get up, but Virgil shoved him

right back. "I'm goin' to talk. You're goin' to listen."

He smacked a piece of newsprint onto Klein's knees—the story of Beauty and the Beast.

"Geez, Virgil, I thought I got rid of all these."

"You're talking, Chief."

"Sorry."

"You've been mopin' around lookin' sadder than your dog. And I for one have had enough. For a smart man you are sure actin' dumb. Take a gander at this."

He folded the paper so that the headline was no longer visible, then he pointed to Isabelle. Klein shrugged. "What?"

"Moron," Virgil muttered. "Look at her eyes. Look at her as she looks at you and tell me what you see."

Klein did what Virgil asked. All he saw was Isabelle, and he missed her.

"No one has ever looked at me like that," the old man continued. "I'd give everything I have for it, and you're throwin' it all away."

Confused, Klein studied her again. What had Virgil caught that he did not? "I'm sorry," he admitted. "I've never seen that expression before, either."

"That's because it's love, fool. She loves you."

"No, she doesn't."

"Idiot."

"Could you stop calling me names and tell me why you think Isabelle Ash is in love with me?"

"Because I got eyes, dimwit. I've watched enough women look at men that way, but never has one looked at me the way that she's lookin' at you."

Klein shook his head. "What about you and Miss Dubray? Thirty years of shared mint juleps can't be for nothing."

"Mint julep means sex, boy. Get with the program. Miss Dubray doesn't love me. Heck, I don't even get to call her Peg during."

Klein winced. He had never told Virgil that he had overheard the secret code for just this reason—he didn't want to listen to the details.

"What she and I have is sex. Great sex, but sex is all it is. She loved once, and when she lost him it nearly broke her. She swore she'd never love again."

Something in Virgil's voice made Klein ask, "What about you?"

Virgil shrugged. "I took what she could give me."

"You love her."

"Yep."

Klein went silent at the thought of loving someone for thirty years and knowing she didn't love you back. He sighed. He could imagine it very well.

The deputy shook his head, disgusted. "You need to get that stick out of your butt and get that butt into town."

"Why?"

"Because Isabelle collapsed at work today. They took her to Doc's. She's okay, but—"

The rest of Virgil's words were lost as Klein vaulted over the porch railing and sprinted for the squad car.

"I don't think there's any call for a code three," Virgil murmured as the red lights and siren began, scaring Clint so badly he dived underneath a chair. The old man smiled. "But then, suit yourself, Chief."

"Exhaustion," Doc Meyers pronounced. "Bed rest. No work for two weeks."

Belle nodded. Now that the pilot was in the can, she could take time off. For all the good it would do her. She couldn't sleep.

She missed Klein every instant—so much so that she physically ached. Pretending to be someone else was the only way she could keep from thinking of him. She'd thrown herself into her work, becoming Sheriff Janet Hayes. Janet would never allow herself to be anything less than completely in control—of her world, her life and her heart.

They'd finished the pilot today, and a minute after "Wrap" was shouted, Belle fainted. Talk about out of control. She was mortified.

Doc Meyers patted her hand. "Why don't you take a catnap here before you go home."

She nodded, and as he went into his office and closed the door, her eyes slid closed. Almost immediately, they snapped open when someone opened the outer door.

Cass Tyler stood on the threshold looking as if she expected Belle to throw something at her, which wasn't like Cass at all.

"Do you need the doctor?" Belle asked.

"What? Oh, no. No. I need to see you."

"Me?"

The two of them weren't exactly pals. In fact, Belle hadn't seen Cass since they'd all gone searching for T.B., what seemed like a lifetime ago. It *had* been another lifetime—one where she'd been happy.

"I'm no good at this," Cass began. "I'm just going to show you and then you'll know."

Cass crossed the room and upended the contents of a manila folder onto Belle's lap. Pictures poured out—pictures of Belle and Gabe. Like a kaleidoscope of the happiest days of her life, the images sifted across her body. Belle lifted her gaze from the stills to Cass's pinched, pale face.

"I wanted more than this place, this town, my rinky-dink paper, earth-shattering feature stories on missing dogs. I thought I could get there like this."

Belle picked up a picture of her apartment, shadowy except for the bed and the two figures entwined on it. Below that one were three different shots of Klein being safety-conscious at the drugstore.

Belle's face heated, but she forced herself to look Cass in the eye. "You could have gotten anywhere you wanted with these. Why didn't you?"

Cass stared at the floor. "The entire time I was sneaking around, creeping up your back stairs and taking pictures through the window, from the building across the street from the five-and-dime—"

Understanding dawned. "Not lightning," Belle muttered. "Camera flash."

Cass flicked a glance at her and sighed. "I even listened underneath your window one night. The two of you were arguing. Klein said you were Beauty and the Beast.''

Belle rubbed her tired eyes. So many things made sense now—too late to matter.

''What I was doing made me sick,'' Cass confessed. ''But I kept doing it. I mean, people do this, right? I figured I'd get over my squeamishness once I saw my pictures in a national magazine. And… and I was jealous of you. You're so beautiful and perfect. You have everything you want.''

''No, I don't.''

And she never would. But she couldn't be too angry with Cass. Belle could understand wanting more out of life and doing foolish things to get it. Besides, if Cass hadn't blabbed, someone else would have. Sooner or later Belle would have discovered that Gabe didn't trust her, that he couldn't love her, that his past would never be the past.

''Why didn't you sell them everything?'' she asked.

''I was going to. But the more I stared at the pictures, the more I thought about beauty and the beast—''

''Quit calling him that!''

Cass turned a contemplative gaze on Belle. ''I wasn't talking about him.''

''Go on.''

''I had this thought—perhaps the beast could be hidden beneath the beauty…''

''And beauty beneath the beast.''

''Exactly. So I started digging—into your past and his.''

''Swell.''

"And I was right. There's a long history of heroics—beauty, like you said—in Klein's past. He can't seem to keep himself from helping every pathetic loser he comes across."

"I know." He'd found a pretty pathetic one in her.

"He told you?"

"No. But I could tell right away he was the kind of man who just had to help kids, dogs and losers."

Cass nodded. "Once I was done with Klein, I moved on." She took a deep breath. "I found some beastly stuff in your past, Big Belle."

It had been so long since Belle had heard that name, yet it still had the power to make her cringe. Maybe she would never be free of her past, either.

"I can't believe you haven't cashed in on that," Cass murmured.

"Cashed in?"

"Ugly duckling to beautiful swan? Rags to riches? Savior of your entire family? People would eat that up with a spoon. They'd admire you. I know I do."

"What?" Belle shook her head. "I'm a high school drop-out. I was fat and I was poor." She left out her last secret—which appeared to still be a secret.

"You did what you had to do. You took care of people who needed you, and you sacrificed yourself for others. I'm not going to tear that apart. I want to be a reporter, anywhere but here. But not like this." She waved a hand at the pile of photos. "Those are all the pictures and the negatives. Do whatever you want with them."

Belle stared at the photos. Cass was behaving like a friend, which made Belle uncertain what to say or do. "You've made my head spin, Cass. Worse than usual."

"What I'm trying to say is I'm sorry. I know Klein thought you had something to do with the story. I'll tell him differently."

"It doesn't matter."

She was bone weary, depressed, run-down. She was sick, and the sooner she admitted that the better.

"Cass, I want you to write a story about the true nature of beauty and what makes a beast."

"I don't understand."

"You will. You see, it all started when I was sixteen…"

KLEIN BURST into Doc's outer office. She wasn't there. No one was. His heart was beating so fast he felt dizzy. A man of his size really ought not to get this upset.

He ran down Longstreet Avenue. When T.B. got in his way, he jumped over the yapping mutt. Ignoring Miss Dubray's cry of alarm, he sprinted around the corner of the five-and-dime and pounded up the steps to her apartment. Without knocking, he opened the door, to discover her packing.

She didn't even look at him. "I assume you've talked to Cass."

"Cass? Why?"

Now she looked at him, and confusion filled her eyes. "She took the pictures."

He shrugged. Funny, but the pictures no longer mattered. The only thing that did was Isabelle.

"What are you doing here, Klein?"

"I heard you were sick."

Her shoulders slumped, and she went back to folding clothes into her suitcase. He wasn't sure how to talk to this sad and silent woman. This wasn't the Izzy he had fallen in love with. He wanted that woman back.

Klein admitted the truth to himself. From the first moment he'd dubbed her Izzy he'd been steadily falling in love with the bright, brilliant, sweet and uncertain girl beneath the skin of this beautiful woman. But now that he'd allowed his past to ruin the present, would he ever be able to convince her that they deserved a future? Klein had no idea, but he did know that he had to try.

"Let me make everything all right for you."

The anguish in her eyes tore at his heart. "You can't make everything all right, because *I'm* not all right. In here." She tapped her head. "There are some people even you can't help. I have to go away and change how I see myself."

She was leaving. Panic nearly choked him. Gabe Klein who never panicked about anything. Desperate, he took a chance.

"I know that you love me, Izzy."

She dropped her makeup bag on the floor. Tubes, bottles and brushes scattered everywhere. She didn't seem to notice. "Who told you that?"

"I opened my eyes and saw the truth in yours. Open your eyes, Izzy. See me."

Her gaze touched his face like a caress. "I always have."

"Then, you know why I lost my mind and behaved like a complete asshole." She raised her brows but she didn't disagree. "I let the past into our lives. I won't make that mistake again."

Thoughtful now, she gathered the scattered lotions and potions into her bag, then straightened and tossed the bag into the suitcase.

"I wish I could say that I believe you, but I don't. I do love you. But until you believe that you deserve to be loved, you'll always be waiting for me to hurt you. The way Kay Lynne did. The way your mother did. Like countless others have. I can't live that way. And I don't want you to, either."

"So you'll make me live without you? That's not living. I've been wandering for years, searching for a home, wondering what was the matter with me because I couldn't seem to find one. And all along it was because I hadn't found you. This is home. But only if you're in it."

Tears filled her eyes as she crossed the room. She kissed him—sweetly, gently—goodbye. He didn't know if he'd survive her walking out that door, but he knew he couldn't watch. So he moved to the window and stared at the immovable mountains.

"There are some things I've got to work out for myself." She took a deep breath. "I've been sick for a long time now, Gabe, and it's time I admitted it. *I'm* the only one who can make me right again. And until I am, I can't come back."

He spun around. "You're coming back?"

Her smile was a shadow of the one he adored,

but it was a smile, and his heart leaped with hope. "You're the best thing that ever happened to me. Of course I'm coming back. As soon as I truly believe that you want me."

"I do."

"But I don't believe it in here." She tapped her chest. "Because in here, I'm still the stupid fat girl who doesn't have a friend."

He wanted to hold on to her and never let her go. But he could see that she had to learn the truth on her own. Only then would she let the past die.

He had a past that needed to die, as well. He had to trust that she'd come back. He had to believe that she loved him and that he deserved it.

"For me you'll always be the bright and brilliant light that came into my life and made me whole."

"And you'll be the funny, handsome, sexy guy who saw me as more before I ever did."

"Do you know that I love you?"

"I know that *I* need to love me…before I can accept that you do."

The door closed, and once again Pleasant Ridge was just a pretty town in Tennessee.

CHAPTER NINETEEN

ISABELLE ASH RETURNED to Pleasant Ridge as summer faded toward fall. She looked a bit different, but the biggest change was inside her.

She no longer felt weak, out of control, ugly—for the most part. There would always be days when the past sang a seductive song. But over the past few months she'd learned to see Izzy in the mirror instead of Belle.

Of course the tabloids had shrieked all her secrets, but by the time she emerged from the private facility to treat eating disorders, the past was passé. She no longer had anything to hide, and she no longer cared about hiding it.

She'd spent some time in Virginia. Her father was doing well. But the place that had once been home was home no longer.

Home was here; home was him.

Izzy slowed her car on Longstreet Avenue. Everything appeared exactly the same. No doubt because the mayor had been informed it had better be.

The show had been a resounding success, and Chai Smith's plans to remodel downtown were nixed by Danny and the producers. To receive the money for the next season, Pleasant Ridge had to be left alone, at least on the surface. She wished

she could have seen Chai's face when he heard that
all his sparkling plans for improvement would have
to remain just plans.

Izzy drove through town and onto Highway B.
She had taken Klein's words of love along with her
and held them close to her heart. Eventually she'd
come to believe that she deserved to be loved exactly as she was.

But had the months apart shown him the same
truth she'd learned? Or had he wallowed in the past
rather than whittled it away?

She turned into Klein's driveway and got out of
the car. Clint's eager bark greeted her from the
porch. Just like the old days. She hoped.

"Hey, Izzy. Long time, no see."

Her heart stuttered, then thundered. Klein leaned
out a second-story window. His hair was white with
drywall dust, and he had paint on his nose. Obviously he hadn't been idle while she'd been away.

The second their eyes met, she blurted, "God, I
missed you."

His smile told her the same truth it always had.
Everything was going to be all right.

"Come on up here. I've got something to show
you."

She didn't need to be told twice. Clint followed
her mad sprint upstairs at a more sedate pace. Klein
met her on the landing.

"You look exactly the same," he murmured.

She laughed. "Gabe, I gained ten pounds and I
cut my hair."

He stepped closer and ran a big, beautiful hand

over her shorn head. Her hair wasn't much longer than his now.

"What will Danny say?"

"Not one damn thing. How I look has nothing to do with who I am or how I do my job."

"Hmm. Seems I heard that somewhere before."

"Me, too. I just didn't believe it."

She wanted him to touch her, to hold her, to marry her. But she wasn't sure how to ask. She should have known that with Gabe Klein she wouldn't have to.

"I need your opinion on something." He led her to the room next to his and pushed open the door. "What do you think?"

Tears sparked her eyes. She threw herself into his arms.

He'd figured out exactly how to tell her everything she needed to know. He'd bared his heart and buried his past. Their future was plain to see.

"I think yes," she whispered, and then she kissed him.

Clint walked into the room, sneezed at the smell of new paint, circled three times on a rug the shape of a bunny, then collapsed in a heap of skin and bones beneath the brand-new crib.

They'd grown up at Serenity House—a group home
for teenage girls in trouble. Now Paige, Darcy and
Annabelle are coming back for a special reunion,
and each has her own story to tell.

SERENITY HOUSE

An exciting new trilogy
by
Kathryn Shay

Practice Makes Perfect—June 2002

A Place to Belong—Winter 2003

Against All Odds—Spring 2003

Available wherever Harlequin books are sold.

Makes any time special ®

Visit us at www.eHarlequin.com

HSSH05

TRUEBLOOD TEXAS

Coming in June 2002...

THE RANCHER'S BRIDE

by

USA Today bestselling author

Tara Taylor Quinn

Lost:

His bride. Minutes before the minister was about to pronounce them married, Max Santana's bride had turned and hightailed it out of the church.

Found:

Her flesh and blood. Rachel Blair thought she'd finally put her college days behind her—but the child she'd given up for adoption haunted her still.

Could Max really understand that her future included mothering this child, no matter what?

Finders Keepers: bringing families together

If you enjoyed what you just read,
then we've got an offer you can't resist!

Take 2 bestselling love stories FREE!

Plus get a FREE surprise gift!

Clip this page and mail it to Harlequin Reader Service®

IN U.S.A.	IN CANADA
3010 Walden Ave.	P.O. Box 609
P.O. Box 1867	Fort Erie, Ontario
Buffalo, N.Y. 14240-1867	L2A 5X3

YES! Please send me 2 free Harlequin Superromance® novels and my free surprise gift. After receiving them, if I don't wish to receive anymore, I can return the shipping statement marked cancel. If I don't cancel, I will receive 6 brand-new novels every month, before they're available in stores. In the U.S.A. bill me at the bargain price of $4.05 plus 25¢ shipping and handling per book and applicable sales tax, if any*. In Canada, bill me at the bargain price of $4.46 plus 25¢ shipping and handling per book and applicable taxes**. That's the complete price, and a saving of at least 10% off the cover prices—what a great deal! I understand that accepting the 2 free books and gift places me under no obligation ever to buy any books. I can always return a shipment and cancel at any time. Even if I never buy another book from Harlequin, the 2 free books and gift are mine to keep forever.

135 HEN DFNA
336 HEN DFNC

Name	(PLEASE PRINT)	
Address	Apt.#	
City	State/Prov.	Zip/Postal Code

* Terms and prices subject to change without notice. Sales tax applicable in N.Y.
** Canadian residents will be charged applicable provincial taxes and GST.
  All orders subject to approval. Offer limited to one per household and not valid to
  current Harlequin Superromance® subscribers.
  ® is a registered trademark of Harlequin Enterprises Limited.

SUP01   ©1998 Harlequin Enterprises Limited

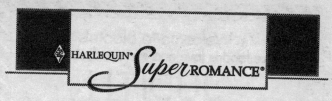